THE SCARLET LETTER OPENER

Linda M. Au

vicious circle publishing

OTHEr BOOKS BY LINDA M. AU

Humor Essays:

Head in the Sand . . . and other unpopular positions
Fork in the Road . . . and other pointless discussions

THE
SCARLET
LETTER
OPENER

SMITH RESIGNS

LINDA M. AU

ISBN-13: 978-1440445811
ISBN-10: 1440445818

Cover design by Rosamond Grupp (BookStudio@comcast.net)
Cover artwork by Mike Ferrin (www.mferrin.com)

Vicious Circle Publishing
PO Box 133
New Brighton, PA 15066-0133
www.viciouscirclepublishing.com
viciouscirclepublishing@gmail.com

For Fara, Lynne, and Mary Beth:
the triumvirate of true friendship

and

For the gang at Crit Club:
for their unwavering support and
uncanny ability to knock some sense into me,
along with a little bit of derailing

CHAPTer 1

A S HOBBIES GO, scouring the aisles of the local Office Depot for great deals on red pens probably doesn't make most people's top ten list. Me? With water, a few granola bars, and a good catheter, I could survive inside an office supply store for weeks and not get bored. I suppose eventually they'd drag me kicking and screaming from the store, clutching a ream of college-ruled notebook paper, some binder clips, and a new slimline three-hole-punch.

Even in my youth, my definition of excitement ran a bit askew. I was the only kid on my block to ask for a typewriter at age nine, fingers barely big or strong enough to plunk the keys of the gray Smith-Corona monster that became a fixture in my bedroom until college. I was the only teen to get excited about the invention of Liquid Paper. And I'm sure I was one of very few grown-ups to get all squishy inside when Post-it notes hit it big.

As an adult, earning my keep as a freelance proofreader meant steady but dull work nitpicking font sizes on cookbooks and bad memoirs. My constant companions were my red Pilot fine-tipped markers and the UPS driver. Despite a few typical bumps in the road of my life, I'd made it to my forties without much of what the rest of the world calls excitement. And I liked it that way.

So, when I walked into the office of the local newspaper's new editor one morning and found him sprawled across his desk—not in a sexy way, but more like a, well, *bloody* way—I reached for my mental dictionary and started redefining the word "excitement."

But I'm getting ahead of myself. Lee Gerber didn't start off dead. Most of us don't. It's just that he had a little help getting that way.

* * * * *

I HAD PUT IN AND TAKEN OUT this same comma three times. Isn't the devil in the details? Suddenly I had a pretty clear idea what that meant as I stabbed three little red dots under the comma one more time and rewrote "stet" in the right margin.

More coffee. I was overdue for more breakfast blend with hazelnut creamer, and it was showing. I wheeled the chair away from the desk, bolted upright, and beat a path to the kitchen with nothing on my mind but my java. Half the distance to the coffeemaker and the phone rang. I detoured to the left, grabbed the cordless handset off the base, and was back on course to the kitchen as I answered it.

"Hello?"

"Maggie, that you?"

It was Helga, from the Brighton *Bugle*. She had this interesting way of calling me and then asking me if it was me. I never quite understood that uber-specific type of flash amnesia, but somehow Helga made it seem not entirely stupid. Not entirely.

"Hi, Helga. Who else would it be? Vladimir?"

She snorted. "That old mutt? No, sweetie, he wouldn't give a rat's patooty about the phone. He probably can't even hear the phone anymore."

"What can I do for you, Helga?"

I didn't mean to be curt with her, but I needed to smell some coffee brewing, and soon. It was a bit of a trick in dexterity to make a fresh pot of coffee and hold the cordless phone against my shoulder with my chin at the same time.

"Have you ever heard of an editor named Lee Gerber? What do you know about him?" Her voice had gotten quieter—which, to be honest, must have been incredibly difficult for her—and she had a distinctly conspiratorial tone to her voice.

"Nothing. Never heard of him. Why?"

"He's taking over editorship of the *Bugle*."

"Since when?"

"Since last week, apparently."

"How did we miss this?"

"No clue, toots. I would have thought someone as sharp as you would have seen this one the second he stepped off the bus. Or out of his sports car, which is probably closer to the truth."

"Really?" I couldn't picture anyone who worked for the Brighton *Bugle* driving a sports car. Not on what that place probably paid. Not even the editor-in-chief.

"Oh, hon, you should see this guy. His suits cost more than my car."

"Helga, you drive a 1989 Escort you got at a fire sale."

"Well yeah, who knew 'fire sale' meant the car'd been on fire, right?"

She laughed, snorting into the phone again. Nice to know one of us thought she was being funny today.

"So, you were saying? He's rich, or what? Because that just doesn't make sense. Rich people don't come here to work for the *Bugle*. They stay wherever the hell they already are and keep making money!"

"That's what I thought too, when I first saw him. I figured he must be here for some other reason, but he came into the office and introduced himself as the new editor-in-chief, and he asked to make an appointment to have lunch with Fiona—and eventually *you*. I just about peed my pants."

"Fiona? Me? What's up with that?" I asked, fascinated at the prospect of this new guy coming in and shaking up our little publishing world here in Brighton. Fiona and I both did outside free-lance work for Brighton Press, of which the *Bugle* was an offshoot. She did the editing, and I took care of proofreading.

"Dunno. She's set up for lunch next Tuesday. You can bet your ass I'm going to watch every move he makes when he comes in here, too. I'll give you the four-one-one after they leave for lunch."

"Ooh, all the juicy gossip. Definitely."

I'd managed to semi-deftly get the coffee going, and it was starting to drip and trickle into the pot now. I focused on the gurgling sound and life-giving aroma.

"Well," Helga sighed, "I'm a bit disappointed you don't have the poop on Mr. Mysterious Lee Gerber for me, but I'll forgive you this time. Just don't let it happen again, sweets."

Toots. Sweets. Hon. I was seriously thinking of wearing a name-tag the next time I saw her.

"Helga, I gotta wrap this up. Second pot's ready and I have some serious copy editing to finish before I can call it quits for the day."

"Willson's essays?"

"The man uses commas like Schwarzenegger uses a machine gun. It's nuts."

"Well, I'll leave you to it, then. Any idea on E.T.A. for the whole project, in case Fiona asks?"

"Including the end notes? At least another two weeks. I have an author manuscript buried on my desk here that I haven't touched yet."

"Fiona's not going to like that."

"Then make something up."

Another snort from Helga. "Yeah, that'll go over like a lead balloon. Anyhoo, get back to work and I'll catch you later when Gerber Baby comes into the office and I get a look at him myself."

"Sounds like a plan," I said. "Java's calling. Gotta go."

* * * * *

I STIRRED THE HAZELNUT into the oversized mug and took a generous, self-indulgent whiff. Perfect. Grabbing the mug, I headed back to the small second bedroom in my apartment that had morphed into a home office. The daybed and trundle at one end of the room and the L-shaped desk and hutch at the other end belied my own state of flux and confusion. In case one of the kids needed a place to stay, I had told myself when I moved in and stubbornly kept the old, wobbly metal-framed daybed. In case Seth or Annie wanted to move back in.

Ignoring the daybed completely—it now had stacks of manila folders neatly piled at one end, with spare outdated dictionaries and style manuals up near the pillow—I spun the highback chair around and sunk into it, mug still in hand, not spilling a drop. Where was I? Oh yes. I had been lapsing into a comma.

CHaPTer 2

BY THE END OF THE WEEK, Mr. Mysterious Lee Gerber—or Gerber Baby, as Helga was already calling him—had been in the office at the Brighton *Bugle* three times. He made a splash every time. Anyone that flashy in a small town like Brighton would have been noticed a mile away. The third time he showed up I was fortunate enough to see him for myself. I was dropping off a thick stack of copy-edited pages on the Willson project for Fiona—a side project we'd been working on with the Brighton Press—when I heard the collective gasp of Helga and Kenny. Now, the Brighton *Bugle* is a small community paper that works without the hustle and bustle of a "real" newspaper. No actual walk-in customers there, which accounted for the Casual Friday look of its employees on Mondays through Fridays inclusive. The sound of the door opening always signaled a welcome break from the tedious work of putting out the little newspaper: a Federal Express delivery driver bringing a happy little package for Fiona or a new columnist or sales person; the driver from the Chinese restaurant down the street bringing the lunch they had all decided to treat themselves to an hour earlier when Helga had asked loudly, "Who wants Chinese?" Or maybe

THE SCARLET LETTER OPENER

even someone like me, coming in haphazardly either to drop off completed work or pick up a new project. I wasn't an exciting new face in the doorway, but I was more than welcome. Someone to talk to for a few minutes, to break up the monotony of scanning photographs or inputting corrections or text into dull screens of white nothingness.

Someone with the newness and flair of Lee Gerber would certainly garner more than a raised eyebrow or slight cock of the head at the Brighton *Bugle*. Even with my jaded view of just about everything, I wasn't immune to the electricity in the air when that door opened. I was just about to hand Helga the latest stack of Willsonbilge when the door creaked open. And, as stupid as we all must have looked, all three of us turned our heads in unison—toward the door, about as choreographed a gesture as I could imagine. Could we have gotten any more obvious? Rhetorical question: No, we could not.

Helga's face adopted a kind of chimpanzee grin, with absolutely no hint of embarrassment or shame about her eagerness. This did not surprise me. And, it didn't surprise Lee Gerber, either. He smiled back at her, warmly, casually—no, *familiarly*. Yes, that was it: It was a downright familiar smile, almost intimate. It wasn't even meant for me and yet I felt myself blushing. Helga, in the line of fire of that smile, wasn't blushing at all. That cagey, bold old bird, she just sat up in her chair a little straighter and hoisted her hand over the front of her desk toward Gerber as he approached. Because there were no walk-in customers like in a regular store or shop, Helga was the closest thing to a receptionist that the Brighton *Bugle* had. Mostly because she was also the closest thing to the front door.

"Mr. Gerber, so great to see you again. And so soon!"

Good grief, the sucking sound of her kissing up could be heard as far away as some small third-world country. Not that anyone had to tell me the woman had no shame. It was usually one of her strengths. Until probably a moment or so ago, I admired her for her forthrightness. Perhaps it was time to rethink that admiration just a wee tad.

"We meet again, Helga," said Gerber, in a low rumbling tone so thick and resonant that I nearly felt it rattling in my own lungs. Nice voice, too. What could this man's weak points be? Was it possible he had none? I tried hard not to think about that too much. Men? Please. My weaknesses were chocolate, poker, Pink Floyd, bad horror movies, and the occasional cigar when no one was looking. Not men. Still . . .

Helga's metallic voice cut through my wandering little thoughts.

"Fiona's in, but it looks like she's on the phone right now. She's all lit up."

Gerber frowned slightly. His eyebrows sure did arch nicely.

"Whatever would she be lit up about?"

"Oh, no, the light! The little blinkety light on the phone, on line two. Her line. It's lit up. You know. These blinkety lights." Helga tapped her index finger on the blinking light under the words "Line 2" and kept tap-tap-tapping the light for emphasis. She was finally a bit flustered by his penetrating stare—I'd never seen her tap nervously like that. And the "blinkety lights" bit was pretty funny. Sounded like she was trying to swear in church or something. Helga was careful about a lot of things, but self-censoring wasn't one of them.

"Ah, I see," said Gerber, nodding smoothly and rubbing his chin. "Okay then. I was in the neighborhood picking up my dry cleaning and thought I'd stop in and ask her to give me the low-down on the freelancer who does the proofreading for the newspaper. I've met my entire staff except her."

Helga's mouth dropped down almost to her ample, artificially upheaved bosom. Wunderkind-wannabe Kenny—way across the room but still well within earshot unless the radio was on too loud—stopped typing and turned his head just enough to make eye contact with both Helga and me. Each of us raised an eyebrow.

"F-Funny you should mention her," Helga stammered. "Heh heh, that would be Maggie Velam, right?"

"Maggie, yes, that's her name."

Helga said nothing, only poked an index finger in my direction and indicated with a sideward flick of her head that yes, I, the very same Maggie Velam, was indeed standing right here in the office, quietly taking up space in the corner by Helga's desk, much as a potted floor plant might do.

Gerber's head smoothly swiveled in my direction, and our eyes met in a most naturally unnatural way—awkward, unsettling, unnerving, and yet, well, almost like fate. A corner of his weathered mouth curled up in some version of a smile, so slight I could have missed it had I not been in an adrenaline rush of heat. All the man did was turn his sandy-haired head and sort of smile. Had Kenny turned up the thermostat or something?

I raised my folderless hand up to my face and managed a weak little-girl wave and sheepish grin.

"Me."

"You?"

"Me."

"You? Maggie?"

"Me Maggie. You Tarzan."

Helga snorted out a laugh behind us and instinctively buried her face in her hands on her desk, trying to keep from giggling like a schoolgirl. Which I appreciated, since she was the only one laughing at my tacky little attempt at breaking the ice.

Gerber—or was I going to find a way to start calling him "Lee"?—let the other side of his mouth curl up too, and a real smile emerged, but no actual laugh.

"Well, hello then, Maggie. I meet my C.Y.A. person at last."

Apparently Kenny couldn't contain his curiosity at this exchange any longer. "C.Y.A.?" he called from his desk across the room.

"'Cover Your Ass,'" Helga announced loudly, trying to talk around Gerber and me and directly to Kenny. "That's what proofreaders do."

"Well, that's what *good* ones do," Gerber corrected, still smiling and now sitting on the edge of Helga's desk, one leg up off the floor with one butt cheek on the corner and the other leg planted firmly on the floor to prop himself up. "Right, Maggie?"

He looked from Helga to me, again that head on a smooth swiveled tilt. He had to practice this crap at home in front of the mirror to get it just right like this, didn't he? And why was that crease in his trousers still perfect in the middle of the afternoon? Did the man have his pants pressed on his lunch hour or something? And why was I sweating like a pig in Arkansas in August?

"Um, yup. Sure do," I said, ratcheting the conversation right back down into a pit of nothingness. Was he really eyeing me up and down? I bet he did this with all the girls. At least, I hoped so. This was becoming unseemly.

"How long have you been doing the proofreading for the *Bugle*, Maggie?"

Oh no, he was using my first name now, and we hadn't even been properly introduced.

"Oh dear," said Helga from behind Gerber's right shoulder, "you two haven't been properly introduced!" She stood at her desk just as Gerber turned slightly in order to include her in our little tête-à-tête. There was that raised eyebrow again. Even Helga was starting to lose her edge and looked a little agitated. It wasn't a good look for her.

"Yes, Helga, please do," he purred. How did he do that? Could a man really purr like that? I mean, one that wasn't gay? This was seriously creeping me out.

"Oh, all right," she said, stumbling for some sort of firm footing here. "Mr. Lee Gerber, new editor of the Brighton *Bugle*, this is Maggie—I mean, Margaret—Velam, freelance copy editor and proofreader extraordinaire." She seemed a bit more relaxed and indicated me standing right there with a flourish of her bangle-braceleted hand. "She's a whiz with that red pen of hers."

"I'm quite sure she is," Gerber said with just a touch of smarm, standing fluidly and offering his hand for me to shake. Shake his hand? What the hell—the rest of me was already shaking, why not the hand too?

"How do you do, Mr. Gerber?" I said, trying to get my wobbling hand into his as fast as possible, if just to keep him from seeing it tremble while it was getting there.

"No need for such formality, Maggie. Call me Lee. May I call you Maggie?" We shook hands briefly, my hand sweaty and his staunch and dry. He'd already called me Maggie. Was I really supposed to go back and tell him no, he had to call me Margaret, or worse yet, Ms. Velam?

"Maggie's fine."

"'Maggie's fine,' what?" He arched the other eyebrow at me—how did he do that?

"Umm, Maggie's fine . . . Lee?"

He grinned broadly, let go of my hand and clapped his hands together solidly. "See? That wasn't so hard now, was it?"

This was starting to feel a little bit weird, not just awkward. Flirting a little bit was one thing, but what was this superiority kick he was on? I wasn't overly fond of being slightly middle-aged, but that didn't mean I wanted people to make me feel like a child. Somewhere in there was a happy medium. But right now, I was just a not-so-happy proofreader. I felt a bit of the ol' spunkiness creeping back in, just in time.

"No, Lee, it certainly wasn't. And now we've been introduced." I managed a weak but deliberate smile in his direction, the folder of papers now on another corner of Helga's desk and my arms now folded across my chest to ward off the shakes and to adopt a stance of firmness. Might as well throw a little solid body language at the guy while I still had it in me.

His smile never wavered but I sensed a slight hesitation before he spoke. Whatever prepared speech loop he'd brought out while we were being introduced had hiccupped just a little bit, and I caught it. It was all the self-confidence boost I needed. I stood a little straighter as he spoke to me, not with a hesitation, exactly, but with a little less smugness than I noticed previously. Fine with me.

"Yes, Maggie, we have. May I ask you a few questions about your work with the *Bugle*?"

"Of course. Ask away." I kept my arms folded. Not ready to let down my guard just yet.

"Well, not here. These fine people probably have a lot of work to do." He glanced around the room, from Helga's cluttered desk over-run with Beanie Babies and pictures of grandchildren to Kenny's bare desk with a complete set of stacking plastic bins with neat little piles of papers in each one. Gerber didn't seem wholly convinced that an office like this could generate actual sweat-of-the-brow work. The look, those eyebrows—it was all so dismissive. Casually dismissive. Oh, this guy was good.

Helga spoke up. "I suppose we do have a ton of work to do, Lee." She was plainly relishing calling the man Lee, despite having not been asked to do so just yet. "I have all these pages of corrections Maggie just dumped in my lap, and Kenny really should be drop-ping graphics into the new ads."

She said this last part past us and toward Kenny, who nodded in understanding, dipped his eyes back toward the computer screen, and tried to look like he wasn't really eavesdropping. Poor kid. He couldn't have found a smaller publishing house than this one to work in—part books, part small-town newspaper—and yet the office poli-tics and corporate ladder hierarchy stuff still existed, albeit in a rudi-mentary form. I didn't envy him the long road ahead of him in this field of work. I bet they hadn't taught him any of this stuff in college.

Gerber merely turned away from Helga and back toward me, making eye contact in an almost deliberate, artificial way.

"As I was saying, Maggie . . . there is a lot of work for them to do and I wouldn't want to interrupt them by chatting with you here. Perhaps we could meet over lunch soon and you could tell me how this all works with your freelancing the proofreading of an entire newspaper."

As he said this, he took his smartphone deftly out of his inner suit jacket pocket and flipped the custom cover open, holding his index finger poised over the screen he'd already turned on. Did he sit in front of a mirror at home and practice this so it always looked so casual? It was seriously starting to creep me out.

"I'll have to get back to you on that," I said bluntly, smiling awkwardly and turning to the door. I barely made it outside before breaking out in a cold sweat.

* * * * *

MY CELL PHONE RANG from somewhere deep inside this thing I called a purse. It was more like a grab bag. I never knew what I would find in the thing when I thrust my hand inside and pulled something out. What prize would I get this time? If you could call an old gum wrapper or a bent bobby pin a prize.

Naturally the phone had sunk all the way to the bottom like a weighted anchor, and every amount of fiddling inside the purse only served to move it deeper and deeper, and to the opposite end of the purse from wherever my fingers were probing. I made a mental note to give the smaller purse one more try one of these days. My mother had gotten it for me two Christmases ago, her not-so-subtle way of telling me she noticed my constant purse-rifling whenever I needed to get anything out. She knew I'd never stand for one of those awful pockets-and-zippers-for-everything purses she was so fond of . . . the ones with a built-in checkbook holder, a built-in mirror, a miniature matching calculator, a key ring that snapped onto the inside lining of the purse, a cell phone pocket on the outside, and probably another zippered compartment that would just fit an Altoids tin. I shuddered just thinking about those purses of hers.

In the meantime, my cell phone continued to taunt me with its random ringtone from somewhere in the depths of my purse. Two more rings and it would go to voice mail. Somewhere mid-ring during the next ring I found it, grabbing it tightly and yanking it out of the purse. I swiped it deftly and let out the breath I was holding.

"Hello?"

"Maggie? This is Lee Gerber . . . from the *Bugle*. We spoke the other day."

Like I was going to forget Lee Gerber that fast. Helga must have given him my cell number. Note to self: Castigate Helga. Soon.

"Yes, of course. How are you?"

Like I cared how he was.

"Fine. Just fine. Hey, listen. I need a favor from you."

"Yes?" I tried not to sound suspicious, but, let's face it: I was suspicious. I was sure Gerber was the sort of man who weaseled favors out of people with his charm and smoothness, simply by lulling them along with just enough logic and truth behind his words to get them to agree with each single step along the way. Then, pow! They've been dragged into something and now can't say no.

"Here's the deal. One of my previous authors from Deerpark Press is coming in to meet with me next week. I'm thinking it should be over lunch, just to keep her distracted a little. She's a little upset about her book being orphaned because I left. If it's just me and her, she'll be a little too focused and I won't be able to get a word in edgewise. I hate that about some authors."

"And?" I asked again, trying to get Gerber to focus at least a little, like those hated authors of his.

"Well, I could use a little company to offset sitting there with Francine for an entire hour, or however long she decides we need to talk."

I saw where he was going with this, and I didn't like it one bit. "Wouldn't adding another person to the lunch only drag things out longer because of all the twists and turns in the conversation? If she's as focused as you say, she'll still want to keep talking till she gets her point across completely. Somebody else in the conversation will just frustrate her more."

He sighed. "It's not really the actual time on the clock that will drive me nuts. It'll be one full hour of All-Francine, All-The-Time that'll make me want to tear my hair out one root at a time. I'll need a distraction. Having someone else at the table will keep me from strangling her, or myself, or both of us!"

Gerber laughed at his own idea of a joke, and I mildly chuckled over the phone, just loud enough for him to hear me but not so raucously that I would encourage him to start entertaining me with that thing he called a sense of humor.

"Anyway," he continued, "since you and I will be working together in the future, and since I won't get to know you through straight office hours like the other workers at the paper, I thought perhaps a business-deductible lunch—on me, of course—would be a good way to at least get comfortable with each other. What say you, Fuzzy Britches?"

Right then, I realized what a huge chance he was taking, assuming I'd seen *Shawshank Redemption* and knew his last line was a quote from that movie.

"*Shawshank Redemption*," I said, confirming to him that I got the reference.

"One of my favorite movies," he tacked on. I wasn't sure I believed that one. I would have thought he'd like *Wall Street* or *Elmer Gantry* or something like that. You know, something he could relate to a little better. Who was he relating to in *Shawshank Redemption*? And did I even want to know?

"Well, Lee, here's what I think: It might be better to have someone from Deerpark Press go along. You know, someone from the actual house that bought Francine's book, to ride shotgun for you. I would definitely be a third wheel, and I'm not really sure I have the time to put into an entire lunch meeting that will only end up being a big part 'lunch' and a small part 'meeting.' I've got a few projects piling up on my desk that are starting to demand more attention and I just don't have excess time for lunches out."

My excuse was close enough for government work, and I held my breath.

"Okay then, how about this?" He wasn't giving up easily. "I meet with Francine from about noon to one. Then I meet specifically with you from one till . . . whenever. If you come a few minutes early it'll at least help me to segue from her meeting to yours without her hanging on too much longer than that initial hour. Plus, she could meet you. I really think you could help her out with some of the specifics of how the publishing world works. She's a fine writer, but her presentation is still a little rough around the edges."

I knuckled under. "Okay, fine. That's a fair enough compromise. When were you thinking of having this lunch?"

"Can you make it for lunch tomorrow? We really should get our talk about the *Bugle* out of the way, and then we can all settle into our regular routines again. Business lunch, of course—on me. Well, on the *Bugle*."

I felt cornered, but then I realized I should just suck it up and get this business lunch out of the way. Plus, I really wasn't in a position to say no to a free lunch.

"Sure. I suppose so."

"Great. One o'clock, at Reeves Garden?"

I wasn't thrilled that he wanted me to have lunch with him to go over my work. I hoped he was simply getting the lay of the land early on in his tenure and wasn't really a tight-ass micromanager. As soon as I hung up the phone, I started calculating how many new outside projects I'd have to take to replace this one.

CHaPTer 3

F OR SOME REASON MY SEX DREAMS never have any sex in them. There's too much other stuff going on. I always wonder if I'm getting gypped or if everyone's sex dreams are this boring. I was pretty sure I didn't really want to know, either way.

This particular morning I awoke in a kind of sudden myoclonic jerk, nearly falling off the bed and having to scramble to remember what day it was and who the heck I was. Tuesday, it was Tuesday. In fact, it was THE Tuesday—the day when I was supposed to meet with Lee Gerber over lunch about proofreading the *Bugle* now that he was at the helm. Panicked, I climbed up off the floor and stole a glance at the digital clock on the night stand: Nine-thirty. Good. The meeting wasn't until one o'clock, so I was still good. Even had time to shower, grab a bagel, and get part of a manuscript marked up before heading out. And, of course, the coffee. The last thing I wanted to do was show up yawning and half-awake at this meeting. The *Bugle* proofing wasn't glamorous work, but it was steady, predictable, and I had it down to a science so I could minimize the time involved. A good thing, since I got paid by the page and not by the hour.

And, of course, there was that whole business with wanting to appear professional in front of Gerber. Why did I suddenly care about that? A game of one-upmanship? To be sure I started off our business relationship on the right foot? Probably the second option, since he had publishing contacts and might go so far as to recommend me to business cronies for other freelance work.

Oh, and there was that whole sexual tension thing. Or was I just imagining that? Or was it just me? And Helga? And Kenny? And how did Helga and Kenny get into my sexual tension scenario anyway? It was way too early in the morning for this sort of identity confusion, and besides, I needed coffee and a shower.

It wasn't until I was freshened up and caffeinated properly that I could sit and think through what was going on with this Mr. Gerber fellow. He was certainly an uneasy, unsettling charmer, but he also seemed incredibly self-aware. I didn't respond well to people, especially men, who were that aware of their own ambiance and presence. They never had any room left over for other people—they were too busy psychologically preening. My guess was that our new Mr. Gerber was what you'd call an alpha male.

I was in the kitchen pouring myself that obligatory second cup of java when the phone rang. Amazingly, the phone was in its cradle where it belonged (a rare thing), and I swiped it up with my free hand, deftly tapping the On button and pressing the handset to my ear.

"Hello?"

"Mom?" It was Annie.

"Hey, sweetie. What's up?"

"I didn't wake you, did I?"

I was grateful for the courtesy, but her unspoken assumption that I was a slacker merely because I wasn't always up this early was one of those little digs I let slide. For now.

"No, Annie. I wasn't up all that late last night, so I'm up earlier this morning." There—a little reminder that her mother often works a lot later in the evening than mere mortals.

"Good. I wanted to ask you something."

It was time to be flattered. The nineteen-year-old wanted to ask

Mom some advice. This could be a good thing. I reserved judgment for now.

"Go right ahead. I'm all ears."

"Okay, here's the deal: Dad wants me to come over there for Thanksgiving, but I don't really want to. He can't cook worth a damn, and I'm pretty sure he's asking me so that I'll come over and cook him something myself. And I don't want to cook his Thanksgiving dinner for him just because he doesn't have a girlfriend this year! Isn't that what Grandma is for?"

Flattery time over. This wasn't exactly the sort of advice I wanted to be giving. Now that both the kids were grown, I tried very hard to let them fend for themselves with their father, but I knew that wasn't always going to happen. Like, for instance, now.

"Annie, you know why he doesn't have holiday meals at his mother's house . . ."

She sighed. "I know, but it's not my fault she feels the same way about him that we do! She's his mother. It's her job to take him in, isn't it? She's most of the reason he's like this. Besides, you let Seth come over every year, and he's a pain in the ass too!"

"Annie!"

"What? You know it's true."

By now I was laughing, just a little bit. "That's just the wrong thing to be saying about your brother. I know you guys don't always hit it off, but honestly—let's not start comparing him to your father, all right? We both know where that will end up. Let's just let it go."

"But what do I do about Thanksgiving?" she asked, and I could tell she was frustrated about this beyond what she was communicating. If she were slightly younger, I would have said she was pouting about it. Then again, she was technically still a teenager.

"Honey, I can't help you there. You're on your own with this one. We did kind of have plans to have Thanksgiving here this year, so you could always tell your father that—that you already made plans with me, your brother, and your other grandparents. Would that help?"

"Maybe. But I think he's finally getting the idea that I'd rather spend holidays with you than over there. It's just so depressing over there. I thought it was bad when he had a girlfriend, but honestly, it's worse when he doesn't." She sighed again. Pouting. But, I couldn't say that I blamed her for it.

"Not sure what to tell you, sweetie. Your father's never been very good at listening—really listening, that is. The best you can do with him is to just lay it out there, tell him what the situation is. If he doesn't like it, there's probably not very much you can do about it. If you end up not going over there for Thanksgiving, he'll figure out something else to do. Probably he'll end up at his mother's house. It's not something you need to worry about. You're not his mother."

Annie laughed at this. And it was, indeed, funny. You couldn't tell ol' George Roberts any of this, though—he most certainly wouldn't listen. But that was part of his charm, his inability to truly listen to any voice in his head except his own. Well, charming from a distance. It wasn't nearly so endearing when I had to live with the man all those years.

"Okay, Mom, that's what I'll do."

"So, while I have you on the phone then, this means you're a definite yes for Thanksgiving?" It seemed obvious, but I still had to ask. She was, after all, technically still a teenager.

"I guess so. Don't really have a choice anymore, do I?"

"Your enthusiasm is overwhelming, dear," I said dryly.

"Sorry, Mom. Didn't mean it that way."

"I know you didn't. I'll have to call your brother to see if he's still a 'go' for turkey too. Besides all that, though, I do have to keep moving here or I'll be late for a meeting."

"Oh, sorry, I didn't know you had a meeting this morning."

"It's later, but I still have things to do here and I have to get there and park and get in the door. . . You know."

"Well, thanks for understanding about Dad."

"No problem. I had to deal with him long before you came along, Annie. I feel your pain."

"Okay."

She didn't get the Clinton imitation, partly because it was so bad on my part and partly because she just didn't give a flying leap about stuff like politics and government. If it didn't have something to do with iPods or whether she'd get overage charges on her data plan, she wasn't much interested these days. I chalked it up to her age and not any sort of inherent shallowness on her part. As long as she didn't end up anything like her father. Anything but that.

* * * * *

THE CHICKEN SALAD I'D ORDERED wasn't bad, but it wasn't anything to write home about. Gerber had a steak—rare—which didn't surprise me in the least. Of course he had a bloody steak at lunch. He was showing off his power-lunch ways. Fake it till you make it, or so I've heard. In any event, I liked my own steaks bloody rare, so his he-man tactics weren't doing anything for me.

I missed the main event—lunch with Francine—mostly because dear little Francine never showed up. According to Gerber, she'd canceled at the last minute and he really didn't have the time to rearrange lunch with me to move it up an hour earlier. So, I'd found him sitting at the bar when I came in, biding his time until I showed up. Why he didn't just buzz me on my cell to ask if I could come earlier is beyond me. Unless, of course, he liked to start his power lunches with good old-fashioned liquid lunches.

At any rate, by the time I got there and found Gerber at the bar, he was already loosened up quite a bit. We were seated almost immediately and ordered quickly. I wanted to keep this moving along. While we were waiting for our food, of course, Gerber made small talk of the usual dull variety.

To his credit, he did ask me a few questions about my work, not just with the *Bugle* but also my freelancing in general. I knew deep down his goal was to foist this Francine woman on me for a little editor hand-holding, to wean her off her dependence on Gerber as her former editor, but as long as I could see what he was really up to at all times, I didn't let his political maneuvering bother me too much.

I nodded a lot while I ate my salad, watching Gerber slice through his dripping steak with the precision of a surgeon. *Nod, nod, mm-hmm, yup yup . . .*

"So anyway," he said at one point, continuing a story he'd started a few bites earlier. I'd been hearing bits and pieces of his jury duty story since he started his steak. I nodded but said nothing. I didn't want to encourage him to talk even more by interacting with him about it, and I just wanted the story to end sooner. It was a typical schmooze-type story.

"Anyway," he continued yet again, swallowing the bite of steak that had interrupted his continuation a few seconds earlier. "The guy was guilty as all hell. We all knew it. But these ass-backwards country hicks I got stuck with just wouldn't convict the guy on the first go-round. I was sure we'd go back into that room, vote once, and be home in time for dinner. Turns out it took us three days of deliberation to come to a consensus. The women all felt sorry for him or something. Like they were all his *mommy*. Made me sick."

He neatly tore into another bite of steak just as I swallowed my last bite of salad. It wouldn't be polite to say absolutely nothing throughout the entire lunch, so I did respond a little.

"So what happened to him? Did you finally convict him?"

He laughed, a bite of steak still wedged in his cheek so he could speak. "Hell, yeah. We fried the jerk. Guilty."

"You 'fried' him? For a bar fight?"

"Well, I don't mean 'fried' as in the death penalty, of course." Aha, so it was melodrama too. "I just meant we all came to our senses and convicted him of assault and battery. Oh sure, he'll probably appeal it and maybe he'll get off, but at least we did our civic duty, right?"

He grabbed for his glass to wash down that bite of steak and drank heartily. I half-expected to hear him call out to the waitress, "Wench! More wine!" Instead he merely put the glass down and went back to cutting the last few pieces of steak into manageable sizes.

"Yes, I suppose you did. Never had jury duty myself."

"This was my third time on a jury. Every time the jerk's been obviously guilty and yet I've had to help sway the whiners. It's like these people go into this thing thinking their job is to be nice to everybody. Didn't they hear the judge's instructions?"

"It sounds like it's a tough job either way."

For a few moments Gerber stopped talking altogether so he could finish up his steak and potatoes. I watched him eat, perversely fascinated to see how someone like him ate in public. At times he seemed to have no awareness of other people around him—as if he were focused only on the bloody, dripping meat on his plate. At one point I almost thought I heard a low lion growl escape his lips, but probably I was mistaken. Mind playing tricks on me, of course.

"Listen, Lee," I said, shifting gears and ramping up for the big finish so I could get out of here and head home to the pile of papers on my desk. "This has been a real pleasure—" A real *lie*, actually. "—but I do have to get back to work on some other projects I'm already behind on. And Brenda's probably sent me new pages from the next edition of the *Bugle* to look at."

"Brenda?" He looked up briefly from his plate.

"The typesetter. For the paper."

"Ah, yes. Brenda." Head bent back to the plate. He didn't have a clue who I meant.

I lifted the starched white napkin off my lap and dabbed at the corners of my mouth, even though they didn't need it. In public, at least, I was a neat eater. I had my Cheetos-cheese-on-the-shirt moments when I was home on the couch watching bad horror movies at two in the morning, but in public I had trained myself to behave in a slightly more civilized fashion. Slightly.

"Maggie, really. We've hardly had time to talk about the *Bugle!*" He sounded genuinely perplexed by this, but honestly—did he think he was fooling me with this ingratiating routine? He probably did. After a while, people like Lee Gerber don't even hear how they sound anymore.

"Well, Lee, whose fault is that?" I chuckled aloud. "You were kind of busy telling me about your ex-wife's bitchy habits and your influence on the firing spree at Deerpark about six months ago. And don't forget the jury duty story. That's a classic in the making. But, we didn't really talk much about the *Bugle*, you're right."

"Then stay and have some dessert and we can talk about it some more." He winked, so subtly I could easily have missed it. And I wished I had.

"Really, no. There isn't a whole lot to discuss, Lee. We have a good system for proofing the *Bugle*, aside from the ad copy, and it keeps me home most of the time, which is how I like to work anyway. I stop in when I need to, and other times when I don't, and nothing's really fallen through the cracks yet."

"Well, this is true. I'll grant you that, little lady."

Now he sounded like he was about sixty, and not my age or younger.

"I don't think we need to lay groundwork for future working relationships. That kind of stuff is for strict W-2 employees who sit behind desks in the same building you do, working under your direct supervision. I just, well, phone it in. Sometimes literally."

He sighed. His plate was empty now, with just a small pool of bloody meat juices gathered in the center of the plate. He let his fork and steak knife drop to the china with a distinct clatter. Not harsh, but noticeable. More noticeable than the wink had been.

"Okay, Maggie. I get it. You're busy. Gotta go. All that jazz. No problem. It was, though, good to get to know you. Now you won't be just a nameless face when you come into the *Bugle* to see What's-Her-Name . . ."

"Brenda."

"Yes, Brenda. And What's-His-Face."

"Ernest."

"Excuse me?"

"Ernest. What's-His-Face's name is Ernest. The other typesetter." He'd been trying to refer to the two main typesetters, Brenda and Ernest, who usually sat sequestered in the prepress room in the back, off the main floor.

"Ah, yes. Ernest. Couldn't think of it for the life of me."

"I agree it's good that we now know each other well enough to be on speaking terms when I have to stop into the office to hand off work. And, this was a lovely lunch indeed," I said, hoping to transition quickly from the initial conversational wrap-up to the final hurrah.

"Yes, even nicer without Francine here to spoil it with her constant bitching and whining."

Somehow I assumed that Gerber's take on Francine's personality was probably a bit skewed, like all things Gerber, but this wasn't the time to challenge him on any of that. Time for me to hit the road.

"Can you stop in first thing tomorrow morning then? I'd still like to go over a little of how you work with us, and maybe doing that on-site would work better. You could bring along a sample of some marked-up pages if you have any."

I sighed. "Yes, I guess that works. I'll see you in your office bright and early to talk *Bugle*-talk. But I won't be able to stay long."

Might as well get that hint in early.

* * * * *

LEE GERBER'S OFFICE hadn't always looked like this. I should know: I knew it when it belonged to Kevin Sparrow, the previous editor. That man knew how to take an otherwise quaint old office building with a lot of character—his own office, in particular—and turn it into something depressing. He had had an old metal desk, bent in on one side, piled high with useless papers that probably should have been filed months ago. An ugly old mug filled with pens and pencils—the pencils with no tips and the pens with half-dried ink and no caps, the ends bitten and chewed. Kevin was a pen-chewer. Nervous little guy, really. Good editor, but a nervous little guy.

Gerber had been in the position of editor for only a week or so and the place was already transformed. He'd had the place painted—a rich, but subtle sage green—and new carpeting put down. A mahogany desk, possibly an antique, and a matching bookcase from floor to ceiling along the far wall. A small stereo on a middle shelf was oozing some smooth jazz through equally small speakers perched somewhere out of sight around the room. The place looked like the Levenger catalog come to life.

I was sitting in a beautifully upholstered arm chair across from Gerber's oversized desk, waiting for him to finish a phone call that had come in the nanosecond I sat down. He was playing with a gleaming sterling silver letter opener, twirling it like a small baton, absentmindedly as he spoke, turning his leather chair to and fro while speaking, paying no attention whatsoever to me sitting across from him waiting my turn.

The desk set of sterling silver—a pen cup, a paper clip holder, a little holder for his business cards (*he already has business cards?* I thought), the letter opener—complemented the rich textured wood of the desk flawlessly. The man was annoying, frustrating, but he certainly had taste.

I tried to keep surveying the room in order to avoid listening in on his conversation, but with his booming, self-confident voice, it just wasn't happening anymore.

"A-a-a-a-anyway, Francine . . . I'm with you on this, really I am. But I'm not at Deerpark Press anymore. I'm not sure how I can help you from here."

As Francine was responding to him on the other end of the conversation, Gerber swung his chair around to face me. He held up his free hand, touched his thumb to his fingertips repeatedly in a yackety-yackety-yack motion, and mouthed "Sorry!" at me. I nodded in understanding. Apparently Francine was a talker, and he was stuck placating her for a while.

"No, I didn't mean it that way, Francine. But once an editor's not there anymore, there's not a whole lot that person can do to keep the publishing decisions where they were before he left. It's just not how the system works. They're moving in a different direction, I suppose. What? Oh sure, it's legal. It happens all the time."

He didn't mean to pause at this point—I could tell he had a lot more to say—but even I could hear Francine on the other end of the phone now. She was obviously quite agitated at what was happening over at Deerpark Press these days post-Gerber.

"I know, I know, hon. I'll try talking to Stein about it, but I can't promise anything. If they don't want you in the catalog this spring, they do have that right."

There was then a lot of silence on Gerber's end of the conversation as he let her talk and talk about her problem. His side was now punctuated only with some "Uh-huhs" and "Mm-hmms" and some head-nodding that she couldn't see. He spun the chair back around to face front, looking as if he were more than ready to end the conversation.

"I realize that, Francine, but I'm sure your contract was quite clear. Have you discussed it with your agent?"

Some yackety noises came through the phone again, followed by an audible click and then silence. Gerber pulled the handset away from his face and shook his head.

"She hung up on me," he said, trying to sound offended and shocked, although it was plain that he'd been through this sort of thing multiple times before in his publishing career. "How do you like that?"

Rhetorical question, so I didn't answer it.

"That happen often?" I asked instead, trying to look as casual as possible despite an intense curiosity about Gerber's work ethics and relationships. If I was going to work with this man, even through a telecommuting or freelance situation, I needed to know just exactly who I was dealing with. How much of a hard-ass was Gerber to work with? Even over the phone or by e-mail? Was the distance between us through telecommuting going to be enough to keep me from going nuts?

Gerber seemed highly successful and competent, but I wasn't overly thrilled about the prospect of working with an alpha male. I'd been married to one for twenty years, and although my ex-husband was mostly an idiot about a lot of things concerning marital issues, he was a sharp-eyed eagle when it came to his work. The bleed-over into our personal lives cost us both a marriage, because he didn't give a rip about me as a person but couldn't admit it to anyone—least of all himself. Trying to get him to address grievances in the relationship was like talking to a brick wall.

Meanwhile, back at the ranch, I realized Gerber was talking, most likely answering my small-talk question.

". . . and when I left, her book got orphaned, as you already know. Not much I can do about it, really. And since I was her editor, not her agent, it's really not my problem anymore. I don't know why she keeps calling me."

I nodded, trying to look like I hadn't missed a single syllable he'd said—alpha males like when you nod a lot and acknowledge their presence all the time—and he smiled in an almost coy way. Or maybe it wasn't coy. I was having trouble reading this man's motives. Alpha males may all do things based on what's best for themselves, but their actual reasons for doing things are as individual as they are. Some act out of love of power; others out of love of lust, or food, or money. Some rare birds act out of wanting all of the above. I'd known men like this all my life, but usually managed to keep them at least at arm's length.

"Maybe she's just frustrated and her agent hasn't been much help either," I offered.

"Well, yeah, her agent's a real nut job too. Met her once at a conference. Almost as frumpy and useless as Francine. They're a good match, really—if you want to go to a craft show. If you want to publish and sell a book, though, not so much. I think Francine may have dropped her by now."

"So why did you buy it? Why were you going to publish it?"

"The book itself was solid. A good mom-lit piece. Good characters, well-paced. She has potential. She just doesn't understand how the business works. Totally green around the edges. And her agent's been no help. Not as communicative as she should be, really. So, when I leave Deerpark and the book gets orphaned by the new transitional staff, her agent just doesn't really make it clear how things work.

"So Francine ends up feeling like she's the only one in the world this has happened to. She's never heard of this sort of thing to begin with, and when I first told her agent I would be leaving at the end of last month—I gave her over two months' warning—apparently she never really told Francine that the book being orphaned was even a possibility. Just damned irresponsible, if you ask me."

Fair enough, I thought. His explanation of the situation, offered almost offhandedly and so smoothly, made sense. Enough sense that no big red alarms went off. I wasn't going to let my guard down just yet, but I could at least wait and hear him out a little more.

"I suppose yes, you could say that," I admitted. "But I feel for the poor woman. She's all new at this sort of thing, and something like this happens. It's gotta be devastating to a new author."

He shrugged and pulled himself forward in his chair, leaning both elbows on the desk and changing gears. "Well, whatever. All I know is, she's not my problem anymore. I should probably give her your name and contact information, though. Her manuscript did need a little bit more cleaning up even by the time I got it. If she's going to be out there hawking this thing again, she'll need to make it even prettier than before."

I wasn't entirely sure he was serious about giving her my contact information, and I wasn't sure I wanted him to. I didn't really need any more high-maintenance clients. She probably wasn't a prima donna, but her lack of savvy on how the publishing business actually worked could easily make her difficult to deal with. Always asking obvious questions, not really knowing what to expect of my services. And on and on. No thanks. I was fine with the client list I currently had, thank you very much.

"You know what? Don't give her my name. I'm pretty well booked solid with regular clients. Not really up for another author who's all green around the edges."

"Fair enough, then. I just thought it might help her feel better to keep moving on the project rather than giving her more time to stew about it. Trust me, she's not really the type you want to see stewing over her own losses in life. Makes her even uglier."

Didn't he realize the irony of his saying that? Probably not. Egotistical people never realized when the rules included themselves. Their egos were always in the way of sound reasoning. Especially about themselves.

"Then she's also not the type I want as a client, either. I don't really want to do any hand-holding right now. Thanks, anyway."

I smiled politely and professionally, looking down at the folder in my lap and hoping the subject would finally get around to the *Bugle* and my freelance proofing.

"No problem. It was just a stray thought anyway. Now, about the *Bugle* . . . What's the usual way this is all done with you? You know: When do we get you copy? In what format? How do we pay you—by the page, by the hour? The usual boring questions."

He grabbed a perfectly sharpened pencil out of the sterling silver cup and tapped its eraser end on the leather blotter under his elbows.

I laid it all out for him: how I got paid, how often, how someone usually e-mailed me a PDF and I'd mark it up in Acrobat and zip it back by return e-mail, nobody gets hurt. He nodded a lot, whipped out a classic Zippo lighter and flicked it on and closed the lid repeatedly as I talked, and murmured "Mm-hmm" a lot too. He was getting harder to read, not easier.

At the end of my dull little speech, I exhaled loudly. "So, I'm curious, Mr. Gerber. What brought you from Deerpark Press to our little dinky daily?" I smiled and even batted the eyelashes at him just once. Not trying to be flirtatious, really. But you catch more flies with honey than vinegar, or so they say. And this was one big mother of a horsefly.

"Don't call me 'Mr. Gerber.' Makes me feel downright old. Definitely 'Lee,' okay?" I nodded. "Good. Now, what gets me from Deerpark to here? Hmmm, it's a bit complicated, really. A lateral move, although I can see why you'd see it as a step down. Small town, small paper, not entirely impressive circulation.

"But my goals are quite specific: I've wanted to move from books to newspapers for a while. Out of college I started out at the university press where I went to school, then got married and stayed where I was to be near Marsha's family. Not that it helped. So when Deerpark's job opened up, I took it, no matter what Marsha wanted. She came with me, but it didn't take long for her to bitch her way right out of our marriage. Fine. It's a lot quieter without her around, that's for sure.

"So, wife's gone . . . no reason to hang around Deerpark Press. Finally, it's time to do newspapers, baby. But, hey, start small, learn the ropes, right? I figured it'll be better to make mistakes and learn the ropes at a small-town paper. One that's more forgiving."

He smiled, still tapping that pencil on the blotter.

"Still, forgive me for being so forward, but you seem a bit . . . overqualified for this job."

He laughed out loud at this. "Oh, you only think so. I talk a good talk, but I still have a long way to go. I'm not afraid of paying my dues, Maggie. Maybe I'd be further along in the ol' career if I hadn't taken that Marsha detour, but, well, young hormones and all that. I took my eyes off the prize for just a nanosecond, and Marsha stepped in and snagged me just that fast." He laughed again at his own young misfortune.

"Everybody makes mistakes," I offered, trying to sound like I understood. In reality, I just wasn't getting this guy. As soon as I got a certain distance down one path in my mind about Lee Gerber, something made me retreat and head back up a new path. And I wasn't getting anywhere.

"True. Too true. And here I am, doing my penance, if that's the way you're looking at it." He laughed at his own characterization of the situation. "And yet, it's just a stepping stone to something else. Don't worry your pretty little head about me, Maggie Mae. I may be here now, but I'm not going to be here forever. I've got bigger fish to fry."

I smiled, and I'm sure it looked as fake as it felt. How was I supposed to take a comment like that? The new editor didn't really want to be here, was just biding his time until something better came along. What did that make us who were here by choice and weren't thinking of going anywhere else? Were we that unambitious, the lot of us?

"Well, how exciting for you then, Lee," I said, emphasizing the "Lee" part, not on purpose, but because that's what people do when they say a person's name for the first few times. It feels awkward and strange, even if you've been asked to use the name.

He continued to smile, and to tap that pencil on the blotter. Oddly, it didn't seem as if he were tapping that pencil out of nervousness, just a sort of high-energy can't-sit-still thing that I personally couldn't identify with. I had no problem sitting still—even for very long periods of time, doing absolutely nothing. In fact, I would have listed it as one of my favorite hobbies on a questionnaire.

"Lee, listen, I really should be shoving off. I have to stop in at prepress and see what they're all up to out there, and check in with the gang about today's edition. My e-mail's been a little squirrelly so I want to give them a second e-mail address to send the PDF to for the rest of the week, just to be sure."

I stood as I said this, and Gerber stood too. He was no doubt taught the ways of gentlemen and good businessmen at the same time and probably often mixed the two together in the right context in order to get what he wanted. And I had a feeling that he often got exactly what he wanted, except maybe with Marsha. Sounded like that was a huge misstep for our little Gerber Baby. It certainly explained why he was at a paper like ours at his age, when by all rights he should have been a few rungs further up the publishing ladder. I knew how relationship detours could slow down a career. Or, as in my own ill-fated marriage and subsequent ugly divorce, could completely derail it for quite some time.

"Let me walk you out," Gerber added, moving from behind the desk to the front and coming up right behind me as I made it to his freshly painted door.

"Oh, uh, no need, really," I assured him over my shoulder, but I knew it was futile and he'd walk me all the way to the prepress room and beyond if he had the time. We walked up the main aisle of the pressroom and I detoured off to the right, heading for the prepress room where two bored typesetters sat and sat and sometimes laid out ad copy while waiting for the main news stories to show up for layout.

I opened the door briskly and Brenda spotted me first.

"Maggie! Hey, I tried sending you the editorial page and the e-mail bounced."

"Yeah, I know. That's why I'm here—gotta give you my other e-mail address for when the service provider suddenly decides not to provide any service."

I grabbed a piece of paper off the corner of her desk and held my hand out in a gesture that was asking for a pen or pencil to write with. She absentmindedly handed me a Bic pen and kept talking.

"You realize you didn't have to come all the way down here just for that. The phone lines still work, Maggie, even though I probably wouldn't have recognized your voice anymore." She winked as I finished scribbling my secondary e-mail address onto the piece of paper.

"Yeah, I know. I was here to meet with Mr. Gerber—I mean, *Lee*—anyway, so I figured this was a good time to give you that address. Besides, I hate the phone."

I handed her the paper and sat on the corner of her desk. She looked directly at me and I silently tried to signal over my shoulder with my eyes, asking her without saying a word if "Lee" was still standing behind me.

"Him?" she asked loudly. "Hell, no, he's gone. He didn't even follow you into the room." She laughed, and I turned to see the door had indeed closed behind me, with just me as the new person in the room. "He never comes in here. I have a feeling he thinks prepress is like some added level of Dante's inferno or something." She whispered exaggeratedly, looking around furtively. "I think he's afraid of us. And I think this room is bugged. Shhhh."

I chuckled and shook my head. Brenda was a trip. And I was gratified to see my general impression of Mr. Gerber wasn't so far off the mark.

"So, he gives you the creeps too?" I asked.

"Not really the creeps. He just doesn't do it for me, ya know? And he thinks he's God's gift to women—well, to everyone, really. If he weren't like that, I could stand him a lot better. But once someone goes all holier-than-thou on me, I get my feathers ruffled pretty good."

She had turned aside from me, back to her keyboard, and was inputting my second e-mail address into her address book. "Wait, what's this? 'Redinkmaggie at gmail dot com'? Aren't you the cute one all of a sudden? What's with the cutesy e-mail address? This your alter ego for those proofreader porn chat rooms?"

She raised an eyebrow at me, and I busted out laughing. "Yeah, Bren. We don't talk dirty all that much, though, because we're too busy proofreading each other's posts."

We both giggled at that one, and Ernest from across the room cleared his throat loudly.

"Girls!"

Snorting with laughter now, Ernest simply peered over his gargantuan monitor and rolled his unibrowed eyes at us. "I'm trying to work here!" Suddenly Ernest cared about getting work done during work hours? That alone was worth laughing at.

I stood. "I won't keep you, Bren—and you, Ernest!" I added, firing the last bit in Ernest's direction. I saw the top of his prematurely balding head shake back and forth, but he didn't raise his head above the monitor this time. Maybe he really was busy.

"I just had a meeting with Mr. Gerber about the proofing and now I'm headed back home to settle in for the day's work. Got anything I can take home with me?"

Brenda shook her head. "Nope. I just e-mailed the PDF to this other address. Should be fun for you today. Got another one of those great letters to the editor from Dirt Boy again."

Ernest eagerly raised his head where we could see it and nodded vigorously. We all loved Dirt Boy. It was our pet name for one particular letter-to-the-editor writer who was regular as clockwork and angry as hell and he wasn't going to take it anymore.

"What's Dirt Boy writing about this time?"

Ernest chimed in ahead of Brenda. "It's about Gerber! He hates the 'new direction' he thinks the *Bugle* will be heading!" The glee in Ernest's voice was unmistakable.

"But Gerber just got here. He's only been running things completely on his own for what? Two weeks, tops?" Both Brenda and Ernest nodded in unison but said nothing. They just grinned and nodded.

"Wow," I continued. "I can't believe even Dirt Boy could find anything to complain about in two weeks. That's fast, even for him." I was impressed. And suddenly this anonymous letter-writer was someone I admired. "I think I want to shake his hand," I added, and Brenda burst out in a snorting guffaw that was hilarious all by itself.

Ernest peered even higher over the monitor. "Gerber's already tried to find out who the guy is. Doesn't like his attitude, he says. Bad for business, he says. Meanwhile, I'm thinking—well, *we're* thinking—what happened to that motto that even bad publicity is still publicity? I think someone like Dirt Boy sells papers, and isn't that the goal?"

Brenda was nodding the whole time, but I shook my head. I was a little further into Gerber Baby's head than these two underlings.

"No, that's not the goal. Because this isn't about the newspapers. Or, it should be, and he thinks it is—but he's too narcissistic to see it that way. It's a personal slam against him, and that supercedes the selling-newspapers thing. Someone like Gerber would always rather sell newspapers on someone else's bad press, not his own. Certainly not his own."

I was nodding now, liking my little theory the more I thought about it. Brenda was seeing my point. "I get it. And you're right—he is awfully self-absorbed. He doesn't really fit in here, does he? Too . . . well, he's just too much for us. He's been around the block a few times—and to be honest with you, he makes most of us feel like a bunch of country hicks!"

Ernest stood from behind his monolithic monitor. "And I went to college, for cryin' out loud!"

"Yeah!" Brenda echoed.

"Yeah!" I chimed in. Suddenly we were all feeling goofy, and we all started laughing.

"Then again, we were all English majors," said Brenda. I smiled.

"So was he, Bren."

"You think so?"

"You think he majored in, like, engineering or something? Something . . . useful?"

Ernest laughed and sat back down quietly. "I gotta get back to work or the paper will be late."

I turned toward the door to leave. "Me too. If I don't get home soon, I'll be up late again tonight with other projects."

"Hey, Maggie, let me know what you think of Dirt Boy's letter, okay? I'm half-convinced it's really Ernest writing from a library computer." She winked.

"Brenda!"

Brenda leaned in toward me slightly. "Shhh, he has no sense of humor when I say that." Another wink.

"Brenda!"

I waved and winked back at her. "Talk to you later. I'll call you if I get home and don't find that PDF waiting for me. And Ernest, get back to work, will ya?" I called over my shoulder. He grunted and tried to sound genuinely peeved at our comments, but I was fairly sure he actually loved the attention, being part of the group and included, even if it meant being included as the brunt of an inside joke. His cueball head bobbed just above the monitor, like a busy worker bee. He had work to do. I should leave.

* * * * *

Back out in the main press room, I ran smack into Lee Gerber, who was schmoozing with one of the press workers who had come up with a press sheet for a book for nits and corrections. The guy was heading for prepress—part of Brenda and Ernest's job was to eyeball the press sheets for errors, nicks in the negatives, other potential problems before printing—and he'd been waylaid by Gerber, whose job didn't involve actual deadlines or actual work. Blue collar meets white collar, and usually white collar wins. And then blue collar has to scramble to make up for time lost while dealing with white collar.

And I made matters worse by literally bumping into Gerber's stray leg hanging out into the aisle. He was trying to stand there casually while talking to the press man, but he'd stuck his left leg out way too far into the aisle, and my foot found it without telling me first.

"Oh, excuse me," I offered, trying to keep going and not get into yet another schmooze fest with Gerber. The press man had a deer-in-the-headlights look on his face, and I genuinely felt sorry for him. I was merely a freelancer and could leave at will (and was hoping to do just that in a moment). But this poor schmoe was stuck in Lee Gerber's world five days a week. The best he could probably hope for was that Gerber himself didn't like to go slumming too often and made his office enough of a refuge that he didn't want to leave.

"Bye, Maggie! See you in the morning bright and early!" Gerber called to me as he saw me pushing open the glass door to the outside world.

"Yup, whatever!" I called back, waving a hand in the air but not turning around fully to meet his eye. Why had I agreed to yet another meeting with Gerber, and first thing in the morning?

As I left the building, I had no clue that this would be the last time I'd see Lee Gerber alive. Otherwise, I might have said something nicer as I left.

CHaPTer 4

T HE NEXT MORNING I AWOKE without the alarm clock. On time today. In fact, a little early. I wasn't keen on dragging my sorry butt out of bed so early just because Gerber wanted to go over more stuff before his day officially started. This was closer to when many of my nights officially ended.

But something had been stirring around in my brain in the moments before I awoke spontaneously, and I didn't have any trouble waking up mentally. The body wasn't cooperating as fully as I would have liked, but a hot shower and hot coffee in a travel mug would probably take care of that.

I padded around the apartment looking for little odds and ends I had to bring with me: cell phone, keys, printout of proofed pages, purse, keys, *keys* . . . just where were my keys? I slipped on my gray hooded sweatshirt and felt around. Bingo—car keys in corner pocket!

The car started up without a hitch this morning—another small treat for me—and I made it over to the *Bugle* offices in record time. So this is what it felt like to drive around before rush hour. If I weren't an avowed night owl, I might have wanted to try this more often.

* * * * *

THE FRONT DOOR TO THE *BUGLE* OFFICES was open, but when I got inside I could easily see that the rest of the staff wasn't here yet. Only a few lights were on. No one was around. None of the computers were humming, and I didn't hear the familiar sound of people's fingers tapping on computer keyboards churning out all the news that's fit to print—plus a lot of it that's technically fit to print but totally useless and dull to print.

Although I had become overly fond of silence once I began proofreading full-time, somehow the unnatural silence in this place was, well, unnatural. Awkward. I could heard my Chuck Taylors squeaking and squidging on the smoothly tiled floor, almost echoing through the eerie early-morning silence. A stray light along the far wall lit my way down the main aisle and then left to Gerber's office.

Gerber's office door was open and the light was on, leading my way the last few steps. Might as well let him know I was coming.

"Mr. Gerber, it's me, Maggie Velam. We have a seven-thirty appoin—"

At this moment, anyone with faster reflexes and mental acuity for such things would have screamed bloody murder. I, on the other hand, merely stood still and felt my heart pounding wildly somewhere in my throat, making it difficult to breathe properly. There in his desk chair, slumped over his desk facedown, was Lee Gerber. I might have thought he was simply sleeping, taking a quick cat nap so early in the morning while waiting for me to show up for our appointment. At least, that's what *I* would have been doing. And that was my initial knee-jerk reaction to the sight that greeted me. Well, except for the sterling silver letter opener that was freakishly lodged just at the base of his neck, sticking straight up in the air, blood all around it on Gerber's neck and back and shirt collar, as well as also pooling a little on the desk just under his head.

Nope. Probably not napping.

At that point, I finally screamed, just for good measure.

* * * * *

ONCE THE SCREAM DIED OFF MY LIPS, I stood shaking in the doorway of Gerber's office, quite unsure what to do. No one else was on this floor of the building that I could see—though they were probably due in soon—and so no one heard my bloodcurdling shriek of terror and panic. I'd never really screamed before, not a real, honest-to-God scream like in the movies. It felt weird, and for one sick moment I had the grotesquely funny thought that maybe I should also run through a graveyard in high heels, constantly looking behind me for a werewolf and, of course, tripping over nothing and then just lying there sprawled out and screaming, screaming, screaming, helpless prey for the monster on the prowl.

When my own scream finally died down, I realized that whatever real-life monster did this to Lee could easily still be in the vicinity. Now I really didn't know what to do. All I'd managed to do with my screaming was send up a signal of exactly where I was. Great.

I caught sight of the phone on Gerber's desk, a few inches from the top of his head, off to the left. Blood had splattered a little on the handset, and without thinking I looked right back at Gerber's upper back with the otherwise flawless letter opener sticking up out of the back of it. I shuddered and looked away, back specifically at the phone. Knowing I shouldn't touch anything in the whole room—and thankful for that because the last thing I wanted to do was touch anything!—I thrust my shaking hand into my purse and sifted around till I found my phone. I'd never watched my hands shake so much as when I was dialing nine-one-one on that thing . . . not even when George had called me from a motel phone to tell me he wasn't coming home and that he wanted a divorce. I'd trembled uncontrollably that day too, and for similar reasons: My life was about to turn upside down through what seemed like no fault of my own.

CHaPTer 5

I REMEMBERED POLICE OFFICERS scurrying around, stringing stereotypical yellow crime scene tape around the room like an over-zealous new mother stringing crepe paper for a first birthday party. It was sickeningly heady, all of it, and I stood off to the side, across the main room of the press offices, watching the buzz of activity from a respectable, safe distance. It wasn't even fascinating in a way I might have predicted if I were making predictions from the outside looking in. Now that I was indeed forced to be here, to stay here, to go through the highly ritualized process that is crime scene investigation, it didn't seem nearly as fascinating. Not even remotely. Bummer, really. It would have been interesting to journal about this later and remember all the subtle nuances of what everyone was doing. But I had a feeling my later memories of this particular event would be emotional, raw, and, frankly, one big blur.

I stood still, staring at the scene around me, fighting hard to keep the bile from rising in my throat. The last thing I needed or wanted right now was to draw attention to myself by puking in the middle of a crime scene. I had a momentary flash in my mind of some poor cop being forced to string yellow tape around a small pile of vomit, marking it with some sort of small numbered placard and taking photographs of it from every possible angle.

But, this really wasn't about me, despite the fact that it certainly felt that way. Amazing how you feel only your own pain during a crisis, how very difficult it is to properly sympathize with the real victims without thinking, "Wow, I'm glad that wasn't me." Then again, there wasn't really any point in trying to sympathize with Lee Gerber, the victim. He was deader than a doornail, whatever that meant. I wondered fleetingly where "deader than a doornail" started. *I really should dig out that book my mother got me last Christmas that gives phrase origins from all over the English-speaking world.*

My mind was wandering on purpose, trying to get itself as far away as possible from the prospect of a dead and bloody Lee Gerber slumped over his desk just a few feet away from me. And, even as I thought that, I watched the EMTs wheel a gurney out of Gerber's office, with the almost-stereotypical sheet covering Lee's now-horizontal (but probably still bloody) body. His neatly shined black oxfords were sticking out of the bottom of the sheet. The EMTs were at either end of the gurney, focusing on their task and not making eye contact with anyone, least of all me. They maneuvered the wheeled cart of death around the desks and chairs just outside Gerber's office and finally made it to the main aisle heading toward the front desk and out the door. I stood rooted in one spot, waiting for someone to tell me it was all right to go home (which I desperately wanted to do). I stood on one foot and shifted nervously to the other back and forth like someone at the wrong bus stop.

"Miss?"

I looked around, turning a full one-hundred-eighty degrees to see a rather important-looking police-officer-slash-authority-figure standing behind me. I hadn't a clue how he got there without me noticing, since I had a feeling my whole body—ears included—was on high alert. Perhaps I was on hyperhigh alert and was responding to the wrong stimuli on the wrong level. In any case, he was there and I hadn't heard or sensed him coming.

"Yes, officer?" I tried to sound as overly respectful as possible without sounding panicky. Hard to do when you feel panicky, but I tried.

"You must feel pretty panicky right now."

Okay, now that was scary.

"A little," I fibbed, coughing to clear my throat and sounding anything but convincing. As long as I didn't sound like I knew something about what had happened, though, I didn't much care what this person thought of me.

"Perfectly understandable. And you probably want to get the heck out of here too." He put his arms on his hips and stood waiting for me to answer. A perfectly obvious answer, so I half-wondered why he needed me to say anything in the first place. I was noticing that my voice sounded awfully wobbly and jittery. I was either upset as hell or guilty as sin.

"I certainly do! Can I please leave now?" I begged, giving him my best forlorn look and hoping he'd take pity on me for standing here lost in the shuffle for this long already.

"We have your contact information already, and it sounds like you just were in the wrong place at the wrong time here. If Mr. Gerber's first appointment had been someone else instead of you, we wouldn't be having this conversation." He smiled perfunctorily, and I returned the favor. I could tell a standard answer when I heard one.

"Don't remind me, please," I said, trying to sound as inconvenienced as I possibly could. "I barely knew the man." Had to get that in there for good measure. "Just met him a week or so ago." One more reminder. "I was only here about some proofreading, for cryin' out loud." Nail in the coffin, so to speak. Perhaps that was a bad choice of figures of speech to think about right now.

"Got it, Ms. Velam. As I said, wrong place at the wrong time. And we do appreciate the time you've taken this morning to help us out. At this point I'm sure you can head on home and if we need any more information from you, we can simply contact you later."

He oversmiled. Again with the smile. I reached down to my purse on the floor at my feet, whisked it up, and slung it over my shoulder, looking very much like I was about to run out the door at full speed.

"And don't leave town!" the office called after me. I stopped in mid-stride when I heard that, turning to face him full on. He was grinning stupidly at me. He was kidding. My hyperhigh alert hadn't picked up on that subtlety either. Obviously the whole high-alert thing wasn't working right. Needed some fine-tuning.

By the time I got outside of the newspaper offices and stood in the crisp morning sunshine, I took a deep breath and stopped rushing. And, looking around me, I saw that the ambulance that had been sitting outside the building with its red lights flashing had already left. A few police cars were still parked out front, but all the officers were still inside collecting forensic evidence. I headed for my car, purse over one shoulder and my folder of notes for the meeting with Gerber under the other arm.

As I watched a small pocket of onlookers eyeing me as I came out of the building and headed for my car, though, I could think of only one stupid thing: The meeting was probably canceled.

CHAPTER 6

Y APARTMENT BUILDING WAS A WELCOME SIGHT as I drove onto my familiar, no-murders-committed-here-this-morning street. I lived far enough away from the *Bugle* offices that, the farther I got from the *Bugle* and the closer I got to home, I felt as if I had left some surrealistic nightmare. I turned off the car and sat quietly for a few moments, mentally regrouping and trying to catch my breath. I was panting as if I'd run a marathon and couldn't seem to calm myself down sufficiently to get the keys out of the ignition and into my trembling hand. A few of those deep cleansing breaths I learned decades earlier in childbirth classes, and I felt marginally better. After that I was calm enough to risk getting out of the car and finding my way up to my second-floor apartment.

The apartment key shook in my still unsteady hand, but after a little bit of effort I managed to get it in the lock and I felt the door lock open and come free of the jamb. Glorious! At once I was inside and closed the door, not a moment too soon. Dropping my purse on the floor by the door and pitching the keys onto the side table just inside the door, I headed straight away for the couch, collapsing into it with a huge sigh of relief that sounded more like a muffled whimper from an injured dog. There wasn't much to be done with what happened. All I had to do was go on with my life and hope the authorities didn't call me about anything. I wasn't really up for dealing with questions and inquiries and anything else having anything to do with the grisly scene of Gerber with a letter opener shoved in his neck like he was some human ventriloquist's dummy gone bad. I was suddenly glad I was sitting on the couch because I felt dizzy just thinking about it.

"Vlad!" I called, wondering briefly why the mangy mutt hadn't met me at the door as he usually does. "Vladimir!" I called again, and this time the oversized Cairn mix clicked his little paws out into the dining room area and sheepishly skittered toward me, his head down and looking quite guilty. If he weren't impeccably housebroken I would have worried about that look of shame on his little furry doggy face.

"What's up, boy? Did you do something bad?" I asked facetiously, trying not to fall into the baby-waby voicey-woicey that other small-dog owners use all too frequently. He hopped unceremoniously onto the couch—something that was getting harder for him as he aged and developed a bit of a doggy paunch in his midsection—and nestled his nose right into my outstretched hand, asking forgiveness and licking the palm of my hand.

"Did you? What did Vlad do today?" I scritched him under his chin and he immediately flopped himself over onto his back, belly vulnerable in the air and open for some tummy rubs. Apparently his guilt didn't take long to dissipate when he sensed the opportunity for a free tummy rub. Dogs, despite their tendencies to guilt, have no shame. Especially mine.

As I was rubbing his tummy dutifully, allowing the simple routine pleasures of my life to soothe me back into some semblance of normalcy, I thought I heard a noise coming from the back bedroom, my office now that Annie had moved out somewhat permanently.

Before I had a chance to panic about who might be lurking back in the office, rifling through my papers or stealing all my best—well, my *nonexistent*—jewelry and valuables, I caught the familiar sight of my son, Seth, popping out of my office and into the back hallway. So, it wasn't one of the police officers looking for evidence of my murderous ways after all.

"Mom! Hi! You didn't answer the door this morning so I just came in anyway. Vlad was barking on the other side of the door and I came in partly to shut the dumb mutt up. He's loud when he wants to be."

"I know," I agreed, wondering if any of the neighbors were going to say anything to me later. Mrs. Nutley might click her tongue at me in the elevator or out near the mailboxes, but Mr. Nutley would just say something nice with a flirtatious edge to it. Awkward either way you look at it.

"Well, honey, I'm glad you came in then," I agreed, standing rather shakily just in front of where I had been sitting on the couch and waiting for Seth to come to me. He rounded the back of the couch and came to hug me, which he did fiercely.

"Didn't mean to scare you, Mom. I didn't hear you come in until Vlad got up off the daybed and ran in here wagging his stumpy little tail. I figured it had to be you if he wasn't barking."

I snorted. "Ha, don't assume anything with Vlad. It could be Hannibal Lecter coming in the front door with a bottle of Chianti and some fava beans and Vlad would still come running with his tail wagging. He barks at people outside the door in the hallway but once they make it inside he assumes they're friendly and leaves 'em alone."

I sat back down on the couch slowly, trying not to draw attention to myself and my constant shaking. Grabbing a throw pillow from one end of the couch, I clutched at it, giving both my trembling hands something to do to keep them from twitching too noticeably in front of Seth. He took my lead and flopped onto the other end of the couch, with Vlad neatly wedged between us. He took over tummy-rubbing duty while he talked.

"Wasn't sure what you'd be up to right now, but I'm between apartments—until the first of next month when I can move in with Sean again—and I thought maybe I could crash here for a week or so."

He paid close attention to Vladimir's tummy, and I wasn't sure if he was trying to avoid eye contact with me or not. He knew he was welcome here any time, but it was probably still tough for a twenty-five-year-old to admit he needed help, even Seth, who was otherwise a reasonably laid-back guy.

"Sure. You know you can stay here. Just make sure you let me move my own stuff off the daybed and make sure you're not in there when I'm working during the day. I don't really have regular hours right now—jobs are trickling in funny and . . ." I hesitated.

"And *what*?" he asked, looking up from the dog's tummy.

". . . and the daily work from the *Bugle* is, well . . . unsettled right now."

"Why? The new editor?"

"Oh, you heard about that?"

"Yeah, it was in the paper." He chuckled, most likely at the irony of the paper carrying an article about itself. He'd find that funny. "Some book publishing guy coming in to replace Sparrow, right?"

I let out the breath I had been holding. "Yeah. Lee G-Gerber," I said, stammering just a little on his name now that I was saying it out loud. I was clutching the throw pillow to my chest so hard I must have looked incredibly out of sorts.

"Mom, you all right?"

I nodded—quite unconvincingly, I'm sure—and sniffed as I clutched my guardian pillow. "Fine, Seth. I just had a tough morning, that's all."

He furrowed his brow for a moment. "I can't imagine the life of a proofreader going so horribly wrong that she ends up sniffling and shivering on her couch. Something *else* happen?"

Okay, so maybe I wasn't so convincing as the strong, independent type.

"You mean, besides the fact that Lee Gerber was m-murdered?" I rocked back and forth a little on the couch as I said this.

Seth stood up, looking and sounding as if he personally had just been offended. "Murdered? You mean, like, well, *murdered*?" he repeated. Flummoxed. He wasn't offended; he was flummoxed.

I looked directly at him now, realizing by the look on his face that he was genuinely, well, flummoxed. It started to hit me all over again that this wasn't the kind of thing that happened every day. Or even every other day. Or month. Or lifetime.

"Yep." I stopping rocking, trying not to look too Rainman-like. "Dead as a doornail," I added, wincing as I said it because I realized as soon as it was out of my mouth that it was a highly inappropriate thing to say. But I was definitely going to have to look that up later. I covered my mouth with my hand in an "Oops!" gesture, but Seth was having none of it.

"Wait, are you serious or not? You almost had me there for a minute," he finally said, deciding for himself that it was indeed one of my sick jokes and not something that had really happened. He began to turn away from the couch. My guess was that he was going to head for the kitchen for a bite to eat, which in Seth-speak meant I wouldn't have anything left in the fridge once he was done. I had learned years ago to keep a stash of meatball Hot Pockets in the freezer for his fridge raids. Seth couldn't visit without eating a Hot Pocket. Or twelve.

"Wait," I said, stopping him in his tracks. He turned back to face me as I looked over my shoulder and shrugged. "It's true. He's dead. Murdered."

"Really?" He didn't move. "Murdered? When? What happened?" Too many questions, really, to narrow it down to just two, but those two covered a lot of territory, so it was just as easy to start there as anywhere else.

I patted the couch and waited till Seth made his way back and sat down next to me. Letting out a ridiculously exaggerated, but probably understandable sigh, I let up on clutching the pillow just a little and tried to catch Seth up on what had happened this morning.

". . . and I knew as soon as I saw him slumped over the desk that he was dead. That he'd been murdered. It was horrible." I looked down at my feet, where Vladimir was now curled up on top of my shoes, and let it sink in—for me as well as for Seth.

"Just because he was slumped over a desk doesn't really mean he was murdered, though, does it?" Apparently Seth wasn't ready to give up on this being some natural part of the course of life.

"Well, maybe not, except for that big bloody letter opener he had sticking out of the upper part of his back," I said, letting go of the pillow with one hand in order to gesture behind my own head in an effort to give Seth a better idea of where I meant. He made a face.

"Ew," he said simply. Then he thought a moment and continued. "Wait, a letter opener? Just a letter opener?" Seems he wasn't so sure you could kill someone so easily with a letter opener.

"Well, you should have seen this thing," I answered, playing devil's advocate for what I beheld with my own eyes. "I mean, I saw it the other day on his desk. Part of a gorgeous sterling set of desk accessories. Really nice. The whole set has these etchings in the silver, plus his initials in everything too. Maybe it was a gift or something, but it really was a lovely matching set of—"

"Mom!" Seth interrupted. "I get it. A nice set of stuff. Still, who stabs someone in the back of the *head*? Wouldn't, like, the skull get in the way?"

I guess I hadn't explained it well enough. "No, no. Not in the head directly. Sorry about that. It was sticking straight up in the air even though he was bent over the desk. Like this," I said, and dropped the throw pillow into my lap completely so I could give Seth a little reenactment of what I found this morning. I bent over and used one hand behind my own head to show the angle of the letter opener at the base of my neck.

Suddenly the whole thing creeped me out horribly and I sat straight up and stopped what I was doing. Seth was nodding.

"Oh, I see. The bottom of the neck. Yeah, that would do it." He made the icky face again and shook his head. "Sounds like a nasty way to go, actually."

"I'm sure it was. I wouldn't know. I just found him once he was already dead."

"You what?" I'd forgotten that I had never mentioned the part where I was the first one who had found him quite dead.

"Oh yeah. It was me. I had an appointment with him this morning so I was the one who found him. The appointment was really early so I was the only other person in the building."

Seth sniffed. "Apparently you weren't the *only* other person in the building!"

I blinked.

"Mom, you could have been hurt! What if the guy was still in the building when you came in? He could have killed you too!"

I blinked again. "Well, there weren't any other cars in the lot or out front, so . . ."

"Yeah, like the murderer's going to just drive his car up to the building and park in a space like a normal person and then go in and murder this guy and leave. Yeah, that's how it happens." Dripping with sarcasm, that kid.

"Okay, okay, I get it. But how was I supposed to know it would be dangerous to go into the *Bugle* offices in the morning? I mean, really, Seth. Hindsight's twenty-twenty, you know? If I had misgivings about anything, it would have been whether or not Lee Gerber was a lech, not whether or not he was dead!"

I was shaking terribly, and Seth noticed. "Mom, sorry. I didn't mean anything. I'm just, well, stunned, you know? It's all right." He patted my hands, which had already grabbed the pillow again and were squeezing the life out of it in an effort to keep me from hyperventilating. "I'm sure you weren't in any real danger. Probably a murderer would leave right away, right?" He nodded. I wasn't sure if he was trying to convince me or himself. Probably a little of both.

"Moot point, Seth. I'm here now. But at the time, all I could think about was how horrible it looked and how I'd just spoken with him about the meeting yesterday. He seemed like a royal pain in the ass in a lot of ways, but he seemed so . . . vital, alive, too. You know what I mean?"

"I know what kind of person you mean. It's just hard to believe he's dead. Just that fast." He snapped his fingers to indicate the quickness of Gerber's passing.

"Yep, that's it," I said, sighing and getting up from the couch and onto my own two feet. A bit unstable but otherwise I was okay to walk. I made a beeline for the kitchen, heading straight for the coffeemaker. "Want some coffee?" I asked over my shoulder. Seth followed me into the kitchen.

"Yeah, that sounds good. I'm not quite awake yet." A small yawn escaped his mouth and he stretched and then overstretched behind me. I kept half an eye on him in the small kitchen, hoping he didn't whack the—

Clank!

Too late. He'd banged into the pots and pans hanging over the small butcher block island that made the kitchen feel too cramped, certainly for stretching. Immediately he grabbed the two pots that had crashed into each other when he stretched and steadied them so they wouldn't continue to clank back and forth until inertia stopped them. I blinked as they slammed into each other one last time before Seth got them under control.

"Oops, sorry."

"That's okay, Seth," I said, reaching for the coffee canister on the refrigerator door. "I still had one nerve ending left to spare." I smiled weakly for him, to let him know it was all right for him to behave normally. He smiled back.

"So," he said, switching gears to more normal guy-curiosity now that he saw me smiling a little and making coffee like the "real" me. "What happened after you found him like that? Did you call the cops? What did they do? What did you see? It must have been gross."

I tried not to let it worry me that he sounded excited about the gross part, chalking it up instead to a typical male reaction to disgusting things like this. The boy watched too much HBO, I was convinced of it.

"Seth, calm down, really. Stop drooling. It was just a dead body," I said, sounding as casual as I could so as not to stir up any more eagerness on his part now that he knew I was all right and we were beyond the initial reactions. I was pretty sure I didn't sound nearly as casual as I wanted to, though.

"*Just* a dead body? Well, honest, Mom, in all my twenty-five years on the planet, I'm not sure I've *just* run into a dead body lying about anywhere. It's not the kind of thing you run into all that often. Look at you. You're almost twice my age, and this is the first time *you've* run into one, right?" he asked, turning this into one of his semi-pointless bantering sessions where the point was to win a war of words and not necessarily to prove anything of any real value. The boy took after his father too much, although at least he was nicer about it than his father had ever been. Plus, he was better at it. I never could figure out why his father insisted on arguing beyond the point of making his point, except that his goal was to crush the spirit of the other person and not really to persuade anybody of anything. What a jerk.

"Seth, dear," I said dryly, "I'm not twice your age. Don't rush me. I was twice your age a few years ago but not anymore and it won't happen again—"

He frowned, wrinkling his brow in an effort to do the math to figure out exactly when I had been twice his age and why I wasn't twice his age now. It was something I'd calculated a while ago— probably all parents do—but I'd kept it to myself at the time because it hurt bad enough to think of it that way. Now that I was beyond that point, it still hurt but not in such a starkly mathematical way. If that even made sense. Math hurt.

"Seth, stop trying to do math in your head. You know how much you hate math," I condescended, patting him on the chest as I went around him back to the fridge to get the creamer for the coffee. "Hazelnut okay? It's sugar-free." I held it up for him to see the label.

"Oh, uh, sure, yeah," he said, still frowning and slowly giving up on the math.

I was feeling a little stronger now and continued. "Besides, I wasn't commenting on how often I find dead bodies lying around. You're right—I don't. I was commenting on the fact that, rare though it is for most people, myself included, it's still just a dead body. Not someone I had any real attachments to. Mostly it was inconvenient, horrid to think about if you're projecting it back on yourself, and a little scary to think the cops might still have to talk to me about stuff because I happened to be the first one in the building after it happened. That's the bitch about all this. I'm glad not to have to look at Gerber's body anymore, I'll grant you that much. But otherwise, well . . . I'll get over it."

I reached overhead into the cabinet above the coffeemaker and took down two mugs, including Seth's favorite, the Harry Potter mug that changed images when hot liquids were poured into it. We'd never figured out how it did that. Maybe it was magic. Or math. Or worse yet, science. Who really knew for sure?

"Don't give me any of that crap, Mom. You were shaking like a leaf when you first came in." He pointed back into the living room as he scolded me.

"I came home to find some strange intruder had charmed my watch dog into playing coward. Of course I was scared."

I turned away from him to fuss over the mugs and spoons, when in reality I was trying not to show him I was smirking.

"Mom."

"Okay, okay. Yes, I'm still freaked out about it, if you want to know. But I'm glad you're here. It's helping me get perspective back. I drove the whole way home in the car with nothing to do but think about it and think about it some more. It was nice to come home and find another living, breathing human being here waiting for me."

"Well, now I'm glad I'm staying here for a few days. Frankly, Mom, once it hits the paper that you were the first on the scene, I wonder if the killer's going to worry that you saw something you shouldn't have seen."

I spun on my heels and stared directly at him. "What? What do you mean, in the paper?"

"Well, the news. You know, once it hits the news. Will there even be a paper today?"

I shrugged but was unsettled just the same. Aside from having to slip past the onlookers outside the *Bugle*'s office building, I hadn't really thought much about the outside world and how they would come to find out what had happened to their newest newspaper editor so soon after arriving in town for his new job.

"Shit." Couldn't really think of anything else to say, and "Shit" just kind of summed it up better than anything else anyway.

"Oh, sorry. I just assumed you'd thought about that part already."

I laid out two spoons next to the two mugs, over-arranging everything neatly to the point of obsession. "No, not really. I was too busy this morning just watching all the weird stuff they were doing inside the building, running around with gurneys and two-way radios and forensic equipment and stuff. And then a few of the cops talking to me, asking questions, then re-asking the same questions, and then other cops coming over and asking the same questions the first cops asked. It was a nightmare having to tell the same sick story a hundred times. Don't these guys believe in smartphones or Dropbox or what?" I sighed, watching the coffeemaker splutter and churn out coffee downward into the carafe and steam upward into the air under the cabinet. I closed my eyes and inhaled some of the strong brew, enjoying the sensory experience at hand.

Seth tried to soften the blow of his revelation about the news media. "Well, maybe you're not going to be that big a part of the story. I mean, you didn't really see anything happen. You didn't get involved. You just found him."

"And I was probably the last person to see him alive. Don't forget that part," I added helpfully.

"Yeah, and that par—hey! Really?"

It was obvious he hadn't thought about that part.

"Yup. As far as they know. No one else has stepped up yet to take that honorable position. Then again, who would? 'Wait, officer, it was me! I was the one who saw him just before he died! Look at *me* suspiciously now instead of *her!*'"

The coffee was done spluttering and brewing so I poured the two mugs full and slid one down the counter to Seth. I plopped some creamer into my mug and slid that down the countertop too. He took the mug and dumped some creamer into it without thinking, splashing a little onto the counter next to the mug without noticing he'd done it. I tried not to let it bother me and mostly succeeded.

"Oh, Mom, I'm sure no one suspects you. Were you the one who called the cops?"

"I dialed nine-one-one, yeah. I just stood there in the doorway to his office, staring at him, calling nine-one-one. I knew I should go in there and check to see if he was breathing or something, but you know—he was dead. It wasn't even close."

"Didn't the operator want you to check?"

"I told her he was definitely dead and told her about the letter opener. Then I think I freaked out a little bit. She asked if I took his pulse or anything, and then I had this image in my head of touching him, and I started shaking. That's when it just got weird."

"I can imagine," he said, although I'm not sure anyone can imagine something like this unless they've been through it themselves. And it wasn't something I would have wished on Seth just so he could say "I can imagine" and mean it. It was a nightmare.

"Anyway, I don't think anyone right now thinks I did it, no. But they still have to ask all those same questions. It just sounded so much like they were, well, accusing me of something."

"Cops probably don't have to be trained on bedside manners or anything, so I wouldn't expect them to soften the blow for you. Still, you didn't do much but walk into the building, see something, and call the authorities. Sounds like you did everything you would have been expected to do. I wouldn't sweat it beyond that. I didn't mean to throw you off with the media coverage stuff. I mean, it'll be there, but beyond the first story or so, I'm betting you won't be the focus of it anymore." He nodded a lot while he said this—a lot—and it seemed mildly amusing that my son was trying to make me feel better about being part of a murder mystery that would show up in the local news stories.

"Thanks, dear. Now, drink your coffee, would ya?"

He nodded but somehow for once knew not to say any more right now. He dipped his face into the oversized mug and slurped loudly, probably trying to convince me he was more interested in the yumminess of the coffee than the goriness of the newspaper editor.

I wasn't the least bit fooled. This wasn't over yet. Not by a long shot.

Chapter 7

Seth was down in the basement of the apartment building doing a load of laundry—having swiped almost all of my remaining laundry detergent and two dryer sheets—when the phone rang. Despite the coffee, I had just settled in on the couch for a quick nap in the vain hope of regrouping mentally after the morning's escapades, and naturally the phone decided to go off at full blast as soon as I had passed the point of making to-do lists in my head and ventured into the corridors of sleepyland. It sounded like a three-alarm blaze was going off inside my head, and I bolted upright off the couch, blinking myself back to the reality of the apartment. Vlad had been lying tucked behind my bent knees while I was prostrate and didn't budge much when the phone rang. He barked at doorbells but not phones.

I knew people probably answered the phone during inconvenient and jarring times like this out of habit during their numbness. I answer the phone during inconvenient and jarring times merely to get the stupid thing to stop ringing.

"What?" I blurted rudely into the handset before realizing I hadn't made the proper transition back to wakefulness and had just communicated clearly my total annoyance in a single word.

"Gee, hi to you too, chickie." Helga. At least I hadn't offended someone to whom I would have to apologize properly later.

"Helga, it's you. Good. Sorry about the 'what?' thing. I was trying to take a nap."

"Yeah, because, like, your day's just been so boring, right?" She let out a snorting chuckle at her own sarcasm.

"Tell me about it. So I guess you heard everything then."

"Gee, ya think?" She was a real charmer when she wanted to be.

"Hey, it's not like I'm sitting here sucking in all the news I can. I'm trying really hard to just forget this ever happened. Wrong time and wrong place, you know what I mean?"

"Boy, and how! You couldn't have gotten a wronger time or place, could you?"

"Not really, no," I said, rubbing my eyes and feeling myself return to life, thinking there might be life after death after all. At least, after Gerber's death.

"Besides sounding sleepy, though, at least you sound like you," Helga continued. "Are you doing all right? Is there anything I can do?"

A charmer and a sweetheart. Quirky, but I loved this woman. "Thanks, no. I'm just sitting here in the apartment, taking a self-appointed day off from any freelance work, and trying really hard not to accidentally watch the local news. Or read a newspaper today."

Helga laughed.

"Oh wait," I added, sitting up straight and snapping full-awake. "*Is* there a newspaper today? What's going on down there? What happened when you guys started showing up for work this morning?"

"Girlfriend, you don't even want to know. If somebody had asked me beforehand, I would have said it'd feel like a snow day in school or something. But it hasn't been like that at all."

"I figured."

"Every time someone new showed up, the cops were all over 'em with questions and identification shit, and asking them where their desks are in here, what their jobs are, what they thought of Gerber Baby. The obvious stuff you'd see on *CSI*, ya know?"

"Yeah, that's the kind of stuff they asked me too. But more in-depth stuff too. About Gerber, and why I was there so early in the first place."

"Hell, I'd ask you that too—you're never up before the crack of noon."

"Yes, I am!" I protested, before catching myself and realizing she was ribbing me, as usual. "Anyway, it sounds one way in TV shows, but when they're asking *you* those questions, suddenly it sounds like they're accusing you of something."

Helga laughed. "Oh yeah. Maggie the murderer. How long do they think that would stick?"

"Helga, one more thing here before I forget. What's up with the paper today? I hate to ask the dull practical questions, but am I proofing anything today? I can't imagine you guys still putting out a paper today. But of course, you *are*, right? I mean, newspapers don't just stop because the boss dies."

"He didn't just die, Maggie. He was stabbed. It's a little bit different than something like a boring old heart attack. This is news to anybody, not just us here at the newspaper."

I sighed. She was right, of course. "So, there's a newspaper, but it's also front-page news tomorrow morning. Right?"

"Yup. You got it, chickie. Sorry. You might want to be on the lookout for a phone call from someone here at some point today. They're going to want some statement from you."

"No," I groaned. "Can't they just leave me alone?"

"I suppose they could, but do you really want them to?"

"Umm . . . *yes.*"

"No, you don't. If you don't talk to someone directly, they'll just put in some hearsay instead. Thirdhand stuff. It's probably better for you to talk to someone so you can at least explain your role in the whole thing. They probably can't keep you off the front page, though."

"Gee, that's helpful."

"I'm serious!"

"I know, I know. And I appreciate it. Honest. You're absolutely right, too. If I don't talk to whoever calls, I lose any control over the content. Maybe I can schmooze my way off the front page. I don't mind so much being part of the 'continued' page, but I'd love to be off the front page if possible."

"That's probably a long shot."

"You're just one big bundle of hope and encouragement today, aren't you?"

She laughed. "Sorry. Just trying to be honest about this. It doesn't help you any if I sugarcoat any of it and then you end up shocked and surprised when the paper comes out tomorrow morning."

"I should probably enjoy my last day of anonymity while I can, then?"

"Too late, chickie. Someone said they saw references to you on a news update snippet on channel four at lunchtime. Be careful walking around your neighborhood from now on. You're semi-famous. Oh, do you have caller-ID on that landline of yours?"

"Yeah, got it last summer when I was having the car payment problems. I'll be sure to be a little more discriminating about incoming calls then. Thanks for the heads-up on the news blurb."

"Okay then, so you're all right with some proofing later this afternoon . . . or no?"

"Yeah, that's fine. Tell Brenda to go ahead and send stuff over. I'm sure I'll feel a lot better doing something normal anyway."

"Good. I'll tell her. Do you mind proofing the cover story too, or would you rather we do that one in-house today?"

I hadn't thought about that, and offhand I wasn't sure whether I wanted to read the story or not. It's not like I needed the news update. I already knew more than I was going to read in the story. But still—did I want to be reading it officially and seeing what it was going to look like in print tomorrow morning?

Then again, it wasn't like I wouldn't *ever* see it. What were the chances I'd live out the rest of my days having never seen this story in print? As part of my proofing services, I had a free subscription to the paper, so it was going to show up on my doorstep tomorrow morning no matter what. Would it be easier on me to see it today under more businesslike circumstances, rather than being hit with it tomorrow over my morning coffee?

"Maggie? You there?"

"Oh, sorry, Helga. Just zoned out there for a minute. You know what? Go ahead and send it along with everything else. I think I'd rather see the article today than get hit with it in print tomorrow morning like the rest of the world."

"Good idea. I was hoping you'd say yes. Better to just look this thing square in the face, right?"

"Something like that."

"Now, I have one teensy question for you myself. Totally off the record, of course."

"Go ahead."

"Who do you think did it?"

"What?"

"You know, who killed Gerber Baby? Who stabbed him like that? I mean, we know it wasn't you. And it wasn't suicide. So, somebody is out there who stabbed the schmoozer right in the neck and then ran out."

Fair question, I had to admit. After all, that very question—the one at the heart of this whole episode—had been subtly nagging at the back of my thoughts since it happened this morning. I had been reacting too personally to my own experience and hadn't let that little voice creep to the forefront. And eventually it would. Because I had been part of a murder scene. I had found a murder victim. I hadn't just stumbled upon a dead or wounded animal. This was a human being—a very dead one, a very deliberately dead one. With blood and everything. A murder victim. Which implied a murderer was still out there somewhere. Which led us back to the real question, the one lurking behind all my petty personal questions. Who killed Lee Gerber, and why? The age-old question in any murder mystery: Whodunnit?

"Maggie? Earth to Maggie!"

I veered back into the conversation with Helga.

"Oh, sorry, Helga. I was just trying to think through that question myself. I mean, let's be honest about this: Did anybody here actually *like* Lee Gerber?"

"Offhand, sweets, no, I can't think of anyone. Most of us thought he was a real putz, you know?"

"Yeah, me included, unfortunately. Not good when the finder-of-the-body dislikes the person too."

"That doesn't make you a murderer, dear. Everybody dislikes a *lot* of people."

I sighed. "I know. And even though a lot of people weren't that fond of Gerber, that doesn't mean they want him dead, right? It's a huge jump from thinking he's a putz to stabbing him in the neck with his own letter opener. I mean, how un-freakin'-stable do you have to be to kill someone just because he annoys the crap out of you?"

Helga tittered, and I giggled in response. Serious though the topic was, there was that impulse in both of us to laugh at the outrageous aspect of the thing. It was easier to laugh since neither of us really knew the guy all that well.

"So, that means you don't think it was Brenda then? Or me?" She laughed at her own sick humor.

"No, I don't think it was you, Helga. Or Brenda. And probably not Ernest either—although I'm reserving final judgment on him till later. You know how typesetters are. He did give me a weird look yesterday when I came in to see you guys."

We both chuckled again. It felt good to laugh, even if it was at the expense of a dead guy and a coworker all at the same time.

"I tell ya, Mags, I wish I could have picked the brain of one of the cops who talked to us this morning. Because personally, I'd like to know if whoever did this is, like, sitting somewhere on the main floor here with me. Ya know?"

"I don't know. I have a gut feeling it's not someone new in Gerber's life. That just doesn't make much sense to me. None of you guys there have known him long enough to hate him enough to risk everything to kill him. Even if he was a sucko boss, he just wasn't a sucko boss long enough to warrant cold-blooded murder."

"Well, Little Miss Jessica Fletcher, aren't we the sleuth now?"

"I'm serious. I think you're all fine there, Helga. I wouldn't worry about some wacko there at the paper. If I were the police, I'd be looking at Gerber's past more than his present. I have a feeling there are more than enough enemies in his past to go around."

"You know, that makes a helluva lot of sense, Mags. Thanks, because I was really starting to feel a little creeped out sitting here at the front door with my back to everyone. And, just in case, I hid my letter opener in a bottom drawer when I first sat down."

"You didn't."

"I did."

I laughed. "Of course you did. Hey, listen. I have to grab some lunch here. And I have to scrounge up something for Seth too."

"Seth is there?"

"Yeah, he showed up at some point while I was out this morning. Scared the shit out of me when I came home and found someone in the house, but it's actually good that he's here. Feels better to have someone here to bounce stuff off of, even if it's just normal day-to-day stuff."

"Well, good. Then I feel a lot better about you being there in that apartment if you're not alone. Got that big strappin' boy with you. Good, good."

She sounded relieved. I hadn't truly realized till now—hearing it from someone else—that perhaps I should have been worried about my personal safety in my own home. It had occurred to me fleetingly at first, but since I worry about everything and analyze everything to death, I hadn't lent a whole lot of credence to my own concerns. Until they were echoed by Helga, who was usually a grab-life-by-the-scruff-of-the-neck type of gal. At the bottom of everything, there was indeed a killer still out there. Didn't matter whether he was from Gerber's past or his present—he was as yet uncaught and running free.

"Helga," I said, changing topics, "I think the main thing I have to communicate to any reporter the *Bugle* sends my way is that I didn't see or hear anything. That I came in well after the fact, and that I didn't help them in any way with any evidence or information. They know absolutely nothing more because of me than they would have known had they stumbled on Gerber's body themselves."

"Aha, yes. This is definitely an important point, girlfriend. You know *nussink*," she said, doing a passable imitation of Sergeant Schultz from *Hogan's Heroes*.

"Precisely. Not that our culprit necessarily reads the *Bugle*, but if he does, at least it'll be clear that I shouldn't be a target. I'd like to fade into the background as quickly as possible, thank you." I paused. "Am I officially whining now?"

"No, why?"

"Because I feel like I'm obsessing about this, that's all. Am I?"

"You? Obsess about something? *Please.*" She couldn't hide the sarcastic laugh, and I joined her. If I was known for anything around that office, it was my obsessing and nitpicking over absolutely everything. It was the very characteristic that made me a good proofreader. But it also made me a real bear to get along with or argue with. Just ask my ex-husband about that.

"Okay. I get it. Very funny."

"Actually, I don't think you're obsessing at all, given the nature of the circumstances here, Mags. I mean, you act exactly the same way when you're talking about the wrong typeface on an ad on page twenty-seven, for cryin' out loud. At least this time you have something to obsess about. Enjoy it for once."

"So, you don't think I'm, like, the boy who cried wolf or anything?"

There was a long pause. She was obviously thinking about this one. So it was possible that this was true then. Great. Just great.

"No, I don't think anyone's going to think of you that way, Mags. I see your point, but I think we all think of you as someone with . . . well, umm . . . a really *really* good attention to detail. That's all. I don't think anyone's going to think any worse of you if you fret about this a little more than usual. I know I would!"

"Helga, I think it's time for me to skedaddle. Seth'll be done with his laundry soon and he'll probably be ready to raid the fridge after that. Plus, I do have a few other things to straighten up around here before the PDF of the paper comes in. I really ought to shove off."

"No sweat. Listen, if you need anything, or if you just need to talk to someone, feel free to call, okay? I think most of us feel bad that you were the one who found Gerber Baby in his office like that. Not that any of *us* wanted to be the one to find him, but it just seems unfair that it was you. You just help us out a little bit each day, that's all."

That might be how she saw things—me just helping out a little—but to me the proofreading of the newspaper was one of those regular freelance jobs that helped keep me grounded in a basic income each month. The book proofreading was iffy, with some months seeing three or four books and other months with virtually no extra work at all. So, ongoing, regular jobs like proofreading the paper were good, steady income.

"Thanks, Helga. Do me a favor and call me if anything exciting develops down there."

"You mean, more exciting than having the editor murdered in his own office?"

"Well, more like, stuff you guys find out or overhear about what's happening with the investigation."

"No prob. Give that big strappin' Seth a hug and kiss from me."

"Consider it done. Just try to keep the gossip about me to a minimum."

"Consider it done."

CHaPTer 8

I KEPT MY SANITY THROUGHOUT THE AFTERNOON, with only occasional attacks of panic and cold sweats over the ongoing mental image of Lee Gerber slumped over his desk with a piece of shiny metal sticking out of his back. Seth, once his laundry was done, was a big help to have around the apartment, despite my nagging fear that he'd still be living here when he was forty and working the overnight shift at a local 7-Eleven. We watched some bad sitcom reruns on a low-end cable network and snacked on microwave popcorn that Seth nearly burned because he wasn't used to using a reliable microwave. Once we got the smoke detector to shut up, and once Seth finished wiping down the inside of the microwave—which was now permanently tinged an oily beige instead of its customary white—we sat on the couch while I waited for the PDF to come in.

Normally I did my laundry and cleaning during the early afternoons, since the PDF's arrival was unpredictable, varying slightly from day to day depending on when Brenda and Ernest could get it completely ready for me. I left the e-mail program open in my office, with the speakers on, and waited to hear its familiar *.wav* file ding at me, alerting me to any incoming mail needing my attention. Until then, it was popcorn and *Full House* time for me and Seth. The show was horrid, but much funnier now in reruns, although for very different reasons.

"Hey, Mom," Seth said during a commercial. "Have you given much thought to who might have killed your boss?"

"Seth, please," I urged, not ready to bring it up again.

"I don't mean to get you all upset or anything. But really—you've got to have some opinion about what happened, don't you? What did you know about the guy?"

"For one thing, he wasn't really my boss, per se. I just do freelance work for the paper, and he happened to be the new editor. We hadn't even really worked together in any capacity yet. That's partly what the morning meeting was about—getting us off the ground working together. I was hoping he could throw me some contact names from other book houses for more freelance work."

"So, who would want to kill someone like him?"

"You mean, besides *everybody*?"

Seth laughed. "What do you mean, everybody?"

"I mean, everybody. The man was a real pain in the ass, if you want the truth, Seth. He didn't seem to have much of a kind word for anybody—people he used to work for, people who work for him now, authors he used to represent, defendants he put away on jury duty. He's had jury duty three times. Three times! Who has jury duty three times in one lifetime? What are the odds? Even letters to the editor were already ganging up on the guy. And he had the stereotypical relationship with his ex-wife—or should I say, non-relationship? Because yes, of course he has an ex-wife. Do I need to go on?"

Seth crunched on a kernel from the bottom of the popcorn bowl. "Nope. I get the picture, loud and clear. A bastard. Got it."

I laughed, nearly snorting Diet Coke out my nose. "Yeah, that pretty much nails Lee Gerber in a word, I think. Don't get me wrong: I feel bad that he's dead, but it'll be quite a trick to narrow this down to just one person with a motive."

"Any idea who the cops think did it?"

"Not a clue. I only talked to them as long as I had to this morning and then I was out of there. And I have a feeling they aren't going to be telling me any of their pet theories on who did this."

"Mom, you know you're sharper than any of them anyway. And you know more about the situation already. At least it sounds that way to me. You could have this case solved in a day if you put your mind to it."

He was reaching to dig the last few kernels out of the bottom of the big plastic bowl, so I just handed it to him. "Thanks, dear. But I really don't want to put my mind to it. That's the point. I want out. I'm already in too deep. I happen to like my little routine, adventureless life, thank you very much. I don't want to start playing Monk in my spare time."

He laughed. "Monk. That's probably not too far from the truth, is it?"

"Very funny," I scoffed, whacking him on the head with one of the puffy throw pillows at my end of the sofa. "Did you leave me any laundry detergent?"

"Maybe just enough for one load—if it's not too dirty."

"Figures. Well, no problem. A little grocery shopping won't hurt tonight after the paper's done. I'll make up a list, so you be sure to tell me what you want me to have in the house. Every time I try to buy stuff I think you like, you tell me you haven't liked it since fourth grade."

"Just get Hot Pockets and show me where you keep coupons for Pizza Joe's. Nothing fancy."

"And Diet Dr. Pepper."

"You know it."

"Easy enough. Although it wouldn't kill you to eat a salad every once in a while."

"Yes it would. I don't think I'm quite finished building up an immunity to greens, so until then I'm not taking any chances."

I downed the last of my soda and slowly crunched the aluminum can in one fist. "Someone from his past. Not now."

"What?"

"It has to be someone Gerber knew before he came here."

Seth sat up straight, putting the empty popcorn bowl on the coffee table in front of him. "Meaning what? What?" Suddenly he was more than a little interested.

"I mean, just what I said. Whoever killed Lee Gerber probably knew him before now."

"Mom, I can see the wheels turning in that nitpicker brain of yours. You know more than you're telling in there. Cough it up!"

He turned directly toward me now, one leg up on the couch and the other planted firmly on the floor. To him, of course, this was mostly an academic exercise. For me, it was more about keeping *me* on the back burner in terms of the police and their theories about who did this. Knowing it was foolish to think someone like me could have killed Gerber—someone who had absolutely no personal stake in the man and not even enough time with him to develop a solid hatred—left only one other option: someone else, someone not from around here.

"Mom, what if it was some weird random act of violence?"

"What, like a drive-by stabbing or something?"

"Well . . ." he stammered.

"Because, of course, it makes perfect sense that someone broke into the building early this morning, knowing there was one person in there alone, made their way into his office, probably unarmed but wanting to kill someone randomly, and—"

"Why do you say unarmed?"

"Because Gerber was stabbed with his own letter opener. If someone had brought in a gun or a knife, wouldn't they have used that instead? Seems to me it's iffy at best to try to stab someone with a letter opener, even if it is a really nice sturdy one."

Seth smiled and shook his head slowly. "See?"

"See what?"

"You *have* been thinking about this. Without even knowing it. It's like it comes naturally to you. You can't help but proofread everything in life, even a murder."

"Proofreading a murder? What does that mean?"

"Just what it sounds like, Mom. You're nitpicking every little detail of this just like you do words on a page. You notice things. You can't help it. If I asked you where I dropped my left shoe when I came in and took off my shoes this morning, you'd know, wouldn't you?"

"It's sticking out from under the back of the recliner."

"See?"

"Seth, that's a mom thing, not a proofreader thing. My mother could do that too, and she's not a proofreader. All moms do it. It's part of that eyes-in-the-back-of-the-head thing we get during childbirth. That, and an extra twenty pounds of ugly fat we'll never get rid of."

"No, with you it's more than that."

"Hey!"

"That's not what I meant."

"I know."

"Seriously, I think you should see if the police want any help."

"No, no, no. I'm not getting involved in any of that, Seth. They know what they're doing, and I'm sure they're much further along than I am in all this. They get paid to think through this stuff. They don't ask for help from civilians."

"That doesn't mean they always get things right."

"Seth, *no.* I don't have any interest in being an amateur cop. Not this time. I just had that *one* thought about the killer being not me, being someone far away from me, probably literally."

"That's enough, though. It'll stick in your mind after this. I know you. You won't be able to let this go until you figure it out. You're the one who searches for your spare reading glasses for three hours straight, because you just have to see everything through to its logical conclusion."

He had a point. I did have a stick-tuitiveness that drove everyone around me crazy. But honestly, did I want to tackle a murder investigation, even in my spare time? Even if it was one that got me involved personally right off the bat?

"Seth, listen. I don't want to deal with this. Just because I can, just because I might be able to do it well doesn't mean I want to. This is just a little too close to home for me. I don't want to be involved in this any more than I am now. I just want the police to find the real killer and convict the bastard, and then we can all get on with our lives. That's the goal for me—to get beyond this, not to get involved."

Seth stood up, grabbing the empty popcorn bowl off the coffee table and heading for the kitchen. Vladimir woke suddenly, bolted off the couch to follow Seth. When anyone headed for the kitchen, Vlad was in it for the possible food involved.

"All I know," Seth called from the kitchen, "is that you won't be able to let this go. You might keep it to yourself, but you'll be solving this one in your head all the time now. Until you come up with who did this. And I predict you get it done before the cops do."

I heard the big plastic bowl hit the sink and then Seth's footsteps coming back my way. I sat still on the couch, one hand on the warm spot next to me where Vlad had been moments earlier. Vlad was still tagging along behind Seth, hoping for food or a treat, as Seth appeared back in the living room, now standing to the left of the recliner, arms akimbo.

"You know I'm right," was all he said.

I looked at him blankly, not wanting to engage him in this particular conversation any longer. I feared he might be right, and the prospect of not being able to let this go terrified me. It was the last thing I needed right now. Life was going well for me lately. Jobs were coming in steadily. Both kids were doing all right—well, until today when Seth showed up at my door. But at least he was healthy and reasonably well-adjusted, if gainfully unemployed and semi-homeless.

"Mom?"

Ding-ding-dong! The computer speakers down the hall alerted me to incoming mail. Probably the PDF of the day's newspaper.

"Seth, that's the proofreading I was waiting for. We're going to have to continue this conversation later. The sooner I get this particular job done, the better off I'll be."

"Okay. I'll just . . . hold down the fort out here till you're done."

I looked around the mundane living room. Aside from the scenes skittering around the television screen, it hardly looked like anything ever happened in this room. Nothing to hold down a fort over, really. And that was a pretty accurate assessment of my entire life. And I liked it that way.

"Okay. You do that," I chuckled, standing and heading down the hall to my office, Diet Coke in hand. The PDF was waiting for me as I suspected, and I double-clicked the attachment icon on Brenda's e-mail and it was onscreen in a matter of seconds. There, taking up my entire twenty-five-inch monitor screen, was tomorrow morning's headline: "*Bugle* Editor Slain in Office: Proofreader Finds Body."

This not-getting-involved thing was going to be a little harder than I thought.

CHAPTER 9

B Y THE END OF DAY TWO of my little adventure in homicide, I was beginning to understand what Marlene Dietrich was all about. I secretly wondered if I could buy a pair of dark sunglasses in western Pennsylvania in November. It was probably hard enough to find a good pair in July, let alone this time of year. Then again, a ball cap and sunglasses were probably more obvious than just winging it and going out in public like normal. I was grateful the newspaper hadn't put a picture of me anywhere in the story on Gerber's murder—they wouldn't have, of course, but the fear was still there—and so no one who didn't already know me would recognize me if I was out in public. Especially if I paid for things in cash. Being a minor celebrity wasn't all I would have guessed it to be before this all started. Who knew I could find a sympathetic soft spot for Tom and Katie or Brad and Angelina among all this confusion and personal fear?

Seth fielded phone calls for me deftly, and I appreciated his presence a little more with each passing hour during those first few days. When his sister Annie called, though, he mistakenly thought I'd want to talk to her and quickly let on that I was indeed there and available. He didn't see me standing across the room waving my arms wildly, indicating that no, I didn't really want to talk to Annie right now.

"Sure, she's right here. No, she's fine—just avoiding any extra press coverage and trying really hard to crawl under a rock and hide." He laughed at something Annie said. "I know. I thought the same thing. Anyway, here she is."

And with that, he finally turned in my direction, as I continued to wave my arms frantically. Then it hit him that I hadn't any desire to talk to my daughter right now. He gave me a look of "oops!" and sheepishly held out the receiver in my direction. As I came closer and swiped the handset out of his hands with a bit of a miffed snap, he mumbled a low "Sorry, Mom" and walked back toward my office to get away from what he saw as a possible mental explosion on the horizon.

"Annie! Hi!" I gushed into the handset, hoping I sounded as cheery as I needed to, to keep her from worrying beyond her usual fretty condition.

"Mom, are you all right?"

"Fine, dear."

"Why didn't you call me? I had to find out about this by reading the newspaper? *Online?*"

"Sweetheart, it's not my fault you're too young to get into watching the evening news each night just for the weather forecast. Wait till you hit forty. You'll understand." *That's good. Make light of things; change the topic a little too. Act and sound normal.*

"Mom, I'm serious. So Seth's there then too? So, what? You called him, but not me?"

"Annie, no. He showed up here all on his own while I was, well, while I was . . . you know . . . being interviewed by the police yesterday morning."

"And yet you still didn't call here. Mom, didn't it occur to you that your own daughter might want to know if you were involved in a murder?" The sound of nineteen-year-old indignation was almost comical. Like nineteen-year-old college students had anything to be really indignant about yet.

"Annie, let's get this clear up front: We don't say your mother was 'involved in a murder,' okay? I wasn't involved in any murder. I just happened to stumble on a crime scene . . . before anyone else did. It could have happened to anyone. It just so happened, that it happened to me. It's nothing more than that."

When I put it that way, it sounded downright dull. Too bad I had a feeling Annie wouldn't be easily convinced by such shallow argumentation.

"Sorry, Mom. That's not cutting it. I read the article—the *whole* article. You're in this up to your neck. I know it, and you know it."

"Meaning what?" I insisted. It sounded like she was accusing me of something.

"We both know how you are. How you get. Once you get latched onto something, you can't let it go. Remember that time with Dad?" I hoped she wouldn't go bringing that up . . . again. It was her favorite "told-you-so" story with me, and I wasn't in the mood for a lesson-learnin' from my younger child right about now.

"I'm not latched onto anything. In fact, ask Seth: I'm trying really hard to just get myself forgotten so I can go back to my lovely, boring life. I like boring. Honest."

"So you say, but I don't believe you for a minute. You're probably already playing little CSI games with yourself trying to figure this out on your own, aren't you?"

Was this a conspiracy against me?

"Annie, really. I desperately want things to go back to normal around here. I don't like the idea that I have to hide from my neighbors when I'm grocery shopping because everyone wants to talk about the dead, bloody body I found first thing yesterday morning. I like things dull and boring and lifeless—well, not *lifeless*. Poor choice of words. Let's just say I like things dull and boring. I mean, hey—look at your father!"

Annie and Seth never appreciated the ex-husband jokes, for some reason. I had a sneaking suspicion they still liked their father a smidgeon more than I did after all these years. They didn't begrudge me the George-the-ex jokes, but they didn't really laugh at them, either. They weren't overly talkative about their dad with me—they'd long since learned I didn't really find him the fascinating topic of conversation they still did—and so I rarely got a good response out of them whenever I tried to pass off the ex jokes. But hey, a girl needs a defense mechanism, right?

"Mom, I'm serious," Annie said, and I could hear her clicking her tongue in a judgmental "tsk-tsk" noise over the phone. She had definite opinions on this and I had a sneaking suspicion I was about to hear most of them. "You know you're going to start making charts and lists and stuff trying to figure this all out. I just don't want you doing any of that stuff."

"But I'm not doing any of that 'stuff,'" I protested. "Seth keeps saying the same thing, but honestly, I haven't really made any lists or anything. I'm just thinking about it a little bit—but give me a break here. That's just natural under the circumstances, I think. Isn't it? Wouldn't anyone in my shoes think at least a little bit about who did the horrible thing they saw? You'd have to be some kind of cold-hearted monster not to care what the heck happened to someone you found stabbed like that!"

I sounded a bit defensive, but she was going to launch into finger-wagging mode—even on the phone—if I didn't find a way out of this conversation.

"Mom, listen to me: I don't want you to get any more involved in this than you already are. It started out as an accident but I don't want you deciding you know more than the police do on this, okay?"

"Why would I think that?" I said, challenging the ongoing assumption that I was going to dive in and become the local Kojak (minus the lollipop and plus the hair). This was definitely beginning to feel like a conspiracy. And I was quickly running out of television detectives with which to compare myself.

"Mom, I don't want you getting hurt! Promise me!"

"Promise you what, exactly?" I was one of those mothers who disliked when her offspring tried to turn the tables on her and play mommy in return. I was over forty, for crying out loud. Plenty old enough to make at least some of my own decisions. Meanwhile, she wasn't any closer to picking a major, so I wasn't sure she should talk. Kids.

I was just about to launch into a little mommy tirade on her—a relatively good-natured one this time—when the doorbell rang. Phone still glued to my ear, I looked down the hallway in desperation, hoping Seth had heard it too. I needed him to run interference for me with the doorbell even more than with the phone. At least the phone had caller-ID on it to give me a heads-up on whether or not to answer it if he wasn't available. But the doorbell was a completely different matter. I was in a second-floor apartment and the bell rang from the outside front door—which I couldn't see clearly from any window in my apartment. Our building was small—only four apartments—and we didn't have any sort of intercom system. So, answering the door was always a crap shoot of fear if I had a potential "guest" I was dreading. Like today.

Seth came dashing out of my office just as the doorbell rang the second time. I pointed to the door and he nodded in understanding. Good.

"Annie? I have to cut this short. The doorbell just rang."

"You're not going to answer the *door*, are you?" The sheer indignation in her little high voice was comical.

"Well, not *me*, no. Seth's on his way down the steps to answer it for me. He's been screening the phone calls for me too. That all right with you?"

"Mom, don't get all sarcastic on me. I'm just trying to help."

"But, sweetie, you're not helping if you're just accusing me of things and getting upset on the phone. I can take care of myself. Honest. And Seth's here for a while yet, so that should be a load off your mind, right?"

She wasn't Seth's biggest fan, but surely even she could see the value in having him here right now, especially if her concern was for my safety. She sighed.

"Fine."

"I do have to go, though. I want to see who's at the door and see if Seth's doing all right down there fending them off for me."

"No way. I'm waiting on the line until you tell me who it is at the door."

I sighed. "Okay. Hang on." I took the cordless handset with me and leaned out the front door of my apartment, which Seth had inadvertently left wide open. So much for trying to hide in the apartment.

From downstairs I could hear Seth talking to two people he'd encountered at the front door, a man and a woman. I quietly leaned a little further into the hallway, cupping my hand over the mouthpiece of the phone and listening intently to whatever words I might hear wafting up the staircase from the first floor. After only a moment I leaned back into the apartment and walked back toward the kitchen, away from the still-open door.

"Annie? You still there?"

"Yes, Mother. Waiting to hear if it's the police or the serial killer at the front door," she said impatiently. The girl had no sense of humor. Must take after her father, I thought.

"For your information, it wasn't a serial killer, Annie. Probably just someone who was really mad at Mr. Gerber, that's all."

"So? Who's at the door?" Still impatient. She was probably late for another class-missing opportunity or a nice long nap or something.

I chuckled. "No need to worry, hon. It's just your grandparents. Probably here to bitch-slap me for getting my name in the newspaper for something other than writing an article myself."

She didn't laugh or even chuckle. Definitely takes after her father. "Well, if they don't slap you for it, I certainly will!" Her frustration—and dare I say loving concern?—was evident in her quivering voice.

"Well, now you know I'm safe. Grandma won't let anything happen to me. She'll just beat up the guy with that lead-weight pocketbook of hers and the guy'll die of a massive cerebral hemorrhage."

"Mom . . ."

"You know what I mean. I now have half the known world here at my door, Annie. You can come home if you want this weekend, but don't come all the way up here just because of me. I'm obviously being well taken care of. In fact, so well taken care of I'm probably going to go nuts by the weekend anyway."

There was a noticeable silence at her end of the phone. "Okay," she said finally. "I'm not really happy about all this, but at least the family's there keeping an eye on you."

"Thanks for the vote of confidence, dear."

"Just make sure you call me if anything else happens."

"Like . . . a dead body in the bathtub or something?"

"Mom . . ."

"Lighten up, Annie. It was a joke. Try to remember what a joke is before you call again, all right? I'm fine. And yes, I promise to call you if anything new develops."

"Promise?"

"Promise."

She hung up just as I turned to face the front door and saw Peter and Vicki Velam stride through the door like two people on a mission. And, in their own minds, at least, they were. And, as I would have guessed, my mother was carrying food.

"Mom, hi!" I said preemptively, hugging her, but this didn't stop her from launching into a conversation as though we'd started it hours ago and had only been interrupted by a cough or a sneeze somewhere along the line.

"Maggie, darling! We saw the newspaper this morning. We went to bed early last night and didn't see it on the eleven o'clock news, so imagine our surprise to get up this morning and find you in the front page story! A *murder*! Are you all right? Seth tells us you're all right . . ."

"I'm fine, Mom. Really."

"Food. We brought you food. Nothing quite like a good casserole to warm the soul. You know what I mean?" She shoved a nine-by-thirteen casserole dish at me, with a blue plastic cover on it. I took the handles in my hands just before the dish would have slipped between us and landed on the floor in a million pieces. One whiff told me it was probably her chicken and rice casserole.

It would be nice to skip cooking tonight. I leaned in and kissed her quickly on the cheek.

"Thanks. This'll definitely help ease the pain and suffering of being a hometown celebrity today."

My dad wedged himself between me and my mom and hugged me fiercely. "Only our Maggie would use up her fifteen minutes of fame by finding a dead body in an office building. Way to go, kiddo." We both laughed. My parents were the kind of people who instilled tension and stress in their children just by being themselves. But on those rare occasions when the stressors and tension-inducers were things outside of my relationship with them, then suddenly they were sources of peace and stability. Amazing how they managed to turn the tables like that, but they always did. I guess that was part of being a parent: being able to rally and get behind the offspring in their time of need.

I moved several plastic containers around in the fridge, making a mental note to deal with one or two that looked particularly suspicious, and made room for the glorious life-saving casserole.

"Where's Seth?" I asked.

"Oh, he's in the living room with your father. I think they're going through the 'look how much you've grown' thing they always do whenever your father sees him."

"But he's been the same height since he was seventeen," I counter.

"I know that. And you know that. And I think your father knows that. But it's one of those time-honored rituals that makes your father feel like the patriarch he secretly thinks he is." She smiled. She constantly made disparaging remarks like this about my dad, but she adored him and it was always done with a ridiculous amount of affection behind it. I wondered, as I often did when I saw them together, how such a stable marriage could have produced such a neurotic progeny. But that was a pondering best left for the therapist's couch. Too bad I couldn't afford a therapist.

My mom came over and put her arm around my shoulder. "Was it . . . horrible? Yesterday morning?"

I sighed and nodded. "It was pretty bad, yeah. Messy." She winced. "Bloody." She winced again. "And downright gory, if you really want to know." She winced again.

"I'm not sure that I *did* want to know, now that you put it that way."

"Sorry, Mom. Didn't mean to gross you out. Let's just say I'm glad it's over, and I hope it never happens again."

Her eyes widened. "Why would it happen again? Who finds *two* dead bodies with letter openers in their necks? It's just not something that happens twice in one lifetime!"

"Couldn't agree with you more, Mom. Once was plenty for me."

She moved in closer and, in a confidential whisper near my ear, she asked, "So, who do you think did this awful thing?"

Apparently I wasn't going to be able to get out of this predicament any time soon. As much as everyone in my family talked about wanting me to stay uninvolved and to get as far away from this situation as possible, they were all doing their level best to make sure I stayed intrigued and fascinated by it all. And knowing how I was about nitpicking things to death, it was only natural that I'd end up overthinking the situation at some point. They were all fanning the flame, even if they swore up and down that they were merely trying to keep me out of harm's way. They all wanted to know whodunnit. It was unavoidable. *Everybody* found this sort of thing fascinating. That's why murder mysteries sell so well, and why the whodunnit thriller is always a hit movie.

And if the average citizen couldn't help getting involved in the story and trying to figure out what happened to Gerber, how was a person with my personal involvement and attention to detail going to avoid it? I was doomed. I was going to follow this story through to its conclusion whether my parents liked it or not. Whether my children liked it or not. Whether my coworkers liked it or not. Whether *I* liked it or not. And right now, I most definitely did not like it. But somehow I had a feeling that what I liked or didn't like about this whole situation didn't really matter anymore.

CHAPTER 10

D
AY THREE OF MAGGIE'S BIG ADVENTURE found me getting in my car and meandering around town for at least a half hour before I got up the nerve to drive to the *Bugle* office and park in the parking lot. Then it took me another fifteen minutes to muster the courage to open the car door, get out, and walk to the door to go in. Small things I used to take for granted but probably never would again.

The last time I'd been in this office, it hadn't been filled with the normal array of people, all sitting at their desks and working, or milling around doing some important errand related to their work. Hustle and bustle now. Quiet and foreboding then. Today it seemed more, well, *alive*, without the obvious implications. I was glad to see all the people back in their usual spots.

Well, all in their usual spots except one. Down at the very end of the main aisle was the door to Lee Gerber's office. The door was closed and I could see through its side window that the lights were off. There was yellow crime scene tape strapped across the door frame to ward off any would-be curiosity seekers. I stood just inside the main door at the other end of that aisle, hoping to catch Helga's eye while she chattered on the phone with a client. She saw me and offered a little fluttery wave with one hand while she continued to chat.

I shifted the manila folder I was carrying to my other hand and sat in one of the chairs that marked off a small waiting area at the front of the expansive main room. I tried not to look down the aisle at that closed door and dark office. But, of course, it was all I could look at. The light made it look like there was a small shiny puddle of dark red blood oozing out from under the wooden door. Most likely it was a trick of my mind and not really the light. There was no puddle. I was just overreacting in my usual way.

"Pssst. Mags! Over here!"

It was Helga, motioning to me over the top of the counter that separated her desk from the rest of the world. Some previous editor, long before I did freelance work for the paper, had decided that having the high countertop along the outside edge of the main desk just inside the door made the place seem more businesslike and professional. I think it just made it easier for Helga to make faces behind her desk without getting caught. She would probably agree.

I hopped up from my seat, grateful for the distraction from my obsession with Gerber's office door, and leaned over the high counter.

"The cops have been back here off and on constantly for two days now. They won't tell us anything! They just come in, go back to the office, fiddle around, and then carry out a paper bag all stapled shut. What's up with that? Or sometimes they'll come in and call one of us aside and talk to us in the back room. Whatever it is they're thinking in those little starched uniform brains of theirs, they're not telling. Frustrating as hell."

"Wow, and I thought I had it bad. They haven't really contacted me except on that first day. Looks like I got off easy compared to you guys. Who'da thunk it?" I grinned, and it felt good to be back among the living, the silly, and the Helga. She was a real balm for the spirit today.

"Hey, no kidding. Here we were all worried that they were going to haunt you for weeks, and they figure out right away you're a total pushover who wouldn't say 'shit' if her mouth was full of it. Meanwhile, we poor lowly schmucks get pushed around by the powers that be for days, all over some boss we barely knew."

"Sucks to be you guys," I said. Helga clicked her tongue at me sharply, but I ignored it and continued. "Listen, I have to go see Brenda about this one ad and two of the articles. The markups got a little weird and I thought, since I had to go out and run a few errands anyway, I'd stop in and go over all the scribbles with her in person to make sure they're clear. Is she in?" I glanced back and to the left toward the prepress room—the only separate room on this floor besides Gerber's office. The door was closed, but that door was usually closed. Neither Brenda nor Ernest was overly social by nature, and they both had trouble doing any serious work with the typical noise level of the main floor. All they liked to hear was the tippy-tapping of their own fingers on keyboards and the subtle sound of computer mice edging around their mouse pads. Weird birds, both of them, but really nice people to work with. Easy, straightforward, clear-thinking. This would be a quick meeting, at least. And productive. I liked productive. It made me feel empowered, especially after a few days of feeling horribly powerless and out of control.

Helga glanced over her shoulder to the prepress room. "Yup, both of them are in today. And they're really keeping that door ultra-closed too. I don't think either one of them has come out of there since this morning, not even for lunch. I think they both figured out that if they pack their lunches, they can stay in there all day."

I found this perversely fascinating. "Why wouldn't they want to come out all day?"

She stole a glance around the main floor, as if someone might actually be eavesdropping. I was pretty sure it was more for effect—to add a certain level of mystique to the idea. "Because they're hiding from the fuzz."

I snorted. "I don't think anyone calls them 'the fuzz' anymore, Helga. And why on earth would someone like Brenda or—even worse—Ernest need to hide from the police?" The mere thought was absurd.

"Have you taken a good look at that guy lately? He's quiet. He's a loner. He's shy. He probably has a stalker-crush on Miley Cyrus or something. You know . . . pictures of her all over his room, lives with his parents, real serial killer profile all the way." She was talking in a low whisper now, exaggerating everything she was saying by look-ing around furtively but trying to look as obvious as possible.

"Aha, I see. Serial killers. Gotcha. Well, that was easy."

"What? What was easy?"

"Figuring out this murder. Everyone in my family is convinced that I shouldn't try to figure out who the killer is on my own *and* that I'm going to try to figure out who the killer is on my own."

She laughed. "You can pick your friends, but you can't pick your family. And—"

"No, Helga. No nose-picking jokes, please. They're beneath you."

"Ha! No joke is beneath me, toots. You should know that about me by now."

I did. "Don't even go there. I'm going back to catch Brenda be-fore you make me forget why I came here." She made a kissy noise as I walked past her desk and off to where the prepress room sat locked down tight like a submarine. I knocked on the door before opening it and peeking my head inside.

"Yoo hoo. Just me. Is Brenda here?" I said into the room, to no one in particular.

"Maggie! Come on in!" Brenda called from behind her over-sized computer monitor. "I was just wondering when I was going to hear from you. I thought maybe those pages got lost in the e-mail ether or something."

"Got 'em right here with me. I wanted to explain some of my little red scribbles to you. There was one page in particular that had so much on it that by the end it dawned on me to just come on in here myself and show them to you in person."

"No problem. Most outsiders these days are, well, you know—in blue uniforms. It's good to see a familiar face that dresses in civvies." She winked.

"I tried talking to Helga about everything that's been going on here, but I think she feels a little exposed out there at the front desk. She joked a little about whispering and conspiracies and such, but I didn't really get a good handle on what's going on with the police. I'm dying for a little gossip—as long as it doesn't involve me!"

She smiled. "First off, there isn't much happening back here, and Ernest and I like it that way." She indicated quiet, serial-killer-material Ernest sitting across the room behind his own mammoth monitor, tap-tap-tapping away, probably on corrections I'd sent in earlier before leaving the apartment on those errands. Ernest quietly indicated his own presence with a small wave of the hand and kept his eyes glued to the monitor.

"I will say this, though," she continued. "They came in here the first day and asked for copies of all the newspapers ever since Gerber Baby first came here a few weeks ago."

Apparently everyone in the office was calling him "Gerber Baby," not just Helga.

"And then, yesterday morning, three of them came back to question some of us some more. And they came back in here to talk to Ernest and me. I was hoping we'd get out of it since we barely knew the guy and really, we live in our own little world back here, you know?"

I nodded. "So why did they need to talk to you guys?" My mind immediately sprang to images of Ernest sewing girls' skins together to make a suit and carrying a little white poodle around the office. I shook the image out of my mind, but it tried to linger in a vulgar, nasty way. I had to stop watching so much cable TV.

"It wasn't really about us, per se. It was about what we might know. About that letter-to-the-editor guy. The disgruntled one who writes in here all the time. Remember?" I did remember. The guy hadn't given Gerber a moment to breathe in his new job as editor before he was writing letters to the editor bitching and complaining about how the paper was being run. But, we knew he did this with every editor the *Bugle* ever had, so none of us took it personally. We weren't so sure Gerber knew not to take it personally. My guess was that no one wanted to spoil the fun of watching Gerber squirm over unhappy readers. But, from what little I knew of Gerber's personality, he probably wouldn't have taken someone like that very seriously. At least not for long, and at least not publicly. Better to put on a good solid front for the huddled masses.

His monster ego might have felt vulnerable knowing a detractor was putting out false negative information about him, but it seems he never let on if it bothered him. He never tried to pull any of the letters or censor them in any way. My best guess was that it did bother him but he realized it was better to stay professional about the whole thing. He might even have heard or figured out that this one guy in particular had an ax to grind with every other editor before him.

"So, you think the cops have an eye on the letter writer?" I asked.

She nodded, "Yeah, at least from back here where I sit. I'm not saying they don't have anyone else in mind, but I know they at least have him in mind. Maybe he'll be out of the running in a few days, who knows? I guess it depends on whether or not they talked to him, and what they found out when they did."

"But he usually publishes his letters as 'Anonymous,' doesn't he?"

"Well, yes, but we don't publish just any letter that comes in here. The person has to at least sign the letter when it comes to the paper, even if they don't want their name on the letter when—and if—it gets published."

"And you guys just gave out that information?"

"We had to. This is a murder investigation. Of our own editor. And, we kept our word: we didn't publish the guy's name! Hey, I just handed over the letters file. I didn't peek inside!"

I laughed. Close enough for government work, I guess.

"You and Ernest don't really think he did it, though, do you?"

She shook her head forcefully. "No, not a bit. He's harmless. And he wasn't any more pissed off at Gerber Baby than he was at any other editor before him. In fact, by this point in time with Sparrow, he really had a good head of steam going and was writing us letters at least once a week—sometimes more."

"Within the first month of Kevin getting here?" I asked. It hardly seemed possible. Kevin Sparrow was such a good, even-tempered editor with good instincts and a fair sense of business.

"Yup. Hated Kevin with a passion. Don't get me wrong: I think Gerber was well on his way to rivaling that position in short order, but for some reason this guy started out a little slower than he did with Sparrow. I just don't see the guy actually making a physical appearance anywhere to do the guy in. He seems like a strictly behind-the-scenes, low-level stalker conspiracy theorist. He might publish a newsletter or have a blog or a website, but he's not venturing out of his own house to stab someone." She shuddered.

"I see your point. And I think you're right. Someone with a history of this sort of letter-writing, over the course of years and several editors in rapid succession, doesn't start on a killing spree all of a sudden. There's no rhyme or reason to it."

"Anyway, that was our excitement back here. Huh, Ernest?" she said, calling over her shoulder back to Ernest. His eyes just barely peeped above the monitor and he nodded his little tufts of hair in agreement. "So, where are these red-inked pages you're dying to explain to me?" she asked, eyeing the manila folder with way too much curiosity for her own good. These typesetters needed to get a life.

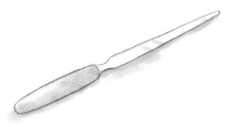

CHaPTer 11

I STOOD AGAIN AT THE FRONT DESK small-talking with Helga for longer than I probably should have. I still had things to do at home—including whipping one adult son into shape before he drove me crazy—but it felt good to chat with Helga, an eternal beacon of delight when I needed a distraction from the frustrations of everyday life. She started on a litany of gossip updates on everyone seated on the main floor of the *Bugle*, and it was fun to listen to her go down each row systematically, giving me the dirt on each person as she understood it at the moment. Her take on everyone else was certainly enlightening, and I secretly wondered what it would be like to work with her on a daily basis, sitting at one of those desks and being just another in her series of gossip-names for others coming in from the outside world. More likely, I'd be back in the prepress room with Ernest and Brenda—now there was a scary thought—and then Helga's gossipy tongue would have a different slant to it. She was slightly kinder to Brenda and Ernest, but more than likely this was solely because she didn't see them as regularly and therefore just didn't know them as well. They were both also a little quieter than many here at the paper, so that alone could have accounted for Helga's lack of information about their worldly exploits. In any case, I had fun with it because she did. Nothing scandalous—well, hardly—and nothing vindictive. Just the fun sort of stuff that made stopping in at the *Bugle* office less than the chore it should have been for a freelancer like myself. In this age of so much technology, I had to do a lot less foot travel to get projects done, but every so often a face-to-face was still necessary. Especially with the speed and clamor of a daily newspaper.

I still did a lot of my book projects for publishers across the country by Federal Express or UPS Next Day Air—hard copy wasn't fading as fast as a lot of the technology pundits had thought in the earlier, headier days of declaring the future of the paperless office. A few clients had transitioned to PDF markups or Word's Track Changes feature, but many editors still liked the tried and true feel of hard copy, real paper and real red ink on that paper. I had to agree. There wasn't anything quite like taking a three-inch stack of paper and slowly but systematically turning page after page, marking up mistakes, highlighting and red-flagging items for the editor to look at, and watching the "done" pile slowly creep up and the "to do" pile slowly go down. It was probably why some writers still used typewriters: Sometimes you just have to see the paper move. You have to see the words appear on the page—an actual page, not a white screen with shadowy features to make it seem like a page.

At some point I came out of this meandering reverie about proofreading, realizing what such musings must say about me as a person, and and Helga was just finishing up her laundry list of who did what with whom and at what office party they did it.

"Helga, I really gotta go. Seth's holding down the fort at home, and he can do his own laundry, but I'm still the one doing mine. I gotta get back and get a load in the washer before I run out of clean jeans."

"That'd be a disaster for sure."

"Would you do me a favor and give me a buzz if the cops come in here again asking questions? I'm curious where they're going with this, and they're obviously not going to be stopping at my house to update me. In fact, the only reasons they would come to my house to talk to me all seem like bad ones, so the less I see of them, the better."

"No sweat. And if there's too much excitement going on, and I can't be blabbing things out loud over the phone, I'll quietly e-mail you instead."

"Wait, I have a better idea. Since I'll be working on the computer off and on for the rest of the afternoon, we can text each other if something happens here."

"Yeah, that works better. Less paper trail that way, too."

"I doubt that. You'd be surprised just how much of what you type on that little screen—on any phone—can be found later if someone knows how to look for it. Be careful online, too, Helga. There really are people watching you. Especially at a big place like this one . . . during a murder investigation, no less."

"True. I'll phone if at all possible. And if we text, I'll try to be as discreet and innocent sounding as possible."

"Good. We have a plan then."

I swear, as God is my witness, I was going to leave at that precise moment—I had every intention of walking through the front door and heading for my car. I would have been home in a short while and safe and sound in my little dull apartment, content to go on with life and getting it more and more back to normal.

But, at this precise moment in time, a rather frumpy middle-aged woman came into the front door of the *Bugle* offices and landed right at Helga's desk, panting, mostly likely from climbing the bazillion front steps outside the building. Fascinated by the prospect of someone in the building who wasn't getting paid to be there—and who obviously wasn't a police officer or a reporter from elsewhere trying to get a scoop or a lead on the Gerber murder story—I had to stay and see who this fish out of water really was.

I stood slightly behind the woman, facing Helga as she herself did, and shrugging subtly at Helga as if to say, "Beats me who this creature is." Helga looked from the woman to me and back again, taken aback slightly herself by the presence of what Helga fondly called an "outsider."

"May I help you?" Helga finally asked courteously, trying to look and sound as professional as she could given the fact that she rarely got to practice her people skills except on the telephone. I stood stock still behind the strange woman, trying hard not to laugh at Helga's obvious jolt back to reality.

"Yes," said the chubby woman. "I'm here to see Lee Gerber. I have a one o'clock appointment with him."

My jaw dropped open, and I could see Helga forcing herself not to let the same thing happen to her own jaw. Well, this was certainly a fine development. Did this woman, who apparently must have had *no* access to local news coverage of any sort, really belong visiting the editor of a newspaper anyway? How had she missed this story over the past couple of days?

"Gerber?" was all Helga could manage to say to the woman.

"Yes, the editor. Mr. Lee Gerber. I'm here for my appointment." The woman looked around, apparently hoping to catch sight of Gerber herself in order to bypass this obviously incompetent woman at the front desk. "Is he here?" She kept glancing around the room, not looking at Helga at all now. Fortunately, she didn't turn completely around, or she would have seen me standing behind her with a smirk on my face the size of Texas. I was desperately trying to maintain some semblance of sobriety and not bust out laughing right into the back of her neck. That probably would have been rude.

"Umm," Helga stammered, taking in a deep breath in order to continue and get the main gist of the story out in one sentence. "Mr. Gerber is no longer with us."

The woman's head turned back around toward Helga now that Helga was releasing something akin to actual, factual information. I turned my own head away from her in order to stifle the laugh that kept building in my craw, and through the window behind me I saw two police cars sitting in prime parking spots right out front. I could see movement inside the cars but none of the officers inside either of the cars made any move toward opening their doors or getting out. Were they having donuts and coffee in there or what?

"No longer with us?" the woman repeated. "Meaning he got fired? Or took another job . . . *again?*" She knew Gerber well enough to know he'd had other jobs, but then again, so did anyone else in this town. It had made a splash when he showed up here, and everyone knew he had to have come from a similar job elsewhere. No surprises there. So if she knew that much about Gerber, why didn't she know what had happened this week?

"No," Helga said delicately. I wasn't sure why she was bothering. It wasn't like her to be delicate in any situation, not even with clients. Was it because this involved death and murder and was just that much more icky than your regular, run-of-the-mill crassness would call for? Seeing Helga treat an outsider so carefully was something I'd remember for a long time. "No, that's not it. He's not elsewhere. Well, technically, yes, he is. He's not here. He's not anywhere. He's . . ."

She was stumbling badly. I couldn't tell offhand if she was embarrassed or upset or just professionally flustered and now frustrated with herself for letting her guard down. In any case, she needed help because she was going to continue to fumble around for the right words.

"He's *dead*," I blurted out from behind the doughy woman in front of me. It felt like I was blabbering it right into her ear from behind, and I immediately felt awful that I'd just hurtled those words directly at her, along with my hot breath on the back of her neck. The poor woman was probably going to faint.

She spun around to face me, her brow pinched tight and her mouth drawn up in an awful frown. "Dead? You mean, as in . . . *dead?*" she repeated.

Was it such a difficult concept to understand? Or did she really not hear me as I blurted it right into her eardrum? That seemed hard to believe. I guess she was having trouble processing what I'd said.

"Yes, he's gone. Dead. Died two days ago, actually." For now I spared her the gore of the situation. With any luck she was an ink salesperson and really wasn't going to need or ask for any of the details of Gerber's untimely death. I looked down at my shoes, scratching behind my ear in a nervous gesture I hoped didn't look too obvious.

"I just talked to him last week. He was fine. What happened?" she asked, still frowning severely. I was worried she'd burst a blood vessel and suffer a horrible aneurysm right in front of me. That'd be just my luck. Would fit right in with the kind of week I was having, wouldn't it?

"Two days ago. He was stabbed back there in his office." I pointed slowly down the main aisle of the big room we were standing in, right toward the door intersected with yellow crime scene tape. I glanced at her briefly, long enough to see she had followed my pointing, but then looked away.

"Stabbed?" she squeaked, nearly dropping her large purse off the crook of her bent right arm. "What do you mean, stabbed?"

I couldn't imagine what was so difficult to understand about the word "stabbed" all by itself, but her question was a natural reaction to hearing this, I suppose.

"Stabbed. Actually, he'd been stabbed in the back of the neck . . . with a letter opener."

She went ghostly pale when I said this. Even without the gory details, it was difficult not to project a mental picture onto a statement like that. It had to be highly disturbing to run an errand like this and then find out the person you were supposed to meet had died violently days earlier. For one thing, on a wholly practical level, what happens with the errand? How far had she come? Far enough, I suspected, that she hadn't heard the news story about Gerber's murder. And now that she was here and there was no Gerber, did that screw up her reason for being here? Or could she meet with someone else and at least make the trip worthwhile?

As I mused pointlessly about the problems of a stranger, she stared at me, distinctly horrified at what I'd just told her. It wasn't a very ladylike conversation to have with a stranger in a place of business. She looked as if she were close to coming unhinged, and I smiled wanly, hoping to set her at ease enough to converse somewhat normally with me.

Through a turned-up nose she asked in hushed tones, "Did you say st-st-stabbed . . . in the neck?" If she had been twelve, I was sure she would have added "Eww" at the end of that question.

"Yes, sad to say. I came in for an appointment with him myself the other morning and I found him dead in his office. It was a horrible mess."

As soon as I'd said that, I knew it was the wrong thing to say. But like everything else that comes out of one's mouth, I couldn't unsay it now. And the frumpy middle-aged woman between me and Helga was suitably appalled.

"Excuse me?" she asked. She was probably hoping she had heard me wrong. What was I to do? Say it again, when it was wrong to have said it the first time? Make up something else to say in its place this second time around, like they do on bad sitcoms? Or something else entirely? Where was Miss Manners when I needed her?

"I meant to say, it was just a tragic thing to find him like that." Yes, far less graphic, and with far less opportunity to create unwanted images in someone else's mind. "Tragic" had just the right tone to it without encouraging ugly mental images.

Her face softened ever so slightly. "I'm sure it was tragic. How horrible for you." Her eyes met mine and I could see for the first time that she did in fact have a softer side. Not all frumpery and middle-aged blah. She seemed to genuinely feel sorry for me in my predicament.

"I'm just glad it's over. These first two days were pretty rough."

"Anyway," interjected Helga, "getting back to why you're here . . ." She had been thumbing through stuff on the desk in the vain hope of finding some extra copies of the date books and planners for Gerber, but to no avail. The police officers had taken with them anything that even smelled like a day planner or a contact book, so Helga was at a loss as to this woman's identity or purpose for being here.

The woman looked back from me to Helga and smiled just a little. "My name is Francine Stettler. Lee was going to publish my book."

Before I could stop myself, my face had already reacted to this news. *Francine!* How many Francines could there be out there? This was the woman whose book was orphaned by Deerpark Press when Gerber left to come here. So now I was faced with the dilemma of whether or not I should let on to this Francine Stettler that I already knew about her orphaned book. If things went one way, she'd be grateful that I knew and would feel a certain odd sense of camaraderie at me having discussed the situation with Gerber. If things went an entirely different way, Francine would feel embarrassed that I knew her business and that Gerber had been talking about her behind her back. Factoring in that the one person she'd ever known here was now dead—and murdered, no less—probably wasn't going to add to her trust. I was at a loss, and so, in my stunned state, I merely stood there and waited for Francine to speak again.

It was Helga who spoke next. "Pleased to meet you, Francine," she said simply and stood up halfway from her swivel chair to reach her hand over the top of the counter separating her from Francine. "I'm Helga, and I'm usually a little more on top of things like appointments than I am right now. It's been kind of insane around here lately, as you can imagine."

Francine reached across and shook Helga's hand briefly. "That's all right. I understand."

"The fuzz—I mean, the *authorities*—took all the day planners and appointment books and haven't given them back yet. I wanted to photocopy some of the pages first for just such an emergency but they said no to that too." She shrugged in a way that communicated, "What can ya do?" very effectively. Francine nodded.

"No problem. Looks like Lee won't be able to meet me anyway." I'm pretty sure she meant that as a way of breaking the awkwardness and tension, but it hadn't worked. I didn't think she was a person with a genuine sense of humor, and so I wasn't ready for a joke from the likes of Francine. I didn't laugh or even get that she meant that to be remotely funny. Until she herself chuckled. Then Helga and I looked at each other, both of us perplexed at this odd behavior. I mimicked Francine's little laugh, and then Helga joined in, finally figuring out that Francine was trying to fit in and probably just be one of the girls. It was funny to think that the likes of Helga and me were suddenly to be emulated and admired, even if it was only by someone like Francine.

Helga managed a small but fake twitter in reaction to Francine's "joke."

"Ha ha ha, no! He won't be able to see you today, will he? Oh dear, no."

Risking startling our little chickadee by speaking from behind her, sight unseen, I said, "Francine, I hope you didn't have to drive far to get here. It's such a wasted trip for you—one that could have been prevented with a single phone call had Helga known you were coming." Francine wasn't overly startled, that I could see, but she did whip around to face me, again putting her back to Helga at the desk.

"I came from Pennwood."

Helga spoke from behind the desk. "Pennwood, Ohio?"

Francine turned back around yet again to face Helga. "Yes, not too far over the Ohio border from Pennsylvania, really. We can almost see Pennsylvania from our house." She smiled at her own humorous statement. She was becoming alternately easy and difficult to figure out. I was beginning to feel ill. Time to change subjects. Sort of.

"So, what were you here to see Mr. Gerber about?" I asked, as casually as I could. I folded my arms across my chest and tried to look as if I didn't have a clue what her answer might be. I haven't a clue if it worked or not. Helga didn't know what I knew so I couldn't really gauge her reaction from over the top of the counter. Since she was sitting, I could barely see her eyes over the countertop from the angle where I was standing.

"Lee and I go way back. He was going to publish my novel." She nodded vigorously as she said this. I looked past her and saw Helga's eyes peering over the countertop, looking incredulous. The image presented a rather unbelievable scenario: Lee Gerber in his impeccably tailored Armani suit, and Francine Stettler in her frumpy Laura Ashley knockoff skirt and ill-fitting button-down blouse of unknown origin. Yeah, they go way back. Like anyone was going to buy that one.

Then again, perhaps she didn't mean it in as friendly a manner as it sounded by her wording. Perhaps in some sense—potential author and potential editor—they did go "way back." I noted that she had failed to mention the fact that her book had been orphaned and now wasn't even going to be published at all. I did, though, cut her some slack on that one. I wasn't sure I would have mentioned such a personally revealing fact to a handful of strangers gawking at me from either side of a desk. It was a fair assumption that she wasn't playing that card because it was none of our damned business. Which, of course, it wasn't.

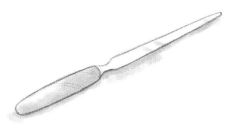

CHAPTER 12

I CAME HOME TO VLAD AND SETH STRETCHED OUT on the couch watching *The Price Is Right*. For the life of me, I couldn't remember a time when I had enough spare time to sit on a couch in the middle of a weekday and watch *The Price Is Right*, but Seth certainly marched to the beat of his own drummer. But I was beginning to think his drummer had called off sick.

At least he was pulling his weight around the house in terms of doing his own laundry and taking care of his dishes—aside from a few empty soda cans in my office that I'd have to remind him about—and I was glad someone was home all the time so I didn't have to come home to an empty house. Vladimir didn't really offset the sense of an empty house since he had a fondness for strangers and a hatred for the telephone. Still, it would be better for Seth if he stopped moving from one transition period to another and simply figured out what he wanted to do with his life and went in that direction. I couldn't tell him what to do, but I was hoping my motherly prodding had come to some sort of fruition by now. The boy was brilliant, but he just didn't have any focus in his life. This limbo was going to have to end. I wasn't so sure he'd realized that yet.

I dumped my keys on the table near the door and slipped off my shoes. I would have to keep the e-mail program open in case Brenda had any questions while going through my scribbles and inputting the corrections. Although I'd explained most of them to her, I hadn't gone over every single detail on every page. There were spots where things probably overlapped—literally—and I had to keep checking to be sure she wasn't trying to get through to me to ask me to clarify one last thing on one last page. I walked past the couch, with the immobile Vlad and Seth, and padded down the hall to my office, moving to the desk quietly and swirling the mouse around on the mouse pad so the screen saver would kick off and the desktop would magically reappear. I then double-clicked the e-mail program and waited until it downloaded all the waiting e-mails. Twenty-seven new ones, but none of them from clients. A good wrap-up to the afternoon.

"Seth!" I called as I came back up the hallway toward the front of the apartment. He sat up slightly, enough so his head peeked over the back of the couch.

"Yeah?"

"Can you please take Vlad out for a walk? His leash is hanging on the coat rack by the front entryway."

"No prob." As soon as Vlad heard the word "walk" in the same sentence as his own name, of course, he was up off the couch, off the warmth of Seth's lap, and was bouncing around near the front door waiting for Seth to get his butt in gear and take him outside. It never ceased to amaze me how dogs and children could go from states of total zonkedness and sleep to absolute wakefulness and eagerness in a split second. It's a great gift to have, one I wish I still possessed now that I was in my mid-forties and as prone to taking naps as those toddlers and dogs who seemed so good at recovering from them. Even Seth, at the ripe old age of twenty-five, was struggling to catch up to Vlad, physically and mentally.

"And while you're out, can you pick up a gallon of skim milk?" As he nodded and walked past me, I handed him a ten-dollar bill. "The mini-mart on the corner doesn't mind if you bring Vlad in with you if you're quick and if he's already peed elsewhere."

"Okay. No problem."

Apparently everything was no problem for Seth today. And this was good. But, now that life was starting to get back to normal for me, it was time for Seth and I to have a little talk about what his future plans were. He had said when he first got here that he was just between housing situations. I didn't exactly know what that meant, but the first of the next month would be here before we both knew it. Is that when his living arrangements—the new ones—were going to be ready for him? I realized just how little I really knew about what he was up to next month.

He and Vladimir were out the door hastily, with Vlad pulling as hard as his little legs would let him and Seth trying to keep up rather than yanking the little guy back and reining him in. Nothing like a small yappy dog to perk one's spirits up. Seth was trying to get one arm in the sleeve of his jacket while holding on to the leash with the other, but Vlad was having none of the attempts to slow him down and keep him in the building one second longer. The apartment door closed behind them and they were gone, for now.

I flopped on the recliner next to the couch and grabbed the remote off the end table between the two pieces of furniture. I purposely hunted for something dull on television, something normal and mundane and not worthy of my precious time. No news channels. No political talk shows. No historical documentaries. And certainly no police crime dramas. This past week I had come to see just how many of these shows were out there. As soon as I told myself I was going to avoid watching crap like that until I could stop thinking about Lee Gerber's dead and bloody body, suddenly it was all I could find on the TV. How crazy was that? Every channel had its own version of either *CSI* or *Law & Order* to offer, and most of them stunk. But they were omnipresent.

I scanned the on-screen guide quickly and found *Ren and Stimpy* on the Cartoon Network. Finally, something totally mindless that I was in the right frame of mind to appreciate. I clicked on the channel and up popped Stimpy's large head and round, squishy cat butt. I sighed in relief and settled in for a few minutes with my two favorite anthropomorphic house pets—living in houses out on their own.

Within minutes, though, I knew I had made a dreadful mistake. Suddenly Ren was scraping his own face off with a cartoon cheese grater and Stimpy was being shown in close-up with his nose dripping some sort of horrible gooey substance. I felt more than slightly ill by this point, and not just because of Ren and Stimpy themselves, although those images alone were enough to make just about anyone a little queasy. For me, the humor had been totally sucked out of the cartoon—well, perhaps the term "sucked out" wasn't really very carefully chosen, since that usually meant one of the two animals using a vacuum cleaner hose to take out someone's internal organs or something equally vile. Something that would actually be funny in different times and circumstances. But today, it was mostly just gross.

I turned the channel up one, settling on the VH1 music channel for now, which was doing a series of specials on funny trends of the 1980s. Much better. Probably very little gore and ugliness in this show, unless you counted Michael Jackson's plastic surgery, of course. I chuckled at my own joke—much funnier than anything Francine had said—and sighed a little bit in sheer relief at being home again and away from prying eyes and ears.

Francine had become more talkative the more Helga smiled at her and played nice, and at one point I had felt as if I was going to be stuck there for the rest of the day if I didn't find a way to extricate myself from the increasingly dull and pointless conversation. Seems Francine had made an appointment with Gerber the last time she had spoken to him. I knew she had insisted on this meeting—that Gerber wasn't really that interested in continuing the working relationship with her now that he didn't work for Deerpark Press any longer. In fact, now that he didn't work for a book publisher any longer. In all fairness, of course, now that he didn't even *breathe* any longer, but that was a slightly different issue altogether. But I kept my lip zipped shut and didn't let on that I knew anything. Not even to Helga. I didn't want to be around there long enough to watch

Francine leave and then stay to talk to Helga, so I made up my mind to excuse myself, leave, and then get back to Helga later with the real scoop on dear old Francine, the book orphan.

Helga wasn't too keen on me leaving her in the lurch like that, but I figured Francine was her responsibility anyway, not mine. I was just passing through—another client of the paper who had temporary business there today but was on her way out the door, when Francine happened to be coming in. Just more bad timing at the *Bugle* office for good old Maggie, that's all. Nothing more. I made a mental note to avoid it a little more often from now on. It was obviously wreaking havoc on my focus. I couldn't keep going there and seeing people I shouldn't and ending up in situations I wanted no part of. I had a life to live—a dull, boring, routine, mundane, listless life.

A life I happened to like quite a bit. And a life a lot more, well, full of life than Lee Gerber's was at the moment.

I was thinking along this line, thinking about Gerber and his stick-up letter opener, when Seth barged back into the apartment with little Vladimir dragging him out in front, panting, tongue hanging out, eyes wide and eager, thinking of nothing but food and sleep.

I meant Vladimir there, not Seth.

CHaPTer 13

I WOKE UP WAY TOO EARLY to the telephone ringing next to my bed. The room was still mostly dark, that semi-hazy darkness that comes not too long before dawn. The kind of darkness that you can look at and know it's going to be morning soon. The last time I'd seen that kind of sky was on Black Friday last year when Annie talked me into going out to Target at five in the morning. We'd stood there in a fog—a literal fog hanging in the air so we couldn't see halfway into the parking lot, and a figurative fog because neither one of us was a morning person by nature but we both had this insane urge to experience Black Friday at least once. And so we'd stood there in line with the other insane shoppers, coats pulled tight around us, looking enviously at those people in line who had had the foresight to stop at a coffee shop for hot coffee, waiting patiently for that last half-hour to go by so we could get inside to get warm. And by the time the doors actually opened, we cared a lot less about all the bargains than we did about simply getting inside where it was warm and not so eerily foggy and dark and dank.

On this particular morning it was that same look outside the window: foggy, dark but not entirely so, dank-looking. At least this time I was inside and snugly tucked into bed. But still, the telephone was ringing. And, that instinct of panic at hearing a telephone ring at such a horrid hour finally kicked in and I grabbed the telephone before the answering machine could get it. It's an odd sensation, really. You want to grab the phone and get it over with—whatever the bad news was on the other end—but you also don't want to know. You don't want to risk it. You have no interest in whatever life-altering news is at the other end of that phone call.

And so it was with me, but my lack of being fully awake came to the fore, and I had reached for the telephone before I had the wherewithal to stop myself. I rolled over onto my side to grab it, and then back onto my back. It was still too dark to see clearly but the On button was easy enough to find and I croaked a small "Hello?" into the handset while my eyes were still closed.

"Maggie, that you?"

Why did people call and then ask if it was me? I'd never understand that.

"It isn't anybody else. Who's this?" Because, of course, at that time of morning, out of context completely, no one sounds like themselves. Female, was all I could make out. And in some small measure of distress.

"Helga! It's Helga! Maggie, wake up enough for me to talk to you. This is important!"

She sounded way more serious than Helga ever has a right to sound, so I did as I was urgently instructed and sat up in bed, pulling myself to a sitting position and reaching toward the end table to switch on the small lamp so I could at least see everything in the room while I talked to her. I had a feeling this wasn't a call telling me she'd just won the lottery.

"Okay, I'm awake," I fibbed, rubbing my eyes and yawning, which she could probably hear at her end of the line. "What's up? It's—" I looked over at the alarm clock on the end table. "—not quite six o'clock in the morning. What's going on?"

"It's Brenda."

"Brenda? Our Brenda?" I asked, knowing already that yes, of

course she meant our Brenda. Brenda, the head typesetter of the *Bugle*. Brenda. Ernest's coworker. Brenda!

"Yes, our Brenda."

"What about her? What happened?" I asked, still not ready to hear it but knowing there was no going back now.

"She's dead."

"She's *what*? Did you say she's dead?"

It wasn't that I hadn't heard her. I heard her perfectly clearly. But I was having trouble processing how Brenda—who couldn't have been any more than thirty years old—was dead when she seemed fine yesterday. I silently hoped Helga was going to tell me she got hit by a bus on her way in to work, but suddenly I knew that's not where she was going with this. As much as we both liked Brenda and her quirks, I highly doubted that even Helga would have called me at this hour of the morning to tell me that Brenda had been hit by a bus. It was tragic, yes, but not something that couldn't wait until the sun was up, at least. Because, if she had been run over by a bus, there was nothing to be done about it. There was nothing to discuss, really. Nothing to regroup about or plan ahead for. It just meant a tragic accident had taken place and someone we both knew had died. That sort of thing happened all the time, didn't it?

But the one thing that would make Helga call me before six o'clock in the morning with news about Brenda's death would be if it were . . .

"Murder!" Helga yelled into the phone, obviously in a state of extreme panic by this point. "She was murdered! Killed! Dead!"

"Helga, calm down," I urged, not awake enough to gauge where she was calling from or who else was listening to her. All I knew for sure was that somehow Helga knew this had happened and it wasn't even light out yet. She could be anywhere, but she probably hadn't been home in bed like me. It was more than a little ironic, though, that I was the one calming Helga down.

"Helga, where are you? Where are you calling me from?" I was sitting bolt upright now, clutching that handset for dear life and trying to maintain a whisper in my voice so that Seth wouldn't awaken and barge in on me. Right now I didn't want to deal with his reaction as well as my own. One person at a time, please. Step in line, wait your turn.

"I'm at the *Bugle* office. I came in early because we've been a little behind all week because of . . . well, you know. Because of Gerber."

"Who else is there? Please tell me you're not alone."

"I am! She's—she's—Maggie, help me! What should I do?"

"Wait, no one else knows? Where the hell are you exactly? Where's Brenda? You haven't touched anything, have you?" There were so many questions to ask her, so many things to tell her to do, not to do—I didn't know where to start.

"I just got here. I saw the prepress room door was open, and it's never open when I come in. So, I went back to see if maybe Brenda had come in early too. We've had a few extra pages in the paper the last few days because of the murder, and she's just had a lot more work to do because of that. And the ads are coming in for Black Friday soon. I just assumed she'd come in to get ahead on some work. Okay, so she doesn't really ever come in early—she's more a stay-late type—but what else was I supposed to think, right?"

"Helga, calm down! Spit it out quick!"

"She was in there, all right. Slumped over her desk just the way you described Gerber slumped over his."

"What happened to her?"

"I'm not entirely sure. I didn't go in any further when I saw the blood."

"The blood?"

"On her desk, under her head. And going all down the back of her shirt."

"Wait, so you didn't feel her pulse or anything to see if she's dead?"

"She's dead, Mags. Her eyes were open and her . . . tongue was hanging out. I just about puked, except I was too scared to puke. You know what I mean?"

Unfortunately, I knew exactly what she meant.

"Listen, even if she's dead and there's nothing you can do for her, you have to get off the phone with me and call the police! Dial nine-one-one right now! You don't want to be there alone for a whole shitload of reasons, Helga, starting with the fact that who knows if the guy's still in the building!"

There was dead silence on the other end of the phone. I could tell she hadn't thought of that.

"Oh, crap. You're right."

"Now, say good-bye to me. Hang up. Dial nine-one-one. Then find someplace more public—like, outside on the front steps—and wait. Tell the emergency operator you'll be waiting outside on the steps so they'll know it's you when they get there. Okay?"

Still silence.

"*Okay?*" I asked, a little more loudly.

"Yeah, yeah. You're right. I should have called nine-one-one first. Oh, God. What an asshole I am. That probably looks bad, doesn't it?"

"Don't worry about it. We've only been on the phone for a few minutes. Just don't try to hide anything, and I'll throw on some clothes and be down there myself, okay?"

Silence.

"*Okay?*"

"Oh, yeah. Of course. But are you sure you want to get involved again? You were just starting to get back to normal and I just realized I dumped this on you without thinking first! I'm sorry, Mags! I didn't think straight. I just called you because you were the first person I thought of to call. Calling you made the most sense of anyone . . ."

She was rambling now. Time to shut it down before she launched herself into a raving panic. I knew how that rising adrenaline felt, and it wasn't any good to let her continue talking.

"Helga. Hang up. Call. Now."

"Right. Sorry."

"I'll see you soon, all right?"

"Yeah. Bye."

We both hung up and I sat in the bed for a few minutes trying to assess the situation a little better now that there wasn't a voice of panic in my ear. It didn't help because I wasn't coming up with anything useful. Although it had seemed like a good idea at the time, suddenly now, with even just a few spare moments to think more clearly, I didn't want to get dressed, go out in the dark and dank early morning air, and get re-involved in this situation. I wanted desperately to climb back under the covers, close my eyes, listen to the soft pattering of rain on the window near my bed, and wake up later—at a normal, decent hour—and find out that this had all been a bad dream and that Brenda was still alive.

Brenda. Dead. It hardly seemed possible. It made no sense at all. Gerber, in some strange way, wasn't as perplexing in theory. *Him,* I could see someone killing. But Brenda? I saw no logic in it. Then again, was there ever really much logic in any murder?

I kept thinking through the side issues of the situation as I got out of bed and started to get dressed. Yesterday's jeans, but everything else clean and fresh. I wasn't going to shower for this— I'd worry about that later once I got back home. I naïvely thought perhaps this would just be one of those little "errands" that you needn't fuss about yourself for, and that I'd be home right around the time Seth was waking up. That sounded reasonable, even if there wasn't anything really reasonable about this entire situation anymore.

Completely dressed except for my shoes, I opened the bedroom door and slipped down the hall quietly to the bathroom, where I brushed my teeth quickly and ran the brush through my hair. I had a wicked case of bed hair but figured this wasn't a beauty contest and I'd have to look all right only for the authorities and for Helga, who wouldn't notice my hair anyway. *Well, she might.* Sometimes you notice all the wrong things in situations like this. You remember smells and sounds that have no bearing on the situation, and you conversely have trouble recalling important data the police officers need to solve the case. So, Helga would probably comment on my hair but not remember what she did first when she found Brenda's head on her desk. It was the nature of memory after trauma, which I knew firsthand.

I tiptoed past my office and out into the living room, only to find Seth standing there in the middle of the room, scratching his head absentmindedly and blinking too much. There was a little more light out here because of the large bay window behind the television entertainment center, so we could see each other even without another light on.

"What's with the phone call?" he asked, now scratching his midsection up under his T-shirt, and still blinking too much.

"Well, you'll find out sooner or later, but I was hoping to get out of here without waking you up. I thought it would be better if at least one of us was on a normal sleep schedule today."

"Why? What happened?"

"That was Helga, at the front desk of the *Bugle*. Seems someone else at the *Bugle* was killed last night. Brenda, the head typesetter in the prepress room."

I grabbed my shoes near the door and walked to the couch to sit and put them on.

"What? Another person? What the hell?"

"Yeah. My thoughts exactly. *What the hell?*"

"Well, who was calling you? Who called to tell you this? And why did they call so early? Did it just happen?"

His questions weren't any more lucid than the ones in my own head right now. "As I said, it was Helga. She sits at the front desk and kinda runs the place. She came in to work early this morning and found Brenda with her head on her desk."

"What happened to her? Not the same thing as the other guy, I hope." He was rubbing his eyes, trying to get his body to catch up and wake up as much as his mind was doing now that it had something outrageous to latch onto.

"Dunno exactly. I don't think it was a letter opener, no. Helga was a little . . . sketchy on the details. Blood, head on the desk. Eyes open. That's just about all I know. I'm going down there now to be with her. She sounded more than a little panicked when I talked to her, and I told her I'd be right down, so I'd better hurry. I know how fast she'll get more anxious and scared. It felt like forever till the police showed up, but it was probably only about three or four minutes."

"You want me to come with you?" He sounded like a typical young guy now—he wanted me to say yes. Curiosity was getting the better of him, and since he didn't know Brenda—or Gerber, or Helga—he could hold a sort of aloof, perverse fascination with the process that I was having a hard time maintaining because of my friendship and relationship with some of these people.

"No. Probably it's best not to have too many people down there right now. Plus, you know what I need from you? Stay here and answer the phone. Because people will call. Not quite sure who I mean, really, but they will. I need you to take the calls—use your discretion on that—and take good, concise messages for any of them that'll need my attention when I get back. I'd like to know that that's being taken care of so I don't have to think about it."

"Okay, Mom, if that's what you want. I can stay here." I could see already that the curiosity was quickly giving way to the need for more sleep. There were down sides to coming with me, and having to get dressed in the dark and go outside in it was one of them. Sleep was good.

"Now," I continued, yanking on my second sneaker and pulling the laces really tight, the way I'd do if I were really pissed off. Was I pissed off? Not sure at whom, but I was definitely miffed about something. "There might be some calls from regular clients—publishers or editors from across the country who don't have a clue about any of this. They'll just ask normal, boring questions about projects, like deadlines or this or that page of a certain manuscript. Just tell those types of people that I'm out for the morning and I should be able to return their calls sometime this afternoon. Be fairly vague but try to sound businesslike. They all know I freelance from home, of course—they hire a whole pool of people like me—but I still don't like the place to sound like . . . well, like I'm actually working out of my house. Does that make sense?"

"Sure. So, no Spongebob blaring in the background and no getting the dog to bark, is that it?" He smirked at me and I let out a tension-relieving laugh that felt good.

"Yeah, that's pretty much it."

I finished tying the second sneaker and wondered if I'd laced it up too tightly in my pissed-offedness. Too late now. I wasn't going to untie the thing and fiddle with it anymore. I had the urge to get moving now—like this morning's phone call, probably just to get it all over with. At this point I had enough information to be scared to death but not enough to ease my mind about any of it. Who knew what was happening to Helga right now? She was alone in the *Bugle* offices when I hung up the phone, and although she was going to call the cops right after that, I hadn't a clue what had really happened. Despite my picturing her standing on those front steps in plain view and the cops swarming all around her, I had no assurance that that *had* really happened. Not until I got down there myself and confirmed it one way or the other. Besides, I was already up, awake, dressed, and ready to go. There really wasn't any advantage to waiting here. I wasn't going to get any more sleep until I got this ugly mess behind me . . . again.

* * * * *

I found Helga just as I had pictured her: standing forlornly on the front steps of the *Bugle* offices, a lit cigarette dangling from one hand, her coat bundled up around her. She was shivering and I could see even from the parking space I'd found out front that her lip was quivering. She wasn't smoking the cigarette. I think she probably just lit it to have something to hold in her hands. And I think her lip was quivering too much to smoke it.

I turned off the car and got out quickly, catching her attention only when I slammed the car door. Her mind had been elsewhere—she had been looking straight across and over the roofs of the smaller businesses across the street. The *Bugle* office had once been a library, and it had these huge steps out front that made it look rather majestic. The library had long since moved to another building in another area of town—something smaller, since the Internet had meant fewer people were going into small-town libraries unless they had no Internet access of their own and wanted to use the library's computers to play around online. This building was way too big for a library like that anymore, and the *Bugle* bought it years ago for a song.

And now I was watching Helga stand on top of those steps and stare out across the rooftops, alone and obviously quite scared. She broke her blank stare when she heard my car door close and looked at me gratefully. She immediately dropped the cigarette, twisted it with the toe of her shoe to extinguish it, and, clutching her purse to her chest, came running down the steps at a panicked pace to get to me.

I passed the police cars at the curb and met her partway up the steps. She threw her arms around me, gasping in gulps of air and trying to calm herself down enough to speak.

"Maggie, thank God you're here!" she breathed into my ear. "They're here—the cops and the ambulance guys are here. They talked to me at first but now they're all inside. God only knows what they're doing in there."

I knew what they were doing in there because I had gone through this very same thing earlier in the week. Only I hadn't had the foresight to stand outside while it was happening. I stood only a few feet away and watched the whole thing, without a friend nearby to commiserate. Watching Helga in such an irritated state made me realize just how serious this all was—and I wondered how I myself had made it through four days ago, with no friend for support and no frame of reference to get through it. I tried not to think about it too much, though. It began to feel more than a little overwhelming if I let it sink in too far.

"Don't worry about it too much, Helga. And don't think about what they're doing. It'll take a lot longer than you think, though, so try to be patient. My guess is that they won't let you leave any time soon, just because you were the one who found her."

"Wrong time, wrong place, huh? Just like you."

"Just like me," I agreed. "You're shivering. Are you cold, or just nervous?"

"I don't even know if it's cold out. Is it cold out? Oh yeah, look, I can see my breath. It must be cold out. It's probably just nerves. I can't even think straight."

"I'm just glad you're all right, Helga. There's no telling what's really going on here, and I was a little worried that you were down here by yourself. How long did it take for the cops to get here?"

She shrugged, hugging herself tightly against the cold and against the recurring bad images and thoughts. I knew exactly what she was going through.

"I dunno. Probably no more than a couple of minutes. The cops showed up first, with the ambulance right behind that. Since I told them I was sure she was dead, they didn't have the sirens on—the ambulance, I mean. They both had their lights flashing, though. And they pulled up real fast and most of them ran toward me first—I was already standing out here like you said—and once I pointed inside and told them where she was, almost all of them ran inside. Except two of them. They stayed behind to talk to me instead."

"Out here?"

"Yeah, out here. They didn't make me go back in there. I told them flat out I didn't want to go back in there, and they were okay with that. So we stood out here on the steps and they asked me all sorts of questions. Sounded a lot like the things you said they asked you on Monday when this happened to Gerber."

She looked down at the steps beneath her and sniffed. She'd been crying; that was obvious now that I looked at her more closely. It was good for her that I knew what she was going through, but it was awfully bad for me to have to relive the whole escapade again so soon after it happened. For Pete's sake, Gerber's funeral wasn't even over yet and here we were already dealing with another death. She and I had been thinking about driving over to Ohio to attend Gerber's funeral—mostly out of a sense of obligation, but I admit, partly out of a sense of morbid curiosity to find out more about the other people in his life. But now, with this happening to Brenda and us mixed up in it, I wasn't sure what we would do. One look at Helga told me she probably wouldn't want to go anyway. She'd be a blubbering mess, and she and I would almost surely blurt things out, and then all hell would break loose—at a funeral, no less. No, that would be a very bad idea.

Once I realized that we didn't need to decide about Gerber's funeral right now, I figured I had time to spend with Helga instead. It was obvious she needed me right now and I didn't want to leave her here at the mercy of the police. They meant well, but none of them were going to be able to help her stay calm and get through this the way I would be able to do. Not only was I a friend and working associate, but I could empathize in a way no one else could. She needed me, and I was glad I could be here for her. Now, if I could only keep the situation focused on Helga and her needs and not let myself slip back into thinking about what had happened on Monday at about this same time, I would probably get through this relatively unscathed.

And, just as I thought that, standing there in the shivering cold with my arm around Helga for both warmth and friendly comfort, one of the police officers came out of the *Bugle* offices and headed straight for us. I recognized him as the same officer who talked to me after I found Gerber's body on Monday. He was looking at a notebook in his hand as he walked but when he looked up he recognized me immediately.

"Ms. Velam, I think, isn't it?" he asked, putting his pen in the same hand as the notebook so he could shake hands with me. I shook his hand lightly, then put my hand back in my coat pocket, leaving the other arm around Helga.

"Yes, that's right. Helga called me to come down here for moral support." He was nodding. "She's a bit, well, out of sorts," I said, for lack of a better way to put it.

"I'm sure she is. And I have to ask her a few more questions, if you don't mind." He got the notebook back out and opened it to a fresh page, clicking the ballpoint pen and keeping it poised over the blank page.

"No problem, officer. Can I stay here, though? Just to keep her from falling over?" Helga shot me a glance and I winked, trying to keep things a little lighter for her sake. She managed a weak smile, and I could see the gratitude in her eyes as I ran some interference for her.

"That's fine. Yes. As long as you're both out here, that should be just fine."

Helga and I looked at each other. Did this guy really think either one of us *wanted* to be inside the building with Brenda's dead body and whatever else was going on in there? I suppose in some cases the people at the scene, even those directly involved, like me and Helga, actually wanted to see what was going on. I think both Helga and I were beyond that stage of misplaced curiosity and instead were more concerned about throwing up on our shoes.

Helga managed to squeak out a few words. "What do you need to know, officer?" she asked, with an obvious air of cooperating but only under extreme duress. The purse-clutching continued and she probably wanted to light another cigarette too. As bad as those things were for her, though, I figured if she ever deserved the self-indulgence of a cigarette, it was now. I didn't suggest it outright, but if she grabbed a new one out of her purse, I decided that I wouldn't rib her about it like I had in the past. This just wasn't the time for it.

"Well, Ms. Smut," he said, mispronouncing her name badly. It was the usual mispronunciation, and in other circumstances, it would end up being the source of a lot of entertainment for us, but right now the last thing Helga really wanted to do was correct this police officer on the official pronunciation of her name. But, she did. It was probably habit after years of having to correct virtually everyone.

"It's 'Schmutt,' not 'smut.' Very German, thank you. You don't pronounce the 'u' like that. It's more like 'oo'—like in 'foot.'" She sounded like she had that answer on a verbal loop that kicked in automatically any time someone pronounced her name wrong.

"Oh, I'm sorry," the officer said apologetically. "Looks like I have it spelled right. But I just said it wrong by accident. Sorry about that." He scribbled something down in his notebook as Helga smirked at him. Definitely not a good time for minutiae like this.

"What do you need to know, officer?" I asked in her stead. Someone needed to move this interview along.

"Sorry about that. Mostly, I just need to go over what you saw, Ms. *Schmutt*—" He pronounced it carefully this time, and accurately, but so carefully that it sounded fake, almost as if he were mocking her for her silly-sounding name. "—when you first walked into the prepress room off to the side there. Did you see anything besides Miss Johnson in her chair, with her head on the desk in front of her?"

"Like what?" Helga asked. It seemed like a straightforward question, but perhaps she'd already answered it because she sounded a little perplexed.

"Like, specifically, we'd like to know what sorts of injuries you saw. Whatever you saw that made it clear to you that harm had come to her."

Odd question, I thought. Surely they knew that themselves by now. Surely the forensics people and the coroner's office had been in there and had much more accurate and definite opinions on whether harm had come to Brenda than Helga did. Helga, who probably looked away quite suddenly as soon as she saw any evidence of foul play. I know that's what I did as soon as I saw that blood and the letter opener perched freakishly in Gerber's neck. And with just that one leap of thought, it all came flooding back and I felt as vulnerable standing here with Helga as I had on Monday when I was all alone. It felt like a never-ending nightmare.

Helga was frowning and still quivering from either nerves or the cold weather that persisted along with the fog. There was more lightness to the sky, though, and it at least felt a lot more like morning and not that ugly predawn darkness to which I had awakened suddenly.

"You mean, like the blood all over her shirt and her desk? Or the gash on the back of her head, like somebody had taken a brick and whacked her head in with it?" Helga was highly agitated now, shaking uncontrollably and taking it out on this officer. He was probably used to it, although he looked a little shaken himself by Helga's sudden outburst.

"Well, actually, yes, things like that. Is that what you saw?" He was scribbling madly now, partly to keep up with Helga's description, but I'm sure it was also partly to be able to look away and focus in on something else other than the Wrath of Helga. I patted her on the shoulder and squeezed her a little tighter, hoping to calm her down—for everyone's sake.

"Yes, dammit. That's obviously what I saw. Dead body. Smashed-in head. Blood. Lots and lots of freakin' blood. Got it?" She stood staring—no, *glaring*—at the officer, who really hadn't done anything except find himself in the line of fire by being in the wrong place at the wrong time. There was certainly a lot of that going around.

CHAPTER 14

AFTER A FEW MORE OBVIOUS, BONEHEADED, and rather pointless questions, Mr. Police Officer decided to go back inside where all the real action was. As he closed his notebook and tucked the ballpoint pen into the spine, he turned toward the double glass doors of the building, only to see two workers from the coroner's office pushing a gurney between them, coming out the door as two police officers held open the glass doors. There was a body bag, mercifully zipped up but obviously with a body inside, on the gurney and a dark burgundy velour blanket or dust ruffle of some sort on the gurney that had "Coroner" embroidered on it in white thread. Looked painfully like what I saw four days ago, although I saw all this from the inside of the building. With Gerber, I also saw them put his body in the body bag and load it onto the gurney.

Several police officers now followed Brenda's gurney out the door and down the steps, and I saw a few people from the forensics unit come out, latex gloves on their hands, carrying stapled paper bags to a waiting car trunk. Evidence.

I turned to Helga to see her following the gurney with her eyes. She was frowning and quite pale, and I didn't know whether to let her watch or to distract her. I leaned forward and asked quietly, "Helga, you all right?"

She turned her head in my direction but kept her gaze focused on the gurney, which was now just outside the coroner's van. The two workers held onto it while the police officers opened the back doors of the van. The gurney slid into the back of the van more easily, and the workers did this quietly, not speaking to each other and looking rather reverential in their work. I, for one, appreciated this—they had acted this way while taking out Gerber's body as well—because I would have hated to see them joking and talking of other things while going about their grisly task. I wasn't naïve enough to think they sat in the van the whole way back with the same quiet looks on their faces. I was sure that they launched into normal coworker talk at some point—if not chatting about this particular body, then about their lives in general, the way all coworkers do. If I had their jobs, I'd probably need that release of common, normal talk as well. Eight hours a day of situations like this and I'd go batty if I didn't have a way to joke and talk normally to another living human being.

"Helga?" I repeated. She nodded and reached her arm around my back to embrace me as I embraced her. Her other hand still clutched her purse.

"I'm fine, sweets. I mean, not *fine*, exactly. But I'm hanging in there. I'll be all right eventually. I think I have it a little easier than you did. I am very glad you're here. I guess I'm a wuss after all." She laughed dryly, probably not the least bit amused at her own joke but knowing there was a distinct irony in her leaning on me for a change. I was glad someone could be here for her, although there were definitely moments I had wished it didn't have to be me.

"How much longer do you think they'll make me stay here?"

"I don't know. That whole morning is really a blur for me. And maybe some stuff will be different this time since it's the second one. I couldn't even guess if that would mean it would take longer, or if it would take less time."

"Me neither," she echoed.

"Damn, I wish I knew what those cops were thinking about all this!" I slapped my leg in frustration. "Now it seems like a matter of safety for the other workers at the paper. It almost seems like they should *have* to tell us what's going on, don't you think?"

Helga nodded. "Especially folks like me who work in the building every day."

As we continued musing in this vein, the same police officer who questioned Helga before came up the steps toward us.

"Uh-oh. Looks like Officer Skippy forgot something," I said.

"Great. Just what I need."

"You didn't steal his pen or anything, did you?" I asked, nudging her in the side good-naturedly. She smiled—a nice thing to see.

"Officer," she called toward him loudly, launching a sort of preemptive strike. "What can I do for you?"

"Ms. Schmutt," he said, taking great care to pronounce it carefully and correctly this time. "I knew I forgot to ask you something before. Got a little sidetracked, I think, when they brought out the body."

Whatever, I thought. *Just get this over with. We'd both like to get the hell out of here.*

"Yes?" She was speaking more steadily, less shaking in her voice. I could still feel her trembling as I kept my arm around her shoulder, but even that was a little steadier than when I first got there.

The officer was right next to us now. "Did you happen to notice Ms. Johnson's clothing?"

Helga frowned, pinching her forehead up really tight. "Not sure what you mean by noticing her clothing. You mean, just what she had on?"

"Yes, that. More specifically, whether what she had on was what she was wearing the day before."

"Why would she wear the same clothes two days in a row?" Helga asked, not following the officer's line of thinking. I was, though.

"She wouldn't," I said. "But, if she's wearing the same clothes we saw her in yesterday, that means she stayed late last night and was probably attacked then . . . and not this morning as if she came in early." I turned to the officer. "Right?"

He nodded. "Precisely."

Helga's face brightened. "Oh yes, I see. I hadn't even thought of that. I just assumed she came in early to get ahead."

"Yes, Ms. Schmutt. You even said earlier that she was more of a . . ." He looked down at the open notebook he was holding. ". . . a 'stay-late' type."

"Damn, you're good," she said, sounding a little more like the real Helga. "Yeah, I did, didn't I?"

"At any rate, Miss, do you recall what she was wearing—either this morning when you found her or yesterday while at work?"

Helga frowned again, thinking hard about what Brenda looked like. After a few moments of silence, the officer spoke again.

"Miss Velam, how about you? Didn't I hear you say you saw her yesterday too?"

"Yes, I did. I came in to give Brenda some pages I had proofed for her, to walk her through my corrections because there were so many."

"Do you remember what she was wearing when you saw her yesterday?"

I felt as if I were getting sucked into this investigation a lot more than I wanted. Once I started giving descriptions and information, I was part of this case too. Even if they were indeed the same case—and it certainly looked that way—I wasn't so sure I wanted to be someone in the forefront of both murders. Stuff like that just couldn't be a good thing.

Now I was the one frowning, pinching my face up and trying to think through things. I could see Brenda sitting at her desk while we went over the corrections together. I could remember her hair—up in a ponytail held back with a burgundy scrunchie—but that wouldn't be much help because, as far as I knew, Brenda wore her hair that way at work every day. At least, every time I saw her at the office.

"She had a burgundy, a maroon scrunchie," I offered quickly, as I continued to try to piece together the rest of her outfit yesterday.

The officer looked perplexed. "A ... what? A scrunchie? Beg your pardon, ma'am, but I don't really know what a scrunchie is."

Helga blurted out, "It's a hair band thing, to tie your hair back in a ponytail." She sounded irritated that the officer didn't know what a scrunchie was. My guess was that he wasn't married and certainly didn't have any daughters.

"Oh yes, I see." He scribbled that down in his notebook. "This was yesterday?"

"Yes," Helga agreed. "She's right. It was like a dark maroon color." She bit her bottom lip and kept thinking. "Because she was wearing that rose-colored sweater. Remember?" she said, turning to me and asking me directly.

"Yes!" I agreed. "That sweater! She's right. It was the pink sweater with the little pearl buttons on it."

"And jeans, of course. She always wore jeans. She was in that prepress room all the time and she could get away with wearing jeans. Her and Ernest." I nodded. I remembered the jeans.

The officer kept scribbling hastily in his notebook. "Okay. Yes. Yes. One last thing . . ." He hesitated when he said this, and I knew instinctively what was coming next. It was obvious based on what he had been asking us just now.

"Yes?" Helga asked.

"Could you both come over to the coroner's van and confirm that the clothing she has on now is what you saw her wearing yesterday?"

He tried so hard to make it sound like a while-we're-all-here-already request, but there was no way to soften the blow of seeing them open up that body bag so we could look inside at Brenda—who would be face up inside it—just to see if what she had on right now was the same clothing as before. I understood why it should be done, but I certainly didn't want yet another layer of involvement tacked on to the several layers I already had piled on top of me. No thanks.

"Do we have to?" I heard Helga ask. It was pointless, though. We were going to have to suck it up and go look. Might as well get it over with, sooner rather than later.

"Yes, I'm afraid so. Once everything starts moving away from the crime scene—including the two of you—everything changes and everything seems harder to keep track of. It's a lot easier to just do this now. Then we can probably wrap things up here and let you two go."

He smiled when he said this, but it was mostly a feeble attempt to set us at ease for the task ahead. I couldn't speak for Helga directly, but to me, his attempt was worse than feeble. The only good thing he'd said was that this would all be over soon. Then again, I had thought that on Monday, too, and look what happened.

CHaPTer 15

ONE OF IT WAS OVER SOON ENOUGH FOR ME, but at some point it really was over and Helga and I were allowed to leave. I walked her to her car first, which was parked not too far from mine, and gave her a big hug.

"Feel free to call me at any time, day or night, if you need to talk about any of this. Who knows? I might need to talk about stuff too."

Helga smiled weakly. "Well, right now, I just want to get home and take a nice hot bath and . . ."

"And take a nap?" I offered.

"Precisely."

"Yeah, that's how I felt on Monday. I needed to crash and forget about everything. I'll warn you, though: falling asleep isn't going to be that easy. Do you have any sort of over-the-counter sleep aid or something? Sominex or whatever?"

"No, should I?"

"Couldn't hurt. They're really mild. I keep 'em in the house because sometimes that night owl thing kicks in and then my schedule gets all screwed up. I only use 'em maybe once every few months, but it's nice to know they're there if I need them."

She nodded. "I'll stop at the store on my way home and pick up something then. You're right—couldn't hurt."

I hugged her one last time and then walked back to my own car and got in. I sat for a while staring straight ahead, and watched as Helga started her car and pulled away from the parking space and onto the street. Sighing, I put the key in the ignition but didn't turn it. Something wasn't quite right. Besides all the obvious stuff, that is. There was something about Brenda's death that didn't jive with Gerber's death on Monday, despite the fact that everyone assumed the two murders were committed by the same person—myself included. It was too big a coincidence to be totally random.

And yet, somehow, the two deaths didn't feel connected. The two victims were as different as night and day and barely knew each other and therefore probably didn't know anyone in common, besides the workers at the newspaper.

This thought concerned me greatly, more so the more I thought about it. I pulled out into traffic slowly and made my way home as I continued to mull over the newspaper connections between Lee Gerber and Brenda Johnson. Perhaps my own sense of safety because most of Gerber's history lay outside our town, outside our state, had been misguided. I would have to rethink my own position on whodunnit quite a bit. Either Gerber had personal enemies here in town that I wasn't aware of or this wasn't about him personally and was instead about the newspaper itself. No matter how I sliced it now, adding Brenda Johnson into the mix didn't quite fit. Even if this were somehow about the newspaper—perhaps its political leanings or its position on a certain specific topic on an op-ed page—there was no sense in including Brenda Johnson, a typesetter, in a list of victims. Offing the editor made a small wee bit of sense if one had issues with the newspaper's stance on something. But why knock off a typesetter? Why not a specific reporter with a byline, or even a salesman who sold a certain type of advertisement? Killing the typesetter seemed to make as much sense as killing the *proofreader*.

I slammed on the brakes as the traffic light right in front of me turned red, and the car just in front of me halted suddenly rather than passing harmlessly through the yellow light. I barely missed crashing bumper to bumper into the car, screeching the tires and skidding just enough to make it plain to everyone around that I hadn't been paying attention. I sheepishly looked down at the steering wheel, trying to find a way to look forward but to not make eye contact with anyone, least of all the driver in front of me as he glared at me through his rearview mirror. Awkward didn't begin to describe it. If a murderer didn't kill me first, I might just do myself in with a traffic accident. I was in a lot of danger, either from some mystery killer or from my own inability to focus and pay attention.

I somehow managed to get home without killing myself, or anyone else. I couldn't say the same for our mystery murderer. He was having a field day—all at our expense, it seemed.

CHAPTER 16

I SAT IN MY OFFICE STARING AT THE PDF PRINTOUT sitting on my laser printer. I had forgotten to swing out the little plastic arm that catches paper when I'm printing more than just a handful of sheets, and a small pile of miscellaneous pages had toppled off the printer and landed in an unarranged, out-of-order pile on the floor by my feet. Unlike other times, this time I let them fall, watching them cascade one by one out of the printer and directly onto the floor once the stack on the printer had gotten too unwieldy. I was tired, and although I knew I'd have to bend over to retrieve the pages, at the moment I just didn't feel like it. It was a proofreading project from a publisher in California. To save the cost of shipping the project in one direction, they had sent me a PDF instead of a FedEx package. I was to print it out to work on it and then send it back to them, my invoice including the slight added costs of paper and toner to print the monstrosity out on my printer.

And so, here I sat, watching their book project tumble onto the floor. At some point I realized I didn't want to sit and reorganize quite so many pages, so I leaned over the right side of the desk and plucked the little plastic arm out of its spot and let it start catching pages. Bending over, I grabbed the scattered pile of pages off the office floor and straightened them out so they were at least all facing the right direction. I would put them back in the right order later, once the whole project was out of the printer.

In the meantime, I wheeled the office chair across the room and opened the small filing cabinet on the opposite wall. I deftly grabbed the file full of job sheets and snagged a new one out for this project, putting the folder back in its spot and slamming the cabinet door closed a little harder than I had to. The cabinet shook a little and the knick-knacks on top wobbled a bit, daring each other to fall off and shatter on the tile floor.

By the time I was halfway done filling out the job sheet for the new project, the printer stopped. I straightened up those pages, tipped in the ones that had fallen onto the floor, and jogged the entire stack by hand, wiggling them first together and then looser so they would fall in straight.

The familiar habits of paper, toner, work sheets, pen and ink all felt good this morning. The mundane points of the morning were glorious in their simplicity. I loved my work, and at times like this I was grateful I hadn't become a philosopher or someone else who had to think about the big questions of life all day long. If that had been so, I would be having a miserable day. But, as God would have it, I had been blessed with an incredible attention to detail, and I had found a way to turn that gift (or curse) into a career. Not a particularly exciting or glamorous career, mind you, but something to put food on the table and pay the bills. And once I got out of proofreading on-site at various jobs and moved to freelancing, my life really settled into a comfortable routine, with me at the helm of my own life for the first time ever.

And so, on a morning like this one, a job like mine—which sometimes included incredibly mundane tasks like paper shuffling and filling out forms—seemed even more comforting. The last thing I wanted to do right now was think about what had gone on yesterday. Well, all this week, really. It was Saturday morning, and although I rarely worked into the weekends, I had had a little too much downtime this week. And so I was forced to sit here Saturday morning with a new project and get caught up. The timing was good because having no work would have meant too much more free time to let the ol' brain engage in meandering thought patterns and bouts of panic and self-doubt. Better to be printing out pages of a book and tipping them in the right order. Shuffling papers felt therapeutic.

As I sat at my desk filling out the rest of the job sheet and getting all the usual supplies in their right spots—Wite-Out at hand, red pencils, two red Pilot Extra Fine Rollerballs, and a packet of small Post-it notes—I could sense someone standing behind me in the doorway. I made a mental note to rearrange my office furniture—a favorite hobby of mine anyway—so that my desk faced the door a little better and I could see people coming in or walking down the hall when I had the door open. I swung the office chair around to face Seth standing there, Vladimir at his feet wagging his tail but with no clue what the humans were plotting now. He only hoped it involved either doggy treats or the leash and a walk outside. Poor dumb mutt didn't realize how little we were going to be noticing him over the next few days. I would have felt sorry for him if I had had the brain space left for it.

"Seth. Hey." Not the warmest greeting I could have mustered, but it would have to do. I felt like crap this morning and was glad to be working normally and functioning. I couldn't be expected to sound good too.

"Hey," he returned. We were both overly talkative this morning. "I took Vlad out already, but I think he wants to go out again. Does he need to go out again?"

I looked at Vladimir, who had started wildly wagging his tail upon the sheer mention of his name. So, the world did revolve around him after all. "Nahh. He'll let you take him out as many times as he can con you into it. If you *want* to take him out, that's always good. And it gives you that nice fresh-air perspective and all. But it's not necessary again till probably close to lunchtime."

"That's what I thought, but he's just been a little . . . clingy today."

"Can't say I blame him, really. He's been thoroughly neglected this whole week."

"By you, maybe. But not by me. I've been here snuggling with the old guy on the couch every afternoon. I'm guessing he usually doesn't get attention like that."

I smiled at Vlad, who continued to wag his tail cluelessly, hoping to catch mention of his name again so he could launch into the upscale "cute" routine he used when he wasn't sure if he was going to get the attention he wanted. "You're right. He doesn't. But that doesn't mean he won't keep using his look-how-pathetic-I-am routine in order to get sympathy. It usually works, too. Just not this week."

I reached down toward the floor and Vlad ran over to meet my outstretched hand. I scratched him under the chin and he wagged his tail furiously.

"Gee, what am I, chopped liver?" Seth asked Vlad, who ignored him in favor of my chin rubs. "Oh sure, I'm fine when she can't take care of you, but as soon as she's around again, you drop me like I'm hot."

We both smiled. It was forced humor. It was totally skirting the real issues of the day. But there was no way either of us was ready to start right in with the heavy, serious topics. And so I was working and printing and proofreading. And Seth was walking the dog more than once and getting overly involved in Vlad's little doggy life.

"Awww, we wuv Seffy, don't we, Vlad?" I said in baby-doggy talk, scritching his chin some more and watching him go all crazy on me because I was paying him some serious attention for the first time all week long. He plunked himself down on the floor, belly side up, and waited for it. I gave in and rubbed his chubby little tummy and his whole body wagged when he tried to wag only his tail. He looked downright funny and I laughed an unplanned, hearty laugh. Felt good. Seth was smiling in the doorway.

"So, what are the plans for today, Momster?"

"Well, first item on the agenda is to never answer the phone again," I said, still rubbing Vlad's tummy and talking in small snippets of doggy talk. Seth didn't laugh, but he was nodding his head.

"And beyond that? Do you have any other . . . obligations today?" he asked, obviously searching for the right word without actually talking about the situation outright.

"If you mean, will the police call me, or will Helga stop by and cry a lot, then I'd have to say I don't honestly know one way or the other. In some ways, I'd like to sit down with her and talk—this time not on the steps of the *Bugle* office and maybe with a nice hot cup of coffee instead—but I'm not sure I'm going to seek her out in order to do that. That just feels like I'd be asking for trouble right now. If she needs me, she knows where to find me."

Seth crossed his arms and leaned on the door post. "True enough. But don't you just want to sit down and vent about this? Run it through the ol' noggin and see what comes out the other end?"

"Ew, that sounds gross," I said, and we both laughed. He hadn't meant it like that, of course.

"Mom."

"I know. I guess there is that raw appeal of sitting around and brainstorming with someone to figure out just what is going on here. But honestly—there's also that element of fear, Seth. I mean, I saw two dead bodies this week—both of whom were people I knew, people I worked with. It's really hard not to personalize that."

"But wouldn't talking through it help you get past it a little bit?"

"I'm not sure I want to keep scaring up those same horrible images just now."

I sat up straight, leaving poor Vlad on the floor with his belly exposed for a few moments until he realized the fun and games were over. He finally surrendered and flipped himself over as gracefully as he could with his short legs and little chubby body.

"Seth, we have to go over all this stuff, you're right. I just am not up to it—today. Unless something happens with Helga and I have to get involved all over again. For now, though, I want to regroup by forgetting any of this ever happened." Seth gave me a look. "Just for a while, mind you. Not forever."

But, as Seth must have sensed, it wasn't going to happen that way. When the phone rang and it was Helga, asking if she could come over right away, I started to have a sinking feeling that I wasn't going to get out of this situation any time soon. I was in it now, as deep as anyone else, if not deeper. I told Helga of course she could come over, and Seth and I sat together on the couch watching pointless Saturday morning cartoons—which were mostly bad anime knockoffs anyway—waiting for the doorbell to ring.

CHaPTer 17

SWEETIE, I SWORE TO MYSELF I wasn't going to call you and get you involved, but hell, all I was doing was sitting home with the mini-blinds closed up tight afraid to answer the phone."

Helga sipped her coffee, closing her eyes and seeming to bask in the hot aroma wafting from the top of her mug. I sat in the recliner across from her, watching her hands shake just a little bit as she held the mug with both hands. I began to realize as I watched her—the real Helga I knew and loved buried just under the surface of this newer, skittish Helga I wasn't as comfortable with—that having her here was the right thing to do, and not just for her. For me as well. Perhaps I did need to talk through this after all.

"It won't always feel like that," I assured her, although where I was getting this information was anybody's guess since I myself hadn't really eased up on the panic and fear, especially after dark. "At some point things have got to change, especially when they catch the creep who's doing this."

"That's the whole dilemma, though," she said, gulping the coffee now that it had cooled. "There *is* some creep still out there. And he seems to like killing newspaper people. And I sit right at the front desk!" Her mug was wobbling badly now in her hands, and she made no effort that I could see to stop herself from losing it on my couch. "I tell you, Maggie, this just has to stop or I'm going to go nuts."

I leaned forward in the recliner, close enough to touch her knee in an effort to comfort her and steady her nerves a bit. "Listen, it'll be all right. I gotta believe there is safety in numbers. For now, nobody works overtime anymore. Nobody stays late. Nobody comes in early. Not until this jerk is caught. Right?"

I looked her in the eye and she seemed to calm down a little bit. "That certainly won't be a hard thing to convince everyone to do, now, will it?" I laughed and she smiled behind the mug she held up to her mouth. "'*No, you have to go home on time! Stop working and leave!*' Yeah, I think that'll fly." She managed a wink and another smile.

I sat back up straight in the recliner. "So what you're telling me is that you're not so much upset about what we saw yesterday as you are about the prospect of having to go about your day with this killer still on the loose."

She looked at me blankly for a moment, and I worried that I had said something enormously wrong and inappropriate. "Well, duh," she said, and I smiled, relieved. "Of course that's it. Besides losing Brenda, who the hell cares what happened yesterday compared to what might happen today? I mean, really. On Monday I have to go back into that office and get my work done as usual and try not to get *killed* before five o'clock. I know I've said this for the past ten years, but now they *really* don't pay me enough to do this job!"

It was good to see some of the old feisty Helga shining through.

"Seth and I had a plan for what you and I should do today," I said, looking up at Seth standing across the way in the open kitchen area. He'd been trying to look inconspicuous and not get too involved in our conversation unless he had been asked, but Helga never really brought it up. I was pretty sure she didn't notice him back there since he was behind her and was extremely quiet.

She turned around on the couch and saw Seth waving a little hello from the kitchen. "What? What should we be doing?"

Seth took the liberty of coming from the kitchen into the living room, sitting slowly and deliberately in the rocking chair opposite the couch. "Here's how I see it," he started, leaning forward and putting his forearms on his knees. "Mom has a great eye for detail. She notices everything. She's good at it. And frankly, most of the time we just tease her about it." I shrugged but he kept going. "But in a situation like this one—which is probably full of little details to be noticed by the right person—that annoying habit could turn out be a real asset."

Helga was nodding. Of course she was: He hadn't gotten to her part in all this yet.

"And you, Helga, have access to everybody at the *Bugle*. You know everybody. You see everybody. Everybody at some point has to go through you for something, even if it's only to pick up their paychecks."

"We have direct deposit," she said simply. Seth and I looked at each other.

"You know what I mean."

"Yes, young man, I do. But I don't want any part of this. Anything I know is something you could probably learn from somebody else. So honestly, I suggest you do that. I won't be that much use to you anyway. Not as much as you probably think I would. How do they put it? I'm low-level functioning right now."

She leaned forward and placed the shaking coffee mug on the coffee table, then sat back and let herself sink into the overstuffed couch cushions. I wasn't sure what to say to her. She was obviously feeling the same way I was: vulnerable, uncooperative, wanting to crawl in a hole and disappear. But she still wanted to come over here to be with me. Was it just that misery loves company, or did she really want to get through this once and for all, much as I did now that Seth had talked me into it?

"Helga, listen," I urged, and now we were all leaning forward on our seats. "We need to get past this. We need to find out who's doing this. I don't have any idea what the police are thinking, but I do know that I'm having trouble sleeping at night. Just like you probably are." She nodded. "And I'm just not the type to let a bunch of strangers keep me safe because it's their job, even if they're experts and I'm just playing amateur detective in my spare time." Seth, to my right, was nodding like crazy, trying not to look overly eager. He was trying to balance the right level of enthusiasm with trace amounts of somberness and seriousness befitting a double murder investigation. I saw right through it.

"I know you're right," Helga conceded, "but honestly, I don't want to deal with it. Can't it just go away? I promise I won't complain about my job anymore. I would give just about anything to go back to that stupid office and sit at that stupid desk and have Gerber Baby sauntering down the main aisle like he did every morning he was there."

She sighed and looked down in her lap. She looked exhausted. She was probably sleeping a lot less than I was lately.

"I know what you mean," I said, feeling much the same way. "But that's not going to happen, so the best we can do is acknowledge that wishful thinking and then move on and deal with it. And find out what's going on before something happens to someone else."

Helga was shaking her head, not in disagreement so much as just a passive acknowledgment of the situation—not liking it but succumbing to it out of sheer necessity. As she sat there, slumped a little now and looking a bit defeated by the whole situation, my apartment doorbell rang. Seth and I looked at each other: early Saturday afternoon and neither of us was expecting anyone. He nodded and I nodded in return: He would run interference yet again.

He got up and left, padding down to the front door with his shoeless feet, leaving me and Helga to sit in the living room staring at the door and waiting for confirmation of who was there. Helga looked overly nervous considering it was just the doorbell—and my doorbell, at that.

"Don't worry," I assured her. "I'm pretty sure murderers don't ring the doorbell first. Not on a bright Saturday afternoon, at least." I smiled, trying to make light of things, but she just smirked a little.

"Sorry, Mags. I'm just way too flighty right now. Just a knee-jerk reaction thing. Nothing serious."

Because Seth had left the front door open, I could hear from up here on the second floor that it was my mother again. She burst into the building as soon as Seth opened the door and I could tell from the increasing volume of her voice and her tippity-tappety footsteps on the stairs that she was already halfway up and was in fine chattering form. Gunning for bear, I think her father would have called it.

". . .And I said to your grandfather, 'Well, that's it, I'm just going to go over there myself, dammit it all to hell, and I'm going to bring her this lasagna myself!'"

And with that announcement of impending food, my mother burst into the apartment. Sure enough, there was a nine-by-thirteen glass dish in her hands, carefully covered with aluminum foil and smelling wonderful. Nothing quite like a mother's comfort food to perk up the day. My mom looked around the room, first to me, then over to Helga, who had dutifully stood up from the couch and was standing there with her arms crossed tightly across her midsection, as if she were clutching herself with a stomachache.

"Oh, I didn't realize you had company!" my mother added, turning to Seth and frowning at him. "You failed to mention your mother had company!" She turned back to us and looked at Helga, smiling overly much, as was her style, and nodding subtly. "I'm Maggie's mother. You'll have to excuse me if I can't shake your hand or otherwise more properly introduce myself." She rose the casserole dish up a little bit until it was nearly level with her chin. "I've got my hands full just now."

She pivoted around away from us and toward Seth, who was hovering between the living room and kitchen area, and held out the casserole dish of lasagna. Not the subtlest hint, but she was right: He should have offered to take it from her. I could see it dawning on him that he was being silently asked to do something, and he stepped forward and took the dish from her by the handles, then turned and walked to the counter and set it down.

"It's still warm, Maggie dear. Not hot, though. You'd probably want to throw it into the oven to warm it up fully if you're going to eat it soon."

"Thanks," was all I said. I knew my mother well enough to know that her gifts of food were a lot like the Trojan Horse: They came with other, more important things inside. My concern was finding out just why she was *really* here. Because it definitely wasn't just the lasagna. She only made genuinely un-motive-laden gifts of food during true emergencies and crises, such as childbirth, death in the family, or major surgery. Or, in my case once, divorce. Since this wasn't any of those, I assumed she was really here on motherly false pretenses. Which was fine. I was a mother of adults myself and I certainly knew well the age-old concept of getting my foot in the door with them if I was concerned about their safety or well-being. In order to snoop around in their lives and find out how things were going, the best way with young adult children was home cooking. Even bad home cooking like mine.

"Thank you, Mom. Definitely appreciated today. And let me guess: You heard what happened."

"Yes, I did," she said, "and I'm not ashamed to admit that's why I'm here." She sounded overly defiant. "So tell me, just what's got-ten into you, young lady? Going around finding dead bodies *everywhere* now, are we? Playing Sam Spade now, are we?" She was trying to sound somewhat conversational, but her voice had that distinct shrillness and quivering to it that she only got when she was extremely agitated.

"Mom, please. I didn't find this other body. Helga did," I said, indicating Helga standing by the couch. "I found the first one, on Monday, but yesterday I just went down to help out Helga because I knew how scary it must have been for her." Helga managed a wan smile and waved timidly. It was an interesting dynamic to see Helga feeling a bit sheepish in front of anyone, and the fact that it hap-pened to be my mother made it all the more odd. I didn't like seeing my mom make someone like Helga cower, even if it was inadver-tent.

"Maggie, I know you're a grown woman, but I do wish sometimes that you would do a better job of keeping yourself out of harm's way. And that would set a better example for your son, too," she added, pointing deliberately to Seth, who stood silently in the kitchen, trying not to get hit with flying verbal debris.

"Grandma," he chimed in, "she's fine. The police were there. I think it's admirable that she wanted to help out a friend like that, even if she was probably still a little scared herself."

I shot Seth a glance that said, *Knock it off*, because mentioning I was scared certainly wasn't going to help ease my mother's worries. I had to put up a strong front to make her think there really was nothing to worry about. But it was too late. My mom turned her head from Seth back to me in a flash.

"I knew you were scared by all this. God knows your father and I are! Now, you really must stop all this nonsense. You're our only daughter and I'm not overly fond of the idea of you getting mixed up with . . . *murderers*. The first time on Monday was one thing: You didn't know what you were getting into and it was the first time it happened. But yesterday was just beyond foolishness."

Poor Helga was standing there looking a little caught in the middle. Her head was turning from one person to the other trying to follow the ongoing volley of words bouncing among the three of us. "Mrs. Velam, I honestly didn't mean to put your daughter in harm's way," she offered.

"I'm sure you didn't. But in any event, you did."

"Grandma," said Seth from across the way, still standing by the open island in my kitchen. "It's really the murderer who's putting people in danger, not Helga, and not Mom. In fact, they're here right now trying to put the facts together enough to figure out just who's behind all this." He nodded, naïvely thinking this fact would catapult the situation into *oh-well-that's-another-thing-entirely* territory. Needless to say, it did no such thing. Mothers in general don't like to hear that their only offspring are sitting around trying to solve murders on their own without the aid of modern forensics and police officers and, well, high-powered firearms. I should know: I was a mother myself, and if this were Seth, I'd be fuming. And I wouldn't have brought such a nice casserole.

I gave Seth another frowning, angry glance while my mother's head was turned toward him and away from me. I shook my head at him, hoping he'd get the idea, which was very simply, *Don't help!* My mother spun her head back in my direction with a glare all her own.

"What is this then? You're sitting here solving the murders right here from your living room? Is that wise?"

"Mom, none of it is exactly wise. But sometimes things that are . . . *risky* . . . are still necessary, given the circumstances." I knew that, thanks to Seth, I had to choose my words extra carefully from now on.

Helga, who had apparently had enough of her own wallflower ways in this conversation, took a few rather self-assured steps toward my mother, holding out her hand. "Mrs. Velam, please, come sit down. I for one would love to hear your thoughts on some of this. I think Maggie and I both are feeling just a mite bit overwhelmed by all this shi—I mean, *stuff* . . . and it would be a pleasure to get a fresh perspective on everything." She beckoned toward the closer end of the couch, trying to get my mother to sit and settle in. I watched my mother's reaction slowly, and I was reasonably sure I had no idea what she was thinking. This was unprecedented for me. I always knew what to expect from my mother, even when she did things in an impromptu fashion. She was predictably unpredictable, at all times. Except for now, when she was *un*predictably unpredictable.

She stood stock still, looking curiously at Helga with no expression on her face whatsoever. It was like all previous emotion had been stripped from her psyche in favor of a *tabula rasa* face. I waited for something to pass before her visage, for something— anything—to register in her eyes. For a smile or frown to cross her lips. For her forehead to pinch tight or her eyes to light up. I was clueless.

Then, without a word, my mother walked a few steps toward Helga, still as expressionless as before. For a fleeting moment I worried that she was walking toward Helga in order to cuff her upside the head, to lay her out flat or at least smack her across the face for getting her only daughter involved in a second murder this week.

But, thankfully, all my mother did was to walk as far as the couch and then sit down. And that was all she did. She watched as Helga slowly lowered herself back down onto the couch to sit beside her. And then they both looked at each other with less emotion than I ever would have thought possible from these two women who were both in such emotional turmoil, even though for different reasons.

I decided to get the two of them jumpstarted somehow, and chimed in to echo Helga's offer. It was probably better to have my mother actively involved and therefore feeling less powerless.

"Mom, yes, please do. We can tell you everything that's been happening, and maybe then you could help us lay out all the pieces of the puzzle a little bit. I think right now both Helga and I are a little too . . . close to the situation to get an objective handle on everything."

Mom turned and looked directly at me, frowning slightly. "What makes you think I can be anywhere near objective in all this?"

"I—I just meant about the evidence. Objective about what the pieces of evidence mean, the facts as we know them so far. That's all."

"Good grief, child. There's no such thing as objectivity here. We're all here for very selfish reasons. *Good* selfish reasons—not evil ones like the wretched killer's reasons for doing what he's doing—but they're selfish all the same. And that means we'll all have an agenda and will want the solution to go in a certain direction. The slant is going to happen whether we like it or not."

"Well, Grandma," said Seth, coming up from behind the couch and slipping into the living room to join the conversation officially. He sat in the rocking chair but slid forward to sit on the edge of the seat. "That's true, but I think the more people we have here thinking things through, the more perspective we have. And the closer we'll be to the truth. I for one highly value your advice on all this."

He shot me the quickest little glance, and it was all I could do not to roll my eyes at his gushing praise of my mother's mental faculties. Not that she didn't deserve it—she was brilliant in a lot of ways—but he was probably the last person in the family to gush over my mother in any capacity. I saw right through him again. I was pretty sure my mom did too, although she didn't let on, probably for the sake of getting through this situation as smoothly as possible.

"Thank you, Seth dear, but we don't need as many people as possible involved. There's not always safety in numbers. In this case, I think it's better to keep your names out of the papers—*both* your names," she added, pointing directly at Helga first and then turning and pointing at me too. "That's the first order of business, laying low."

She was saying that because her agenda was to be protective of me, but she also happened to be right this time. And I knew Helga didn't want to call attention to herself right now, either.

"You're absolutely right, Mrs. Velam," she said, scooching forward just a little on the couch and turning toward my mother eagerly. Her demeanor said, *Now here is a woman with a lot of common sense!* "It's time for me and for Maggie to just be quiet and not get too involved. But I think we should maybe still sit down and figure out what our own opinion is of the murders. Won't that help us both stay safe if we have a better idea of what the hell is going on here?"

Mom nodded, and I sat and watched the proceedings. My mom reminded me of the old days in elementary school when she was our Brownie troop mother and always helped us plan how to get our next troop badge. My mom always had a plan, and this time that was a really good thing. I wasn't ready to give up all control, but suddenly I did want to hear her opinions. So, I sat back and listened to what she had to say. And, the part that didn't surprise me in the least was that she had a lot of opinions on what had been happening. A lot.

CHAPTER 18

AFTER A FEW HOURS IN THE LIVING ROOM, my mother got up and motioned for Seth to follow her into the kitchen. By this point we had the early makings of a suspect list, sketchy though it was, with tendrils of proven facts and possible facts leading off from each one, listing motives (some real, some imagined, some more than a little forced in terms of murder). There were arrows meandering around the paper, several types of handwriting, and more than once my mother had asked me if I had multi-colored highlighter markers. I did, but I pretended I didn't at first. To me, once you started highlighting things in rainbow colors, then the neon-colored Post-it flags would come out next. After that was the dry-erase board wall chart, and beyond that were the Polaroid pictures of suspects taped up on the living room wall like some gargantuan FBI manhunt room. Next we'd be clipping newspaper articles about the murders and researching car tire imprints on the Internet.

But, while my mother and Seth were in the kitchen putting the lasagna in the oven to warm up and setting the table nicely and civilly (the first time all week, now that I thought about it), I looked at our scribbles, doodles and lists and thought maybe different colors on the charts and lists would make finding different pieces of information easier.

"I'll be right back," I informed Helga and stood suddenly, walking past her and down the hall to my office, where I was sure I had an entire unopened pack of highlighters. There, in a drawer where I kept office supplies of all types, was the unopened pack. I grabbed two packs of the Post-it flags too while I was there, and more blank paper, some lined and some unlined. FBI manhunt, indeed. Suddenly my obsession with office supplies didn't seem so petty. Well, perhaps it still was . . .

I went back out to the living room with my arms loaded down with supplies just in time to hear my mother announce, "Dinner!" in her distinctly commanding way. Not that any of us there weren't dying to dig into that lasagna by now. It was nearly five-thirty, and we showed no signs of letting up with our brainstorming session. Helga had perked back up to her usual self, now eager to take control of her own situation and move forward, jettisoning the rest of us with that same eagerness out into the wide world of amateur detectivehood. My mom felt much more in the loop with the information, and felt much better knowing she wouldn't keep hearing what horrible things were happening in her daughter's life by reading the newspaper or watching the local news on television. I assumed it was the lack of information control that unnerved her more than the situation itself. That seemed clearer the more the afternoon wore on.

Seth, of course, was having a great time, considering there were dead people I knew involved. The Cartoon Network really had little left to offer him this week, and my subtle hints of putting on the Food Network in the middle of the afternoon weren't working. He was still asking me what was for dinner every night at about five o'clock. So, after days of complete and abject boredom, with only a sad little neutered dog to keep him company while I alternately proofread cookbooks and stumbled on dead people, Seth was more than ready to jump into this sleuthing business with both feet. It didn't pay very well, of course, but neither did watching the Cartoon Network.

As for me, I was feeling a lot better having three people I knew and trusted in my apartment with me on an otherwise dreary Saturday afternoon. Son. Mother. Coworker/friend. Definitely better than being alone in the house with Vlad, who really wouldn't have been able to mirror my emotions appropriately nor help me solve the mystery surrounding the two poor hapless folks who'd turned up dead this week.

By the time I had dropped the office supplies on the coffee table and made it back into the kitchen area to the oak pedestal table, the three of them were seated and my mother was beginning to offer the others a nice-sized portion of her scrumptious sausage lasagna. For the first time in nearly a week, I felt close to normal. All I needed was a little garlic bread and I would have been in heaven.

Not *literally* in heaven, of course. There were already too many people around me who'd made that trek this week.

* * * * *

AFTER DINNER WE CLEARED THE TABLE, loaded the dishwasher, and decided that the round oak table with chairs was a much better place to plan our strategy and run the numbers than hunching over the coffee table in the living room. So, while the others brought all our supplies and charts and lists out to the kitchen, I threw on a pot of breakfast blend coffee and set out mugs and spoons for some good, life-giving java. Once everything was on the table—papers and supplies and coffee—we each took a seat around the table much as we had for dinner. I think we all felt rejuvenated enough to look at everything with fresh eyes. I looked at my mother, who seemed as eager as I'd seen her when starting any project—gardening or landscaping or crafts—and I was glad Helga had had the foresight to simply invite her into the circle. She did have a sharp mind and a certain kind of objectivity simply because she herself had seen no dead bodies this week.

"I have to call your father," she blurted out as we were all grab-bing a colored marker and popping the caps off.

"Oh geez, that never even occurred to me!" I said, realizing it was well past his own usual dinner time. "What was he going to do for dinner?"

"He's out hunting today, dear, and we agreed he'd stop and have a bite to eat with the boys on his way out of the woods and back home—it's a two-hour drive to get back home—so that's not the problem, really. I just want to leave a message on the machine for him, so he knows where I am and not to worry."

She got up and went into the living room to get the phone, while the rest of us laid out the "Other Suspects" chart on top of all the others. This was, of course, the most important thing we were doing today. We were running through our heads the total list of possible murder suspects in this case. This proved to be a lot harder than we would have thought initially, if only because the cross referenc-ing of Brenda with Gerber brought up so few good leads on people with any real motives for murder. Beyond that, since we hadn't re-ally known Gerber all that well, and he had come here from an-other state, a lot of our list consisted of people without names to us but with general descriptions: Gerber's ex-wife. Gerber's jury duty defendant. Dirt Boy, the letter-to-the-editor writer. We knew who we meant, but we would have felt more professional, I suppose, if we had had actual names for some of these people. At one point we switched "Gerber's ex-wife" to "Mrs. Gerber/ex-wife" and that helped a little, but not much. Besides, she seemed way too obvi-ous a suspect for Gerber's murder and a total blank as a suspect for Brenda's murder.

Despite the lists, charts, color-coding, and Post-it notes, I sud-denly felt as if we were getting nowhere. Maybe it was time to break out the dry-erase boards and the wall charts after all.

CHAPTER 19

THE PHONE RANG, startling me enough that I literally jumped a few inches out of my desk chair, freaking out Vlad, who was, as usual, underfoot and underwheels. A sharp, loud yip of protest and he too jumped a few inches in the air. He was feeling almost as skittish as I was. Meanwhile, the phone was on its third ring, heading for a fourth. I lunged for the receiver in the cradle to the far left of my monitor on the desk and caught it just before the fifth ring, when the answering machine would have gotten it.

"Hello?" I tried not to sound frazzled, which was a lost cause, I realized, as soon as I heard my own voice.

"Maggie, is that you?"

I'd lived alone since the divorce. Frazzled or not, I was sure I still sounded like me. What was it about George Roberts that made him so, well, *stupid*? As ex-husbands went, he had to be one of the stupidest. There really was no other word for him. Stupid. After many years of marriage and five years of divorce, this much about him was clear. Stupid, stupid, stupid.

"Yes, George, it's me. Who did you think it was, the dog?"

He laughed—guffawed, really—as if I had just told the funniest joke in the world. Maybe a better word for him was pathetic. Some-times stupid didn't seem big enough.

"No, of course not!" he added, answering my rhetorical ques-tion the way only a pathetically stupid person would. "You just, well, is something wrong? It sounded like something was wrong. Before. When you answered the phone . . ." He trailed off awkwardly, appar-ently realizing even in his pea brain that I was finding him annoying today. More than I usually did.

"George, nothing is wrong. I'm fine. The dog is fine—not that you care about him, of course. Life is fine. My parents are fine. The neighbors you've never met are fine. The state of the union is fine. We're all fine. Anything else I can help you with while you have me glued to the phone today?"

I was drenched with my own sarcasm, every bit of which was needed if I wanted George to take the hint that He Was Annoying Me and that I Had Better Things To Do.

"Well, the thing is, the guys wanted to get together for a game of baseball down at the campus, and I can't find my baseball glove. I'm starting to think maybe it's still with you. Have you seen it?"

So, this was George's monthly "Have You Seen My [Fill In The Blank]?" phone call. George was under the mistaken impression that, when he and I split up five years ago, I had moved out of his house but had somehow managed to pack up half his stuff without his knowledge and found room for it in this two-closet apartment. In reality, the stuff he called about was usually found weeks later in the attic or basement of the house, tucked away behind an old washing machine or dresser or sitting in a damp unmarked banker's box. It never failed. And yet, he continued to call here first whenev-er he couldn't find something. It was the divorced version of "Hon-ey, have you seen my keys?" The woman always knows where stuff is—it's in our genes—and George falsely assumed that this genetic trait translated into some sort of cross-town prognostication that he could still tap into. Try as I might to explain that the divorce severed any paranormal ties I might have had with his belongings, George remained undaunted and continued to call routinely. I was beginning to think it was a ploy. Since when did he play baseball with the guys? And, just who were "the guys"?

"No, George, no baseball glove here. If I had it here, I'm sure Vladimir would have peed on it by now. You know how he loves to wet on leather."

A few comical beats of silence hung between us. "Really? Do dogs dislike leather?"

I couldn't resist.

"Of course, George. They're personally offended by the presence of the skinned, tanned hide of a fellow four-legged creature. They can smell the death and misery in the leather."

"Really?" he asked, deadpan and serious in his inquiry. "I had no idea."

"Oh, yes. Dogs are quite militant in their animal rights activism. They really have no choice, though, do they?"

"Wow. I wouldn't have guessed that," he said. I could sense the revulsion in his voice. George was not a dog person.

It was time to press on to other topics, before I started snorting with laughter and ruined the fun of having caught him again. I was so glad he'd never really understood this side of me while we were married because it made him so much more fun now that we were divorced. He took me so friggin' seriously.

"George, I don't have your glove. Haven't seen it since the Paleolithic era of our marriage. It's probably in a box in the living room closet, with your golf cleats and tennis racket."

"Oh, good idea. I didn't think to look there."

Why did this not surprise me? Sometimes even I hated being right all the time.

"Is there anything else, George?" I didn't bother to disguise the petulance in my voice.

"No, Maggie."

"Okay, then," I said, hoping I sounded dismissive.

"Maggie," he added quietly.

"Yeah?"

"Are you sure everything is all right? You really sound on edge."

I sighed. How could he tell? Was it so obvious that even George could hear it in my voice? Or, more likely, was it just that even a broken clock is right twice a day? Whether or not he was right, I wasn't about to get into a discussion with him about why I was feeling a little off-kilter these days. There were plenty of up-sides to him living three towns away—and him not knowing about the murders was one of them.

"I'm fine, George. The president is fine. The squirrels in the back yard are fine. Bruce Jenner is fine. Let it go."

"Okay. If you insist."

I sighed again. Where was this easy compliance while we were married? Somewhere else I wasn't going to go.

"Yes, I insist. Now, go look in that closet. I bet you find your glove."

"Okay. Talk to you later."

"Yup," I said curtly, hanging up before he could threaten me with the promise of a future phone call.

The call felt like pulling teeth. Impacted wisdom teeth. And George hadn't mentioned anything about either murder. Either this really hadn't made it to his own local paper, or he was even more clueless than I suspected.

It was time to refresh my java and wrap up the online putzing so I could get ready for Gerber's funeral. Helga, Seth and I were leaving for Ohio in an hour because we thought it best to be there and observe. Suddenly real life was kicking back in with a vengeance. And I'd totally forgotten to firm up my Thanksgiving plans with the kids while I had George on the phone. My brain was officially on sabbatical.

CHaPTer 20

'D ALWAYS THOUGHT FUNERALS WERE UGLY THINGS. Messy. Confusing. Awkward. Obligatory. Uncomfortable. Even if the deceased was someone I didn't know well, and I was in attendance out of a sense of duty to the living, there always came a point where tears welled up in my eyes and I would begin choking back emotion I wasn't even sure I felt. Perhaps it was in some sense that common fear of death every person harbors. Perhaps I was weeping (or trying not to weep) for myself and my own inevitable death. Perhaps I was upset at being reminded of my own mortality—and, worse still, reminded by someone I didn't know very well. Certainly not well enough to impose that sort of emotional stranglehold on me without my permission.

In any event, I sat between Helga and Seth at Lee Gerber's funeral a week after his death in a kind of dazed stupor. I tried not to let either one of them see my oddly personal reaction to the generic religious drivel being foisted on us from the generic religious authority figure behind the generic wooden lectern. It was clear the man had never met Gerber and that he'd been hired by the family to deliver the plastic-coated eulogy emanating from his wholly unaffected mind. To him this was a job like so many others; his delivery was stoic and his words unemotional and flaccid.

And yet I was doing the choke-back-tears thing. What was that all about? And, in situations where self-consciousness and awkwardness set in, having to hide the unbidden emotion from companions made it all the more difficult to restrain it. And so I sat between my son and my friend, trying vainly to will my lips to stop quivering and my eyes to not cast off tears when I next blinked. But it was a hopeless cause, as it always is. The blink came, and three or four telltale tears trickled down my flushed face. I clutched my pocket-pack of tissues in one hand and yanked the top one out in the nick of time, catching the wayward tears before they spilled off the end of my chin. A quick dab and they were gone. In my peripheral vision, though, I saw Seth frowning at me, most likely confused that I was dabbing at my eyes over someone he'd heard me call Gerber Baby. Without thinking, I sniffled at just the wrong moment, and Seth's frown deepened as he nudged me in the side. When I glanced ever so fleetingly in his direction, he shot me a "What is *this*?" look that told me the jig was up, for sure. Caught red-handed. Or, red-faced, in this case.

The prepaid preacher wrapped up his prepackaged eulogy with a reading from none other than Psalm 23. Even the worst heathen could have guessed that choice of comforting Bible passages. I mean, it didn't take a degree in theology to have written this thing. Perhaps I could convince Seth I'd been weeping over the verbal murder of English prose at the hands of our dear Reverend Ridiculous. It was a long shot, but not without merit. My son had already branded me a grammatical tightwad years ago.

"Mom, you okay?" Seth half-whispered into my ear as I thrust the damp tissue into my skirt pocket.

"Fine, dear," I whispered back, hoping that stating it firmly and clearly would make it so. "I'm just bored to tears, that's all." I smiled and winked, which might have won him over, but I also sniffled again without catching myself in time, and Seth's hesitant smile turned directly into another frown. *I already have one mother,*

I thought. Next he'd be bringing me casseroles for the freezer and taking my temperature.

I turned in the other direction to face Helga, who looked just preoccupied enough with her own thoughts to not notice my sniffling. But then she absentmindedly handed me a tissue while staring straight ahead, which made me realize I must have been more obvious than I initially thought. When was the nightmare going to end?

Just as that question passed through my brain, Reverend Lite said a pronounced "Amen," and everyone in the place echoed him stoically. He cleared his throat too loudly, an indication that he had an addendum to that amen.

"The congregation is invited to . . . errr . . . congregate down in the fellowship hall for . . . umm . . . fellowship and coffee. The family will remain later for a meal prepared by the ladies of the congregation. The fellowship hall steps are . . ." He trailed off and looked to the front of the side aisle for some help. An usher pointed to a side rear exit door. ". . . out the back right door. We hope you can join us and greet the family."

I leaned over toward Helga. "Hey, are we going to stick around?" She straightened up, came back from whatever other world she'd flitted off to, and shrugged.

"I don't know, but we should, right?" she whispered. "I mean, don't they say that the murderer sometimes comes back to the scene of the crime? This isn't exactly the scene of the crime, but the murderer could be right here in the room right now!"

"It's cliché, yeah," I whispered back, "but you're right. I suppose it's possible. If it were me, I'd be in Mexico by now, but I suppose I'd make a pretty bad murderer to begin with."

I canvassed the room with my eyes, making mental note of anyone who looked either inherently suspicious or too nervous to be at this funeral as a mourner. Frankly, nobody caught my attention. Everyone looked either mildly bored, obviously in attendance out of a sense of obligation to a past employer, or in some small state of actual mourning, which might have included me if I were being judged merely by number of tissues used and redness around the eyes. Sometimes I despised my wayward tear ducts for rebelling on me at the most inopportune moments.

"See anybody who looks like a murderer?" Seth asked me as we stood in place and waited our turn to file out.

"Not really, no," I said surreptitiously, still darting my eyes around and talking under my breath. "You?"

He shook his head. "Nope. Then again, though, O.J. Simpson didn't look like a murderer in the *Naked Gun* movies, either."

I looked straight at him and blinked. Sometimes I wondered how his synapses fired the way they did. I assumed he got this kind of thing from his father. Or at least, I hoped that was where he got it.

Helga tugged lightly on my sleeve. "Psst. Do you suppose she's the widow?" She kept her grip on my sleeve but let one finger curl out to point to our right and straight on toward dawn. Standing about twenty feet away from us, talking quietly to a few other people I didn't know, was a woman in a modest black dress. She had a black clutch bag tucked under her left arm, buried almost in her armpit, and she looked like a one-woman receiving line, shaking hands with everyone who passed and nodding. She was saying very little. It seemed as if she was receiving tidbits of conversation more than she was giving them.

I nodded. "That'd be my guess, although would she technically be a widow if she was divorced from Gerber Baby—I mean, Lee—before he died?" I frowned at my own question and turned my gaze to Helga and Seth, my co-sleuths at this funeral. They both simply blinked at me; it seemed apparent neither one of them had an answer.

"I'll Google it once we get home," Seth said.

"Good, that's your assignment, although it was partly a rhetorical question, sweetie," I replied. "She just seems to be playing the part to the hilt over there, and yet she wasn't even married to the guy anymore."

Most people had begun to file out the rear right door, and I signaled to Helga and Seth to head toward the back. I thought we'd go out the middle doors and take a peek at whomever had decided to cut out early. Seemed to me a murderer would pop in out of curiosity but wouldn't necessarily hang around for coffee and cake. Unless he was really, really hungry or it was really good cake. Neither of which was all that likely.

I strode at a good clip up the middle aisle, weaving deftly around small pockets of two or three people standing there. I could hear Helga and Seth's footfalls behind me, trying to keep up. I opened my purse as I walked, not slowing down, eyes straight ahead, while fumbling inside the purse for a piece of paper and something to write with. My goal was as many license plate numbers as possible. I wasn't even sure I could get information on people based solely on license plate numbers—that sounded too much like stuff from the movies—but any information I could get on the cars in the lot would feel like some sort of forward motion.

I burst out the main doors onto the top of the concrete stairs in the front of the church building. I saw several people walking slowly to their cars and one single car already pulling out of its space, raising a small cloud of dust from the unpaved parking area on the side of the church building. *Damn!* Looking around the parking lot, I tried to make a snap judgment call on whether to dash toward the moving car—an orange Aveo, I noted—or give up on that car and concentrate on the plate numbers of the other cars that were going to be pulling out soon. As I hit the bottom step and nearly dove face-first into the dirt, I saw the Aveo's right blinker go on, saw its driver look both left and right as he waited for traffic on the main street to pass, and then saw its little orange metal body turn smartly into traffic in an open spot, heading onto the main drag and right toward the junction with the interstate. And I stood there with my hand still buried up to my elbow in my purse, having found no paper or writing implement.

Two more car engines started, one after the other, as I pulled an old pen from the bottom of my purse. Seth and Helga showed up at my side. Helga noticed the pen in my hand and my forlorn look as I gazed at the second car leaving the lot.

"Oh! Paper? Here, I have some!" she said excitedly and reached into her small handbag, coming out with a neat little pad of paper and handing it to me. "How's this?" She blinked at me innocently. There sure was a lot of blinking going on lately.

I snatched the pad from her and looked quickly at the third car, its engine running and its white backup lights already on. "The plate number!" I yelled, a little too loudly, pointing with the pen toward the back of the car. Seth took a few hurried steps toward the car to see better and his lips mouthed the letters and numbers on the back plate of the car. He misjudged the car's backward movements a little too much, though, probably because he was busy memorizing numbers and letters, and the old Impala swung crazily to the left, barely missing a forward-moving Seth, who stopped short when he realized he'd run into the blind spot of the Impala.

The car stopped abruptly as the driver caught sight of Seth, who was now standing on the car's left side, looking directly into the driver's side window. The driver, a younger man, looked directly at Seth as he rolled down his window.

"What's your problem? You trying to get hit or what?" The man—almost a boy, really, not much older than Seth—frowned severely at him and shook his head. He angrily threw the car into Drive and sped forward to the end of the parking lot, pulling into traffic without signaling and disappearing from view. Seth's head drooped and he turned to us, shrugging as he walked our way.

"I got the first three letters," he said sheepishly. "R Z X. And then three numbers and another letter, I think."

"You're sure about the letters, though?" I asked.

"Yeah, that much I got. Just before I almost got hit." He smiled, trying to make light of the incident. I put the pen to the pad of paper and tried to write "R Z X" on the top sheet, but the pen wouldn't cooperate. No ink was flowing, so I scribbled large circles on the sheet, doing nothing but carving colorless lines into the paper. "I hate this pen," I muttered, just as the ink kicked in and the circles magically became visible in glorious black. "Oh, good!"

I scrawled the letters onto the paper and wrote "blue Impala, young male driver" after them.

"What else did either of you notice about him or the car?" Seth looked at Helga, who turned to look at me. I was pretty sure this was all we were going to get out of this enterprise. I sighed. "Okay then, what did anyone notice about the second car—the one that drove out as we were rushing to get information on the Impala?" More blinking. Some shrugging. A little foot scuffling in the dust and gravel. Yes, we were a fine bunch of detectives, weren't we?

"It was blue," Seth offered.

"No, that was the Impala," Helga said.

"The other car was blue too," Seth insisted. "It's not like there's only one blue car in the world."

"Seth," I reprimanded. "Don't treat Helga like she's your sister. No squabbles. We're here for a reason." I wrote again on the paper. "Second car leaving lot: blue. Not very helpful, but I'm going to write down everything. We can always get rid of it, but recreating it later will be . . . well, let's say it'd be challenging." I coughed. "Especially for the likes of us."

Helga chuckled. "Did you get any other plate numbers before we got out here?"

"No. The first car I saw leaving the lot was an orange Aveo," I said as I wrote that information onto the paper. "Signaled properly. Good driver. Cute new little car. My gut reaction is, not the murderer."

"Sounds good to me," Seth said, "but I agree with writing down everything now and sorting it out later. Right now is for information gathering. Later we can interpret it."

"Agreed," Helga added.

"Good," I said. "I'll take the paper and pen and walk around the lot jotting down makes, models, and plate numbers. Maybe you guys could head back inside and join the gang downstairs and see what you can find out. When I get done out here, I'll join you and we can add more stuff to the paper here while it's still fresh in our minds."

I took a few steps into the parking lot, heading first for the car to my right and intending to work my way around the lot counter-clockwise.

"Good idea," Helga called after me. "Just don't look too much like a meter maid or you'll look obvious. Try to look . . ." I turned and saw her scratching her chin.

"Sneaky?" I suggested.

She smiled. "No, the last thing you want to do is look sneaky. Try to look . . ." The chin-scratching continued.

"Surreptitious?" Seth offered.

Helga grinned and pointed at Seth, who was heading back up the steps. "Yes! Nice two-dollar word there, college boy!" She clapped him on the back as he joined her at the top of the steps. "Now," she said, loudly enough for me to hear, "let's go in, have some coffee and cake, and leave your mother alone to do her nitpicky thing. You and me might transpose numbers or something, but a proofreader's perfect for the task!"

"'You and *I*!'" I corrected. "It's 'you and I'!"

Helga burst out laughing. "See? I told you!"

CHaPTer 21

N O ONE ELSE CAME TO THEIR CARS in the parking lot while I scurried around writing down plate numbers as fast as I could. The old pen cut out on me several times, and I made more than a few mental reminders to put a better pen in my purse when I got home—along with a little pad of paper like Helga had been carrying. Not that I needed more junk in my purse, but it now seemed vital to carry paper and pen with me at all times. Surely all good sleuths carried such things. It was shameful that it hadn't occurred to me to have pen and paper on hand today. I chalked it up to my grief and mourning and tucked the pad and pen into my purse as I turned for the steps and headed back into the church.

The steps down to the fellowship hall were to my immediate left as I passed through the main doors into the church, and I could hear the low muffle of many voices coming from the room below. I reached the bottom of the stairs and scanned the room for either Helga or Seth. When I caught no sight of them, I crept further into the room, melting into the small crowd of people who were milling around with coffee cups or dainty plates in their hands, chatting in mostly hushed tones and trying to look sufficiently reverent for the occasion. Several knots of people off in far corners were smiling and joking—nothing too raucous but still noticeable in comparison to the more somber pockets of people standing around the room in what looked like tightly staged still-life shots of mourners.

As I continued to gaze around the room, my peripheral vision caught a small hand waving above the heads of the people between us. Assuming it was Helga, who had probably seen me on the stairs, I walked toward where the hand had been waving, all the while darting my eyes around, sweeping the room for suspicious or awkward activity. I nudged past the last knot of people before reaching the refreshment table and saw Helga motioning me over still further.

"Hi, sorry you couldn't see either of us down here. We were standing closer to the steps at first, but then Seth overheard some guy talking trash about his boss, and off he went!"

"That's okay," I said. "Was Lee the boss he was talking about?" Swiveling my head around and standing on tiptoe to look for Seth's head, I darted my gaze around the room without finding him.

"Dunno. Seth probably figured, what the heck? It's worth a shot. Anyway, I stayed back here after getting a cup of coffee since I could see the stairs from here pretty good." She handed me a cup of coffee, which I took gratefully. I wrapped my hands around the cup and went back to room-scanning.

As we stood there silently, both of us panning the room for any sign of either Seth or someone who looked like a murderer, my ears caught snippets and tails of conversations around us. Although nothing immediately surrounding me sounded like a thinly veiled murder confession, I thought perhaps Seth had a generally good idea. Perhaps we were going about this all wrong to stand here waiting for someone with a big scarlet "M" on his lapel to show up and walk right by us. Perhaps it would be more productive to meander around the room, to mingle a bit and listen to other conversations. Perhaps someone who didn't necessarily look or dress or act like a killer could still say something telling that might give him away. Something we might notice but that an unsuspecting person might not pick up on as easily.

And so I signaled to Helga that I was leaving her company and I slowly slipped into the group, clutching my coffee cup and trying not to have my elbows jostled so I wouldn't end up with hot coffee spilled on me. Even if I could sue McDonald's for spilling scalding coffee on myself, could I sue a church for it? Would I even want to?

I derailed this train of thought and listened intently to conversations around me as I walked. Speakers with their backs to me as I passed by were problematic but not impossible. A little upper-range hearing loss from years of headphone use as a teen didn't help my cause either, but at least I could hear the men's voices fairly well. It was only the women's voices that occasionally lost an end word or dropped the end of a sentence as I passed by slowly.

A few minutes later I looked up from the floor as I nudged my way past a cluster of rather rotund people, and ahead of me I saw Seth standing off in a corner like a wallflower at the school dance. He saw me looking at him and smiled, waving with a hand held close to his chest so as not to attract too much attention. I smiled in return and nodded, indicating I was heading in his direction.

After snaking my way through several groups of people, one of which was all *Bugle* employees, I got entangled between two groups whose current speakers were standing back to back with their shoulder blades nearly touching. I stopped quietly and looked between their heads at Seth, who shrugged as if to say, "No problem, take your time." I stood for a few moments next to the conjoined speakers, waiting patiently, when the group to the left changed speakers.

"It is a shame," said a docile-voiced woman on the far side of the group. "Now I don't know what'll happen to my book." I stood quite still, remaining wedged between her group and the one to my right. The voice sounded vaguely familiar.

"Was Gerber the editor then?" asked the burly man whose shoulder blades were courting those of the man directly behind him.

"In the beginning, yes, he was. But then he left to come here, and frankly, all hell broke loose. All of a sudden Deerpark didn't want it anymore."

I was now sure I'd heard her voice before. Of course it was the author with the widowed book that Lee had wanted me to meet and mentor. Francine something or other. I stopped looking for a way out of the crowd and decided to listen and look a little while longer. Francine was dressed in a simple navy dress cinched at the waist, very low black pumps on her panty-hosed feet. A simple pearl necklace circled her thick neck, her gray-tinged hair pulled back into an otherwise unadorned ponytail along her back. It reached just past her shoulders, the hair itself rather dull and lifeless. Her eyeglasses sat a little too far down her nose—I expected to see her reach up and nudge them back into place higher on the bridge of her nose—and were too big for current fashion. Well, for several decades' worth of current fashion, actually. The frames were the big, mottled, plastic kind that made a person look like a three-dimensional Atom Ant. The earpieces swooped melodramatically from the bottom of the frames and then back and up behind her ears. Ugly, ugly buggers, really, and about as unflattering as her hairstyle and dress. She was neat, clean, and presentable, but wasn't much beyond that.

Although I felt uncomfortable making snap judgments about people I didn't really know, I could see why Gerber wasn't in any hurry to keep meeting with her. She oozed author confusion and lack of experience. And Gerber never struck me as the kind of editor who would have wanted to hand-hold his authors all the way through the process. Their relationship must have been one instance of miscommunication after another—him using his usual off-color jokes with obscure references strewn around, and her feeling overwhelmed, confused, and mentally manhandled. Yeah, this felt a lot like a bad marriage gone haywire.

I sipped my coffee down to the halfway point, noting that it was growing tepid. The conversation to my left had changed yet again, this time with a third party speaking. The topic had apparently changed to Gerber's ex-wife, so I raised my eyebrows in Seth's direction and nodded my head to the left to let him know I was listening in to a particular conversation and wasn't in a hurry to get to his corner of the room. He nodded in comprehension, so

I refocused my attention on the conversation and ever so slowly sidled one or two steps left, waiting for a small break to appear in the shoulder-to-shoulder stances of the six people in the circle. Perhaps I could slyly insinuate myself into the group and become an official participant in the conversation. Or, at least, a spectator. I could nod sympathetically in response to anyone who spoke and hope that Francine got around to expressing more opinions about Gerber. Perhaps someone at Deerpark had been speaking out of school about our dear Mr. Gerber and she'd heard it somehow.

"I don't know why an ex-wife would take charge of his funeral like this, though. Doesn't it seem to you like she's in charge of everything?" a tall, thin, middle-aged man asked the group, who were all vigorously nodding their heads while holding tiny plates and cups that were now empty.

"Doesn't seem right, I agree," said a small woman to his right. "I mean, when I croak, I certainly don't want my ex handling things. Even the thought of Mark deciding what happens to me and sitting in a place of honor or something at my funeral is enough to make me sick." The others all laughed, some a little too loudly. She smiled politely, but there was an embittered look on her face that was all too familiar to anyone who's been through it.

The cluster of people on the right had been dwindling slowly as people moved about to talk to other people. An opening almost the size of the parting of the Red Sea appeared between the two groups, and I jolted back to reality. I glanced in Seth's direction, only to find him missing from his spot holding up the wall in the corner of the room. He was instead heading in my direction, bobbing and weaving between people a little more easily as they began leaving the fellowship hall in groups of one and two. He reached me just as I stepped into the dry sea bed between the clusters that had been oddly conjoined earlier.

"Hey," he said simply when we got close enough to speak.

"Hey," I replied. Why couldn't someone my age pull off the hey-instead-of-hello greeting without sounding even older? I guessed it was a generational dilemma and that I'd never be allowed into the

Say-Hey club unless it involved Willie Mays. I doubted Seth even knew who Willie Mays was.

"So, what were they saying?" he asked boldly, with the two of us still within earshot of most of the group.

"Shhh," I cautioned, taking him by the shoulders and turning him around to face where he had just come from. "Let's talk over in your wallflower corner."

"My what?" he asked over his shoulder as I lightly pushed him forward and away from where I'd been eavesdropping.

"Over here," I said as we made it back to the wall. "I don't want anyone to hear that we're listening in on them."

"Isn't that a little hypocritical of us? We can listen to you but we'll go over here so you can't listen to us talking about listening to you?"

"Yeah, something like that. Now, what have you got for me? Helga said something about a guy badmouthing his boss . . .?"

Seth shrugged. "Not much, really. I thought maybe he worked at the newspaper office and hated Gerber like everyone else, but it turns out he was talking about his boss at some factory somewhere. You know, his supervisor or something. Not a suit like Gerber."

"Okay. Not a problem. Anything else?"

"Not really. That letter-to-the-editor guy is here, though. Is that significant?"

"You mean Dirt Boy?" I asked, turning around to face the entire room so I could scan faces again. "Where?"

"He left."

"He what?"

"He left," said a voice coming from my left. It was Helga, who'd left her post by the coffee pot and had finally joined us. "About a half hour ago. He didn't stay long, but I think it might mean something that he put in an appearance, don't you?" She nodded as she said this, as if her not-so-subliminal efforts would sway me to agree with her.

"Sure, definitely. But did either of you follow him out to see which car he got into?"

"No, we figured you were out there already gathering license plate numbers. You'd see him leave."

I blinked at Helga and paused before speaking. "Helga, how would I have known he was significant? It's not like I know what Dirt Boy looks like!"

"Oh, yeah," she said, excruciatingly slowly.

"So what does he look like?" I asked. It should have been an obvious question, but apparently my judgment on that point was a tad flawed. Seth looked at Helga, whose expression seemed to say, "And now let's throw it back to Seth with the weather! Seth?"

"He's probably about ten or fifteen years older than you are, Mom," he started as Helga nodded.

"At least. At least!" she agreed, as if a simple pronouncement of his age being near mine would offend me in some way.

"And?" I coaxed.

"Hardly any hair left, and what's there is mostly graying. Kinda short, but not as short as you."

"Yup," I acknowledged, not minding the casual reference to my being vertically challenged. At first I thought he'd meant the man's hair was short, so this was a clarification, really. "Did he say anything damning? And, hey, how did you even know it was him in the first place? I don't suppose you checked his I.D. and it said 'Boy-comma-Dirt' on it, did it?"

Seth let out a self-conscious laugh. "No, nothing like that, of course. Your friend Ernest pointed him out to me."

"How would Ernest know it was him?" This was like pulling teeth, only a lot less fun.

"Apparently he introduced himself to Ernest as 'the letter writer' or something once he found out Ernest worked in the typesetting room of the paper."

Helga was reaching in her purse for a lighter, a slender cigarette dangling loosely from between her lips, where it shook awkwardly. Her hand emerged from her purse clutching a yellow lighter, which nervously shuddered in her hand and lit only on the third try. Matching up the lighter's tiny flame with the tip of her cigarette proved to be a daunting task, and watching her, I finally came to the rescue and reached out to steady her hand enough to keep the lighter's flame from missing its target yet again.

"Thanks," Helga said through pursed lips encircling the other end of the cigarette. "Sorry, I'm a bit nervous today after all."

"Can't say I blame you, Helga. I'm not feeling all that sure of myself either, to tell you the truth," I sympathized. "And to think we have to do this all over again in two more days," I said, referring to Brenda's upcoming funeral. Helga nearly bit down on the tip of her cigarette.

"Didn't really need a reminder like that right now, Mags," she said through clenched teeth, keeping the cigarette held a little too firmly between her teeth.

"Sorry." I looked at Seth. "How do you know Ernest all of a sudden?"

Helga waved her hand to get my attention. "That was me," she confessed. "While you were outside gathering numbers and letters, I was down here introducing Seth to all the *Bugle* employees who bothered to show up. That was when Ernest told us about meeting the mysterious Dirt Boy."

"So, what's the verdict then?"

"He's not all that mysterious."

"Bummer."

"Yeah. It kinda ruins all the fun now, to know what he looks like. That, and the fact that he looks like my Uncle Sid from back in the sixties."

"Bummer."

"You have no idea. Oh, and he dresses like him too."

"Also from back in the sixties?"

"Hell yeah," she answered, her hand holding the cigarette a little more steadily now. Banter always seemed to bring out the real Helga.

Seth clapped his hands together lightly, echoing more than I would have thought given all the people in the room. Glancing around the fellowship hall, I immediately noticed that many of the people had cleared out. I looked at those of us who remained—

probably no more than half the number who were here when I first came downstairs—and realized with an awkward feeling in the pit of my stomach that we were likely the only people left who were mere acquaintances of Lee Gerber. And that wasn't even counting the fact that Seth had never met him at all and probably couldn't remember Gerber's first name.

"I think we've overstayed our welcome," I said casually. Seth and Helga tried to look furtively around the room, but their attempts at being inconspicuous were a farce. It was a good thing we weren't being watched. As a crack team of detectives, we sure were a sorry lot. We couldn't even manage a properly surreptitious glance across a room. "Besides, should you even be smoking in a church?"

"It's the fellowship hall, Mags," Helga shot back.

"Still . . . maybe we should skedaddle."

Helga coughed. "Only if you stop using words like 'skedaddle.'"

"Let's blow this popsicle stand," Seth said. Helga and I looked at him simultaneously, and he frowned and said simply, "What?"

"Nothing," I said. "Let's go before we get asked to stay and clean up."

And with that, the three of us headed up the stairs and out the door into the half-empty parking lot. We decided to rendezvous at my apartment after work tomorrow to discuss how to handle things differently at Brenda's funeral. Seth and I got into my car and pulled out of the lot, with me trying to steer the car properly through the tears welling up in my eyes. I saw Seth watching me in my peripheral vision, and I was grateful that he said nothing and turned to face front again.

It had been a long day, and it was only mid-afternoon.

CHAPTER 22

B RENDA'S FUNERAL FOUND US A LITTLE MORE ORGANIZED because we didn't make the same sorts of Keystone Cops mistakes we'd made at Gerber's funeral. But, Helga and I were also distracted a lot more by the event itself. We both knew Brenda and worked with her. There was a more personal quality to the service, and Helga and I were in tears on several occasions as several family members and a college roommate all spoke of the Brenda they knew and loved.

This was so unlike Gerber's service, which seemed perfunctory and shallow to us, almost griefless. In contrast, Brenda's funeral was filled with stunned, stricken people. It was a nobler and yet uglier affair, a dichotomy I couldn't have explained to anyone but which I was fairly certain Helga felt as well. The sheer wrongness of her death permeated the entire service. I think Seth, Helga, and I weren't the only ones who felt her murder was some sort of tacked-on afterthought by the killer. It felt more random than Gerber's murder, and that made Brenda's death so much more senseless and sad. She didn't have to die—a thought not many people were expressing during Gerber's funeral. For some reason, there were plenty of people ready to believe that someone had offed the guy. They were practically lining up out the door to get a crack at him. Seth, Helga, and I were sure that Brenda was simply in the wrong place at the wrong time.

By the end of the service, the three of us were beginning to feel the same way: like we were in the wrong place at the wrong time. I had no sense of foreboding at this funeral—no sense that the killer might actually show up to view his handiwork. There were no angry exes, no disgruntled former coworkers, or anything approaching the feeling that anyone here might have held a deadly grudge against Brenda.

So, Helga and I felt a little freer to participate in the service as friends rather than watching it as sleuths. I, for one, was grateful for this since neither of us had had any real time to process what had happened to everyone this week—no real time to grieve for anything or anyone. Helga's hand reached over and waved in my line of sight as I looked down at my shoes in an effort to hide my wet, red eyes.

"Got a tissue?" she asked in a whisper. This time I'd come prepared with two full pocket-packs and handed Helga a full one from my purse. "Thanks," she said and took the pack, yanked the first tissue out, and blew her nose as daintily as she could, given the circumstances. I couldn't understand why some people never learned how to blow their noses without sounding like a trumpeting circus elephant. George had always been a morning nose-trumpeter, and I quickly became irritated with his apparent inability to clear his nose in a less dramatic fashion. I don't think he realized just how noisy he was. And now I realized Helga had learned the fine art of nose-blowing at the same Dizzy Gillespie School of Nose Trumpeting. Only a few folks nearby glanced our way, and Helga and I quickly turned our faces downward to continue looking at our shoes.

Disperse, disperse—nothing to see here, I thought as another head turned when Helga blew out a second trumpet call with tissue number two.

* * * * *

"No more funerals for a while," Seth said when we got back to my apartment. He flopped onto the couch and kicked his shoes off. He wasn't used to wearing much else on his feet besides sneakers and the occasional pair of sandals in the dead heat of the summer. Wearing dress shoes twice in one week probably felt like a personal sacrifice to someone like Seth. Must be nice to have a life simple enough that going above and beyond the call of duty meant wearing black laces and leather dress shoes.

Helga walked over to that end of the couch and tousled his hair as she walked by. "We're not planning on any, hon. Don't worry about that."

"The only good thing to come out of all this," I offered from the kitchen, staring into the crammed freezer trying to decide what to thaw out for dinner, "is that we're overstocked on casseroles for the next month, at least." I chose whichever glass dish was on top—a chicken and rice dish that had originally smelled marvelous when my mother first brought it over hot several days ago. The eating habits of all three of us hadn't been that regular since this whole fiasco started, and we'd fallen behind on our casserole-eating duties.

"How's a nice homemade chicken and rice number for dinner?" I called out.

"By 'homemade,' you mean Grandma's home, right? Not yours?" Seth asked from the living room.

"Watch it, buddy. Canned soup isn't out of the question just yet."

"Point taken."

"Anything's fine," Helga said, a bit more graciously than Seth. "I'm not overly hungry anyway. A funeral like that sucks the oomph right outta me."

"I know what you mean," I agreed, joining them in the living room now that the microwave was doing its job with the casserole. "I know for Brenda's sake we should get back to our white board and lists as soon as possible, but part of me just wants to curl up on the couch in my sweats and give up for a little while." I dropped into the rocking chair, leaving Helga with the recliner against the other wall.

"I hear ya, Mags. The killer can wait another few hours while we chill out and recharge our batteries. He isn't goin' anywhere." She reached in her purse and kept looking for something she wasn't finding. She must have bought her purse wherever I'd bought mine. I secretly hoped she wasn't searching for her pack of cigarettes. I didn't want to tell her not to smoke in the apartment, but neither Seth nor I would have appreciated it much if she did.

"Well, actually," Seth interjected, "he *might* be going somewhere. The funeral's over. Unless he's got a reason to stick around—like, more killings—he really might just leave. We might be racing against the clock and not even know it."

I frowned at Seth and tossed a throw pillow in his direction. "You're not helping, Seth."

Helga withdrew her hand from her purse, clutching a pack of gum. I sighed in relief.

"We could relax a little while here, eat some lovely chicken casserole, and then get out the spy equipment and solve the problems of the world. How's that?" Helga suggested, unwrapping a single small stick of gum and popping it into her mouth. *Aren't we going to eat soon?* I thought.

Seth rolled his eyes a little like the impatient young buck he was. "That's close enough, I suppose."

"Thanks for humoring us old folks," I said.

"But if this guy gets away with these murders, it'll be on your heads!" he added.

"Wait a minute!" I protested. "Remember, the police are officially on this case, not us. We're just doing this to keep ourselves busy for a while and to keep us from going stir-crazy with fear. And to make sure we're *personally* as safe as we can be."

Helga nodded a little too enthusiastically from her side of the room, chomping on her gum and pinching the small paper wrapper between her thumb and forefinger. "Totally agree. To-ta-lly agree."

"Then why are we investing in dry-erase markers and white boards?"

"Haven't a clue, sonny," she continued, "but I think it has something to do with making us feel a little less helpless."

He smiled. "So, you're *both* control freaks then." He grinned wider.

I didn't have a second pillow to throw, so I merely crossed my arms and harrumphed a little in his direction. The microwave beeped, and I waltzed by Seth sprawled on the couch, trying to look ridiculously superior and making faces only to make Helga snort with laughter.

"You two!"

Seth sat up straight and winked at her. "She really is a control freak, you know," he said to her in a cartoonishly conspiratorial tone. "You should see how organized her sock drawer is!"

Helga leaned over and patted his hand. "Honey, most women have organized sock drawers. It's only the men—the ones who have most of the pornography—who let their sock drawers get . . ." She touched her fingertip to her lips as if trying to search for the right word. ". . . untidy." And with that, she winked at him and joined me out in the kitchen. Vladimir just growled a very unconvincing rumble under his breath, his tail wagging the whole time, giving away his true feelings on the matter.

Girls, one. Boys, nothing.

* * * * *

I LOOKED ONE MORE TIME AT THE HUGE WHITE BOARD hanging on the wall in front of me. I had taken down my cork board—the one I used to tack up current job sheets and invoices—and had hung the white board on the large nail in its place. Helga, Seth and I stood staring at it now, as if we were in a room at the Carnegie Museum gazing at a few panels of Monet's *Water Lilies*. None of us spoke for a while. I stood with my arms crossed against my chest. Next to me Helga was pursing her lips and tapping a toe, arms akimbo. Seth stood loosely to her right, his mouth open slightly, looking as if nothing was registering in that otherwise underutilized brain of his.

"Nothing's adding up," I said. "We have a good list here—almost like we're playing a game of Clue—but nothing's coagulating properly. Why is that?"

For a few moments, no one spoke. Helga switched feet and tapped the other one now, shifting her weight to the left. I doubted this was going to produce any new revelations, though. Seth spoke next.

"Err, because we can't seem to find any connection between Lee Gerber and Brenda?"

I turned to face both of them. "Very good, class!" I said, smiling slightly. "Because there's not one damned bit of connection between the two of them."

Helga stopped tapping her foot. "Maybe we should just stop looking for a connection then. What happens when we run with the idea that there really is no connection? What if we forget about Brenda for a minute and concentrate on Gerber Baby?"

She stepped forward and stood in front of the white board. Taking the red dry-erase marker from the tray clipped to the bottom of the board, she uncapped it and ran a big red "X" over the right side of the board where we had tried—vainly—to list anything about Brenda's murder that might seem relevant. Enemies? We couldn't think of any. Past connections to Gerber? *Nada.* Seth and I blinked at Helga a few times, waiting for her to continue. But, she had no other point besides just telling us to let it go and work with what we had instead.

"Are you sure this is the right approach?" Seth asked tentatively. He stepped forward and reached for another marker, but Helga was too quick for him and she lightly smacked his hand away.

"Yes. Now zip it." She winked. He zipped it.

"Helga, this works for me. And at the very least, it'll narrow our focus enough for now that we can feel like we're making progress. I think we should focus on Gerber's enemy list for now. If we're considering the possibility that the second murder was random or was something the killer did by accident, then that changes how we approach this whole task anyway."

Seth frowned, now tapping his own foot, obviously trying to come to terms with the concept of a man who would commit a second murder merely to cover up a first one—or for some other semi-random reason. Seth was young. He still liked to think the world held more order and reason than it really did. Helga and I knew better. We'd been around long enough to see randomness everywhere. And I, for one, wasn't about to burst Seth's bubble just yet. I kinda liked him like this, despite the drawbacks.

"Here's our list then," I said and we looked at the white board's main list:

—*Dirt Boy*
—*Ex-wife*
—*Defendant from jury duty*
—*Orphaned author—Francine*
—*Disgruntled worker from Deerpark Press?*

Was it a good list? Who knew? Did it actually include the real murderer? We could play detective all day long, but the main question hung there in the air: Had one of these people killed Gerber—and Brenda?

I sighed, frustrated, and walked away from the white board, heading back into the kitchen. Sitting at the table, I drummed my fingers, tap-tap-tapping out a rhythm that fell in sync with the suddenly too-loud wall clock—the clock that was now tick-tick-ticking off the seconds in a slow plodding march going nowhere.

Seth and Helga joined me at the table but said nothing. After a minute or two of my frustrated finger-drumming, Seth clapped his hand over mine, a plain signal that I should just knock it off, and pronto.

"Mom, I'm going to take Vlad outside for a walk, okay?"

He didn't wait for me to answer, but instead left the table without looking back. "Here, Vlad!" he called, and the fuzzy little guy came scrambling out from my office and down the hall, heading for the front door as fast as his short legs would carry him. Seth hooked his leash onto the collar and opened the apartment door.

When the door closed behind him, I turned to face Helga, whose hands shook a little bit as she fiddled inside her purse—this time probably for a cigarette. "Well," I said, grimacing. "At least somebody around here's getting something productive done today."

CHAPTER 23

THE NEXT AFTERNOON I SAT IN MY OFFICE printing out two rebills for clients who notoriously forgot to pay me on time. Ah, the joys of the freelancer! Not only did I get to do all the work itself, but I got to be my own marketing and accounting departments, too.

The phone ringing sliced through my musings.

"Hello?"

"Mags, you check your e-mail lately?" Helga.

"It downloads every minute. Why? What am I looking for?"

"Today's PDF of the paper. You haven't opened it yet, have you?"

"No. Hang on." I swiveled around in the chair and faced the computer, clicking the icon in the system tray to bring the e-mail program to the front. There was the e-mail from Ernest—eerily not from Brenda anymore, of course—with an attachment. A few double-clicks and the PDF began to open.

"Well?" Helga asked impatiently.

"It's coming. Hold on." *Stupid slow computer.*

Within a few more seconds it was open.

"What am I looking for here, Helga? Give me a clue."

"Under the fold. Right-hand side."

I scrolled down to the bottom half of the page and saw it: "Editor's ex-wife questioned in murder."

"Oh, Helga," I said quietly. "Wow."

"I know. Freaky, isn't it? Nobody's talking about anything else around here today."

"I'm gonna read this all the way through and then call you back, okay?"

"Sure thing. You know where to find me."

We hung up, and I enlarged the PDF to one-hundred percent onscreen, soaking it all in. The article wasn't overly forthcoming about the subtler facts in the case. I began to think that Helga and I knew more than the reporter who wrote the story. Either that or the police were incredibly adamant about keeping things under wraps while they worked on the case. In any event, it seemed that the former Mrs. Gerber had been brought into the station and grilled for about five hours the day of Brenda's funeral, which she wouldn't have attended anyway. Even if all three of us found her a bit of a pretentious control freak at Lee Gerber's funeral, that didn't make her a murderer. If merely being annoying could make someone a murderer, then my ex would be a serial killer by now. After the grilling—whether or not she was marinated first wasn't clear in the article—they determined that she had what all television detectives call an "airtight alibi," and they let her go.

I gave Helga a ring after finishing the article and told her I thought nothing was going to come of the questioning. She sounded disappointed, but she agreed with me when I pushed her on it. Seth the Naïve was quicker to think it absolutely had to be Mrs. Gerber, and Helga and I chalked that up to his youth. He didn't yet realize just how cliché it was for the ex-wife to off the ex-husband. Perhaps he was projecting my own situation with his father and assuming all ex-wives wanted their ex-husbands dead. Or, in some other way incapacitated. Was it really that obvious?

"No, Seth," I told him that night at dinner, a veritable feast of reheated pepperoni casserole courtesy of Mrs. Velam. "It makes sense that it wasn't her. When I had my lunch meeting with Gerber Baby—*Gerber*—he mentioned the fact that he was still paying his ex a big chunk of alimony. No smart woman in her right mind would cut off her nose to spite her face like that."

"Cut off her what? To . . . what?"

Some days I hated being this old. "It's an expression, sweetheart. You know, like 'dadgum' and 'what in tarnation?'"

He blinked. I could feel the gray hairs popping out of my head as he stared at me, the little whippersnapper.

* * * * *

WITHIN ABOUT A WEEK I began to hold out hope that life was going to start feeling normal again soon. I adopted the stance that no news was good news regarding the murder case, and on most days I could definitely see this from an ostrich's point of view. Or, better yet, see no evil, hear no evil, speak no evil. Anything that took me out of the equation was a good thing. I'd had enough semi-adventure for one lifetime.

So, it was with extreme sadness that I found out upon entering the *Bugle* office one day to talk to Fiona about that freelance Willson project—the project that wouldn't die, as we were now calling it—that a former employee of Deerpark Press had been picked up on suspicion of murder in the Gerber/Johnson cases. I stood at the main desk peering over the high counter down at Helga on the other side, clutching my large padded envelope of scribbled pages, my jaw hanging probably damned near close to the floor.

"For real?" I asked—always the obvious.

Helga nodded, gazing around as if this was a secret. It wasn't. "We have a short article about it in today's edition, which is probably in your inbox at home even as we speak!"

"Okay, I'll read it when I get home then." I found myself glancing around furtively too. No one really knew Helga and I had been playing junior detective for the past few weeks. "So, do you think it'll stick? Do you think this guy did it?"

She shrugged. "Who knows? I just wish they had a picture with the article. I was kinda hoping we'd recognize him from one of the funerals."

I sighed. "I suppose this should be a big relief, right? They caught the guy. Game's over. Time for everybody to go on home now." I smiled weakly.

"So, you're a little bummed too?"

"I didn't say that," I argued. "Why would I be bummed that they caught a killer? One both of us had almost had a run-in with?"

"Not bummed, really. I guess that's too strong a word. Disappointed?"

"Disappointed with what, exactly?" Oddly, although I was arguing with her, deep down I knew she was going somewhere with this, and that I was going to end up agreeing with her.

"With the fact that the cops caught the guy before we figured it out!"

And there it was. The truth was, the more I thought about it, the more I *was* disappointed that we hadn't beaten the cops to the punch. What did they know that we didn't? What evidence did they have at their disposal that led them to their conclusion? Probably nothing more than the fact that we knew no one at Deerpark Press.

Helga patted my hand, the one still with a tight grip on the envelope. "Don't be discouraged, Mags. The cops had all that DNA and fingerprint stuff, and all we had was a white board and a few funerals to attend." She smiled, and I laughed outright.

"Well, when you put it that way, it doesn't seem so bad."

"And frankly, I'm relieved I can keep working here and finally be safe. It was really starting to creep me out to always be the first person people saw when they came in the door!"

"Agreed. I'm glad we're all a lot safer now. Now my mom can sleep better at night too."

"Now I can maybe give up smoking." She glanced at the pack of cigarettes sitting on her desk and frowned for a moment. "Nahh."

CHaPTer 24

THE NEXT MORNING I EXPECTED TO WAKE UP to a brand new era, one that didn't include wondering if a murderer knew where I lived and what my routine was. But instead I woke up with an eerie sense of foreboding. I hastily chalked it up to my unflinchingly skeptical nature and headed for the coffeemaker.

By the time I had finished the first cup of coffee, it seemed clear to me that it would be a good idea to pay a little visit to Deerpark Press in Ohio. The to-do list today was short—just the newspaper this afternoon—and I told myself a little road trip would do me good. As I showered and dressed, I played a mental tug-of-war with myself about why I was going to spend my entire morning, and possibly part of the afternoon if I hit a bad patch of traffic somewhere, traipsing off to Ohio for no particular reason at all. I reminded myself that I could always use a few more clients, and that Lee Gerber had already suggested Deerpark as a place to submit my name as part of their ever-growing freelance pool of proofreaders and copy editors. I tried to ignore the fact that I'd been saying for months that I really *didn't* need any more clients and that I had more work than I could handle and enough money to live on.

But part of me—the perversely curious side, I admit—wanted to see where Gerber had last worked. Since it was a Deerpark worker who was now in custody for his murder, I felt this overwhelming urge to meander over there and see what scuttlebutt I could glean from the workers. If the place was anything like the *Bugle*, there would be gossip bouncing off the walls like crazy over there by now. I knew it was boinging around the *Bugle* office, and the culprit wasn't even a *Bugle* employee. Imagine the twittering going on in Ohio over this arrest!

Shoes on, purse grabbed—keys, cell phone and wallet all safely ensconced inside, although scattered about the bottom of the purse along with gum wrappers and a few old pens and who knew what else—current work résumé and MapQuest printout of directions to Deerpark Press in hand, I was ready for my solo adventure. Someday I'd get a data plan for my phone so I could use a GPS app instead of relying on MapQuest.

I left a hastily scribbled note for Seth on the kitchen table, telling him there were still Hot Pockets in the back of the freezer somewhere and asking him to take Vlad out as soon as he read the note, and I tiptoed out the door, pulling it closed quietly behind me. I wasn't ready to answer questions from Seth about where I was going or why. He already thought I was half-crazy. Why confirm his suspicions now?

The drive into Ohio was uneventful, as I assumed it would be. I took State Route 51 out of Pennsylvania, where it magically turned into Ohio's State Route 14. Looked like the same road to my untrained eye, but apparently the good people of Ohio felt the road was better served with their own number. A small, wooden Welcome to Ohio! sign, weatherbeaten and uncared for, stood on splintered wooden legs not far past the state line. A dubious welcome at best, I'd say. Perhaps the subliminal message here was, "Go home, you Pennsylvanian freak! We know you come here just to buy fireworks and cheap milk."

My mind continued to wander in these odd directions as I pulled the printout of directions to the top of the pile of stuff strewn about on the passenger's seat. I reached over and smoothed it out quickly so it would lay flat and be readable, keeping my eyes on the road and glancing over every few minutes to see if I had positioned the paper well enough to read it. I really had to get myself one of those little suction-cup clipboards for the dashboard for times like this. Or that data plan. A suction-cup clipboard seemed like something only traveling salesmen would use—not to mention the fact that it'd take up half the dashboard and sorely block my view across the right side of the hood of the car. But right about now one of those babies would be a heck of a lot safer than craning my neck over to the passenger's side of the car trying to read directions in ten-point Helvetica. It was bad enough the whole printout was probably missing a few crucial lines to begin with—a problem I'd encountered before with these sorts of sites—but to then make the font impossible to read while driving was just unconscionable.

I was so busy mentally chastising the good folks at Mapquest that I nearly missed the first turnoff in Ohio. Vowing to pay more attention to my driving and less to my moral indignation at the online world that offered me directions for free, I took a deep breath and headed off Route 14 and closer to Deerpark Press.

After an hour of Turn Left Here and 1.5 Miles There, I saw small posted signs for Deerpark Press and turned onto the long driveway leading up to their main building. It was smaller than I had imagined, assuming someone like Lee Gerber would work only for a large, sprawling publisher's office, even factoring in that they did no actual printing here. I had gotten used to the size of the *Bugle* office building, which also housed the press room downstairs, the largest room in the place by a factor of ten or more. Newspapers were very different animals from book publishers, where the editors and copy editors sat in one building sequestered away from the grittier, dirtier work of printing the books they chose and tweaked so meticulously. I was pulling up to a strictly prepress operation. I realized as I pulled into an open space toward the back of the front lot that I probably would have preferred a larger place with far more employees—a place in which I could get lost in the crowd and observe and listen a little more unseen. Although this place seemed impressive enough given the state of publishing these days, I now began to hope that it housed a lot of hustle and bustle, if not a lot of people. Anything to make me stand out a little bit less.

I turned off the car and sat there for a few minutes, clutching my keys and staring at the building, willing myself to grab my purse and go in already. My nerves weren't cooperating. Just what was I doing here? What was I thinking this morning? Like most mornings, probably not a whole lot. At any rate, here I sat in Deerpark Press's parking lot, and it was time to go in. I figured the worst that could happen would be for me to ask for freelance work and get turned away within two minutes. Sighing and grabbing my purse off the passenger's seat, I tossed in my keys and stepped out of the car.

* * * * *

CHRISTOPHER BELICHICK SEEMED LIKE a nice enough guy. I wasn't necessarily the best judge of character or first impressions—one had only to look at my track record with men to see that much—but from across the desk he looked kind and warm and I felt a little more at ease talking to him than I'd ever felt talking to Gerber Baby. I quickly made a mental note not to call Lee "Gerber Baby" while I was here. Belichick, after all, was Gerber's replacement here at Deerpark Press. I didn't need to come off as crass right off the bat. Better to let him figure that out later, much later.

"I must admit, the last person I expected to see walk into our offices was someone who works for the *Bugle*. The coincidence is a little off-putting," Belichick said over his desk, casually drumming an unsharpened pencil on the paper blotter in front of him.

I smiled, hoping I seemed equally casual. "It's no coincidence, Mr. Belichick. When I mentioned to Mr. Gerber that I'm always looking for extra freelance work, he suggested I check in here and have my name put into the freelance pool." I smiled again—this time a little closer to a grin or smirk, I could feel it—and handed him my now-semi-crumpled résumé. He reached across the desk and took it with his unpenciled hand, squinting at it for a moment and scanning its contents while I sat quietly on the other side of the desk awaiting his reply. I fought the urge to tap my foot or rap my fingers on his desk in anticipation. There was no logical reason for me to be nervous about this: I didn't even *want* any freelance work. So why did I feel beads of sweat beginning to collect on the back of my neck? Was it warm in here? I couldn't believe what a wreck I was. I was beginning to think that the past few weeks had taken a much larger toll on me than I had realized and that perhaps I shouldn't have come here at all—at least, not so soon.

"This is a mighty impressive résumé you've got here," Belichick said, nodding reassuringly from his side of the chasmic desk. "I can see why Gerber recommended you come to us." He put the paper down on the desk and leaned forward slightly, clasping his hands together and putting them in front of him on the desk. He looked ready to say into an imaginary television camera, "My fellow Americans . . ." Why did it seem all these editors felt they had to put on a veneer when talking professionally? Was it something bred into Deerpark people? Or had my perspective changed with the growing amount of sweat on the back of my neck?

"Thanks," I managed to squeak out. I was going to have to get this nervous panic thing under control around editors. Perhaps I'd been freelancing too long and had lost my edge with the face-time thing. I suppose this was one downside to working with clients solely over the Internet. "The *Bugle* proofing and a few other jobs are steady work, but I wouldn't mind a few more supplemental book jobs now and then," I fibbed, relaxing and sitting back in the chair after taking a deep breath.

"Before he left for the *Bugle*, Lee mentioned passing along Francine Stettler's book for someone at the *Bugle* to look at—someone just like you. I don't know if Lee told you what happened with her—"

"Yes," I interrupted. "He did. Orphaned book once he left here."

"Sad thing, really, but these things happen sometimes. A few higher-ups also left when Lee did, and chief among them was the man who'd gone to bat for the book in the first place. No one filling in the gaps wanted to touch it—thought it was already a little risky from a marketing perspective."

I had a hard time imagining Francine writing anything risky.

"I met Francine once when she came to the *Bugle* looking for Mr. Gerber. Risky doesn't seem to describe her."

"Oh, not the book itself. That was pretty tame, actually. It was the marketing that would have been risky. To be blunt, it didn't have enough sex or violence in it. And it wasn't literary enough to pass for lit-fic, either. Nobody here after the shake-up wanted to touch it. Granted, part of that is office politics—everyone wants to launch their own authors and not ride the coattails of the guy before them, especially if he's totally gone."

He picked the pencil back up off the blotter and tapped it again.

"Aha, I see."

"Anyway, I'll admit to you that part of the reason for asking you to help her out would be so that she could find her way again—and could stop hassling those of us who are still here and had nothing to do with her book in the first place."

"Hassling you?"

"Not in so many words, no. But she keeps . . . showing up here, asking about her book and if there is anything she can do to get it back on track. We've tried as nicely as possible to tell her it's not going to happen here, but she's frustrated. I guess I understand that, but she needs a heavy dose of reality in how this business works. It is, after all, a business."

I'd heard this all before from Gerber, and I was beginning to wish I hadn't come here. Instead of hearing juicy bits of gossip about the arrested employee, I was back to square one with good ol' Francine.

"I realize all that, and I'd love to help you out. But I'm not really a book doctor. I'm a proofreader and copy editor almost exclusively. I'm not sure what kind of help I could give her."

He shrugged and sighed deeply. "Just between you and me, Miss Velam, this really isn't about editing her book. Lee had already edited the thing enough for publication. We're thinking of this more as a transition for Francine emotionally—to give her a sense that it's time to repackage the book, revamp it a little bit, and start to send it out elsewhere. Anywhere, frankly, that's not Deerpark Press."

So my hunch was correct: pawning her off on me was just a way to get rid of her.

"I feel for you, Mr. Belichick, but I'm really not the right person for the job here." I shook my head and frowned, trying to look as put-upon as I possibly could. "I was thinking more along the lines of just freelance proofing projects—books going to press, that sort of thing."

"Fair enough, Miss Velam. We'll definitely add you to the pool, and I'll flag your name as coming directly from Lee. That'll help move you up the list for projects, although it could still be a while till you hear from us."

"I understand. That's fine," I said, glad to be somewhat off the topic of Francine Stettler and hoping to get out of Belichick's office and into the main part of the building where eavesdropping might be better served. I stood and offered my hand across the desk. Belichick shook it vigorously, but not overly so. A fair handshake, all around.

As he walked me to the door and out into the main hallway, I saw very few people milling around, and fewer still were actually talking to each other about anything. I felt brave enough to ask Belichick the question that had been hanging above my head since I'd gotten up that morning.

"So . . . dreadful news about the arrest, wasn't it?" I offered, hoping I sounded as offhand and casual as I needed to in order to squeeze information out of him. He coughed into his hand and arched his eyebrows.

"Dreadful hardly begins to describe it, really." He seemed uneasy talking about the fate of another Deerpark employee in front of an outsider. "Devastating comes a little closer to describing it. He was only a mailroom clerk—didn't have that much direct contact with Lee that I'm aware of—but it still puts a black mark on all of us here, as you can imagine." Another cough.

"The *Bugle* hasn't been feeling all that great about any of this either. I think they're just trying to get back to normal again, and they see this arrest as a signal that they can all breathe a sigh of relief. Nobody's blaming Deerpark in general, of course."

"I suppose that's the only way to consider the situation. I'm glad to hear that the blame's falling on the mail clerk and not on the rest of us. I suppose it was just one of those things that happens in this crazy world."

He'd been walking with his head down, hands clasped together behind his back, looking pensive. We came to the front desk, with nary another person in sight, and he stopped and looked up at me.

"It's been a pleasure meeting you, putting a face on someone affiliated with the *Bugle*. And I suppose it represents a certain amount of good will that you'd like to work with us on some projects in the future. No hard feelings?"

"Of course not," I assured him, and we shook hands once again. I took a single step toward the door, having given up on my quest to overhear rumors or gossip, and he took a step back toward his office. Just as I reached for the door handle one step later, he suddenly turned back toward me and frowned as I looked back at him.

"Just one thing keeps bothering me, though," he said, half to himself. Or possibly he was gauging my own reaction—it was difficult to tell since I barely knew him. "None of us here can think of a single reason why that mailroom clerk would have wanted to see Lee Gerber dead. And he had no history of any sort of violence. Don't you find that strange?" His arms were still behind his back, and now his head was cocked slightly to one side. It seemed he wanted vindication that the people working with him at Deerpark Press weren't ghastly criminals bent on murder and mayhem. Although I couldn't offer him the assurance he seemed to want, I certainly agreed on his singular point.

"It is strange," I agreed, pushing open the door. "But it wouldn't be the first strange thing that's happened this month."

CHAPTER 25

DINNER WASN'T EXACTLY A SUMPTUOUS AFFAIR, but it wasn't a reheated casserole, either. By the time I got back to the apartment, the smell of roasting chicken greeted me warmly. Knowing Seth was no cook unless it involved a microwave and individually wrapped packets of food, I climbed the stairs assuming my parents were there. I came in the door and was immediately assaulted by Vlad the fur ball, yipping in glee and excited about the aroma of chicken that he—tragically—didn't yet realize wasn't for him. Dogs are such eternal optimists about food. I wasn't going to be the one to break his little doggy heart, though, so I dropped my purse on the recliner and reached down to pick him up. He wagged his whole chubby body in my arms, licking my face and making me wonder why I hadn't just gotten a dog twenty-seven years ago instead of marrying George. The perks were so much simpler and purer.

"Hi, Mom. Grandma and Grandpa are here," Seth announced as he came into the living room from my office down the hall.

"I can see that," I said, stooping to put Vlad down before he squirmed right out of my arms from too high up. "And she's cooking, apparently." I smiled at him. We both preferred my mother's cooking to mine. It probably made a difference that she didn't despise cooking with every fiber of her being like I did.

"Yeah. Chicken and potatoes—and they brought fresh broccoli too—and cheese to make cheese sauce."

He sounded almost giddy. I was beginning to feel a bit guilty that I was a bad enough cook that the thought of a chicken with a few potatoes thrown on it sounded so exciting to him.

"I don't suppose they just showed up all by themselves, did they?" I asked, raising an eyebrow and pursing my lips.

"No, I called 'em," he admitted. "I got your note and thought you just might want a good meal when you got home."

"Really? So, it has nothing to do with the fact that you thought I might be gone all day and unable to make you dinner?" I winked.

He shrugged. "That too. Anyway, what happened at Deerpark?"

"What makes you think I was at Deerpark?"

He shook his head. "Where else would you have gone? I know you were thinking about it." He said this so matter-of-factly that it caugh me off-guard. "And who's this guy they arrested? Did he really do it?"

I balked at the last question. "What do you mean, did he do it? The police arrested him. They think he did it." I headed to the kitchen to give my mom a quick hug, with Seth following me. "Hi, Mom," I said, pressing my cheek against hers, still turned to face Seth off to my right.

"Hello, dear! How was your adventure?"

Apparently Seth had told them everything.

"Fine. I didn't really find out very much." She stopped cutting up potatoes and looked up. Seth was already staring at me. "The guy they arrested was a mailroom clerk at Deerpark Press. That's pretty much all I got out of the trip. Well, that and the fact that the new editor there—the one that replaced Lee Gerber—doesn't quite understand why this guy got arrested."

"Maybe the police aren't telling him very much," my mom said, going back to her potatoes. "Besides, how much would an editor know about the personal life of a mailroom clerk? The man obviously had everybody fooled." *Chop, chop, chop.*

"The way he put it to me, everybody there at Deerpark is confused by this arrest. Not just him. Nobody can figure out what this guy's motive might have been."

"Perhaps the police are just being rather tight-lipped about the whole affair," she said.

"Mom, I'm not really sure why you feel you have to play devil's advocate on this. Something just seems odd here, that's all."

"Sweetheart, I'm not meaning to play devil's advocate," she countered, stopping her potato-chopping and gesturing with the knife in her hand as she spoke. "I'm merely trying to point out that you've got a head of steam about this murder mystery thing. I think you were enjoying the game so much you're not ready to let it go."

I said nothing. Seth turned to look at me, and my mother was still looking at me, holding that gargantuan knife in midair. "Mom, could you maybe put that knife down while you're talking about murders, please?"

She lowered the knife slowly onto the cutting board. "Yes, dear. But do you get my meaning?" she asked, looking at me intently.

"I see what you're saying, but I don't agree with you. I went to Deerpark today looking for freelance work."

Seth burst out laughing. "Don't think you're going to pull that line on us, Mom."

"Okay, I admit I didn't *just* go there for work. I went to see what I could find out. And frankly, what little I did find out makes me wonder what's going on there. It sounds like nobody at Deerpark Press is happy with this arrest."

"Of course they're not," Seth said. "It makes them look bad!"

I sighed. "I guess that's kinda what Belichick said."

"Who's Belichick?"

"The editor who replaced Gerber when he left. He was worried that the arrest would give Deerpark a bad name. But he also said he couldn't think of a single motive for this guy."

"Give it a rest, Mom. Enjoy yourself for once. You've been wound tight since this all started."

My mother scooped up the sliced potatoes and put them into the frying pan on top of the stove, which was already simmering some oil and sliced onions. The sizzle of the potatoes hitting the oil was comforting in a way. I had to admit that it was nice to have the aroma of good food emanating from my kitchen for a change. She put a lid on the pan and turned back to face us.

"Sit down, have a glass of wine, and put your feet up, dear," she said. "It's time to get back to your real life again. And that includes us." She put her arm around me and led me out of the kitchen and into the living room. With her hands firmly on my shoulders, she edged me around to the front of the couch and gently pushed my shoulders down so that I got the hint and sat on the couch.

"Okay, you guys win—for now. The mail clerk did it."

I closed my eyes and that same sense of foreboding I'd had in the morning crept back quietly. Not quite right. Something was not quite right.

* * * * *

It took me a few days, but I managed to shake off that icky feeling I kept waking up with and made a conscious decision to get on with my life. On Thursday of that week, I gathered up a new manila envelope of copy-edited pages on the Willson project for Fiona to look over and headed over to the *Bugle* to drop them off. I'd also get a chance to talk to Helga while I was there and see how she was doing now that everything was over. I left Seth with Vlad and a recent edition of the paper's want ads—a not-so-subtle hint—and toodled over there on a rare gorgeously sunny and crisp autumn day. Through the glass doors, Helga saw me coming and waved her hands frantically in my direction. *She's amazingly glad to see me*, I thought initially, and waved back in an equally frenetic and goofy way. It wasn't until I'd swung open the door and noticed that Helga had abruptly stopped her flailing and that her eyes were darting furtively to the left and back that I realized I'd misinterpreted her actions.

I smiled weakly and shot a quick glance to my right. There, rising from the bank of chairs stationed up against the wall across from Helga's desk, was Francine Stettler. She rose when she caught sight of me, so I was certain I was her intended target. Helga had been trying to warn me while I was yet outside not to come in, since she knew I wasn't overly enamored of Francine and didn't want to listen to the story of her orphaned novel for a third time. I was pretty sure I'd already heard every version of that story that existed. Stopping at Helga's desk and depositing the manila envelope there, I tried vainly to make eye contact only with Helga—as if simply ignoring someone like Francine could ever make her go away.

"Hey, Helga! Long time, no see!" I fibbed. I kept my eyes facing front, but Francine was now sidling up to my right, where she stopped alongside me and lightly touched my arm. Even though I'd seen her coming in my peripheral vision, I flinched as soon as she touched me.

"Oh, sorry," she apologized, withdrawing her hand quickly. "Miss Velam, I didn't mean to scare you. I could have sworn you saw me coming."

"I did, I did," I admitted, "but I'm just a little jumpy sometimes. That's all." I turned to her and smiled halfheartedly.

"I don't know if you remember me. My name's Francine Stettler." She held out her hand for me to shake and I obliged.

"Yes, yes, of course I remember you. You . . . you're a novelist. You worked with . . . Mr. Gerber."

She grinned—which, for some reason, was a tad unsettling—and seemed pleased that I remembered who she was. "Precisely, yes!"

In an attempt to act like Francine might actually be here to see someone else, I smoothly turned back to face Helga and patted the envelope on the counter in front of me. "I can't stay long today, Helga, but I wanted to be sure Fiona saw these pages. I had some issues with Willson's use of commas and wanted to see if she agrees with how I marked up this chapter." I patted the envelope again and pushed it toward her a little so that it sat hanging over her edge of the counter, teetering precariously as I continued to push it. Helga put her hand up to steady it and then let it slide down onto her outstretched palm.

"Thanks, chickie. I can be sure to get it to her before she leaves today, if that's good enough for ya."

I nodded. But, Francine wasn't finished with me yet.

"Miss Velam, I was wondering if I could ask you something."

Slowly I turned, inch by inch, toward Francine, not wanting to make eye contact, feeling it would seal my fate because I was so horribly bad at saying no, especially to pity cases. But just as I tried to avert my eyes to avoid eye contact, I looked the wrong way and inadvertently met Francine's stare head on, and our eyes locked. With the feeling of a deer in the headlights, I already knew I was doomed.

I heard myself saying, "Sure, Francine. What can I do for you?" Out of the corner of my eye I saw Helga pinching her eyes closed in agony, knowing too that I was doomed. She was going to ream me out for my wussiness later once Francine had left. I was doubly doomed.

"Well, you know my book's been dropped by Deerpark Press since Lee left—God rest his soul—and they had that shake-up in authority."

"Orphaned, yes. I remember hearing that. A shame." I was saying as little as possible so as not to encourage her. It was never good to encourage someone like Francine to talk longer than was humanly necessary. My head might explode from frustration and boredom.

"Lee suggested I ask you to help me polish it up a little bit so I can send it out to other publishers." She thrust a fat manila envelope that looked a lot like mine toward me. I resisted the knee-jerk reaction to take it from her and instead stared down at it as if it were coated in the Ebola virus. Francine seemed a bit confused by my reaction.

I continued to stare at the infected envelope, my brows furrowing tightly. "What about your agent? Shouldn't he help you place this with another publisher?"

Francine held the envelope a few millimeters closer to me, and I felt myself instinctively drawing back an equal number of millimeters in order to avoid physical contact with the envelope of death.

"She. My agent was a she."

"Was?"

"I fired her."

"Fired her?" I repeated. "Why on earth would you fire your agent?" The deadly envelope had made its way ever closer, and I actually stepped back to keep from having it touch my body.

"First off, she wasn't all that enthusiastic about my book. Plus, Lee told me before he left Deerpark that I could just as easily get the novel in with a small publishing house without an agent. So, I figured, why keep the hassle of an agent when I can do this myself?"

She stopped moving the envelope toward me. I straightened. "Well, because agents know the business better than we do, and they keep track of when editors like Lee move from one place to another."

"But he's *dead* now," she said bluntly, almost curtly. "She certainly didn't see *that* coming, did she?" The hostility in her voice was evident, and I realized I'd touched a huge nerve getting too close to the bad outcome of her experience with Gerber and Deerpark Press. This woman was a ticking time bomb of frustration and sour grapes. I reminded myself to not be anywhere near her when she went off. Time to change the subject in order to be safe.

"At any rate, Francine, what can I do for you?" I asked, realizing as soon as I said it that she'd already answered this question for me. And I had a funny feeling someone as emotionally insecure as Francine might have a problem with people who pretend to listen but who really are just playing nice.

"I've just told you," she said through gritted teeth, shoving the envelope at me full speed now, where it stopped dead upon hitting my chest just near my collarbone. "I'd like you to help me with my manuscript. I'd like to finally get it published."

"Of course, yes. I do remember. But honestly, I'm not entirely sure I'm the person you want. Mr. Gerber didn't know me all that well, and I think he may have been under the mistaken impression that I'm a book doctor or editor. Really, I'm just a glorified proofreader and sometimes a copy editor. I don't really work in the larger terms—the broader scopes—you might need in revamping your novel."

I was shaking my head slightly through this whole speech, hoping it was striking the right note with Francine. I wasn't holding out much hope of her actually agreeing with my logic, but a girl can dream.

"I think you'd probably do just fine, though. You have experience at this sort of thing. Where else am I going to find someone I trust with my novel, my *baby*?" She pushed the envelope forward a little bit so it pressed against my collarbone, and I put my hand up and took the envelope just to get her to stop pushing it on me like that.

"Francine, honestly . . . I'm afraid I'm just going to have to say no. It's nothing personal. But I just can't fit in any more projects right now. Totally swamped. I wouldn't be able to do it justice. Either that or you'd never see it again because it would take me so long!" I chuckled unconvincingly, trying to lighten the tension I was feeling all the way down to my fingertips. Glancing at Helga, I could see that she felt the same tension. There was something about Francine that brought out the anxiety in both of us. I thought it might be her obvious lack of humor. People who couldn't muster a decent sense of humor about life made me nervous. Francine made me more nervous than most.

I saw Helga's face full of tension turn into a face full of fear and awkwardness and realized Francine was looking at me. I turned her way and saw that she was frowning at me, eyeing the envelope I was holding out in front of her now. The frown increased dramatically the closer I moved the envelope in her direction. With a supreme effort of will, I kept my outstretched hand from shaking as I held out the unwanted envelope for her to take back. An unspoken battle of wills ensued, with me keeping the envelope between us and her staring at it as if that would make it burst into flames—or perhaps make *me* burst into flames. I wasn't clear which she truly wished to see happen.

After what seemed an achingly, desperately long period of time, Francine gave in and snatched the envelope from my grasp and tucked it under her other arm with a snap. She made it perfectly apparent that she wasn't happy with this turn of events—she'd driven all the way down here fully expecting compliance, I was sure of it—and stood there longer than anyone would find prudent, staring first at me, then Helga, then the envelope, and then back at me. It was an ugly, unfiltered stare, the type a socially awkward person wouldn't have learned how to control properly, so Helga and I became the brunt of her unrestrained pouting and frustration.

"Fine, then. You can be that way. I come here hoping I'll get a little help—after my one good editor is murdered here in your building," she said in an unsettling, accusatory tone, "and all I get in return is more rejection. Not that I'm entirely *surprised*," she added, looking first at me and then at Helga. She sure was good at darting those glances around, and it was becoming more than a little bit intimidating.

"Francine, please. We didn't mean anything by it," said Helga from behind her high counter. I was pretty sure this kind of pleading wasn't going to placate someone like Francine.

"Yes, Francine. I personally am sorry I can't take on this project right now," I said, changing the tone and spirit of the reply to something more businesslike and less personal. "I'd much rather be reading a novel than these ugly political essays from the eighteen-hundreds," I said, pointing to the similar envelope that was still clutched in Helga's hands. "But this project's just eating up all my spare time."

I tried to look at her in my most pleading, sincere fashion, but I was certainly no actress and hadn't a clue how well I'd convinced her of my sincerity. She merely looked at the envelope tucked under her arm, did some sort of combination shrug-and-pout, and turned back to the bank of chairs to pick up her purse. I shot Helga a quick look of "fingers-crossed-that-she-really-leaves" and made sure to look Francine's way in time so that she didn't catch me passing a mental note in math class. By the time Francine had her purse and had turned back toward us, I'd gone back to looking at her as honestly as I possibly could. I managed a weak, forced smile, letting it look awkward since that would have been appropriate given our exchange.

"I guess I'll have to find someone else to help me with this project then. Maybe somebody's more helpful back at Deerpark Press. Maybe that new editor can give me a list of names of *helpful* people."

And, with that threatening yet somehow welcome statement hurled in our direction, Francine stomped to the glass doors and pushed one wide, storming down the front steps without looking back. Both Helga and I let out the breaths we'd been holding and turned to each other, smiling.

"Wow," said Helga. "Can you believe that broad? She's a real trip!"

"I almost didn't get out of that one," I said, laughing nervously and looking over my shoulder and out the glass door, making sure she wasn't watching us from the bottom of the steps. But, mercifully, she was gone.

Helga looked at me more seriously. "Sorry I didn't warn you right when you were coming in. I tried, but I didn't know how to let you know she was here waiting for you."

"That's okay," I conceded.

"I couldn't call you and warn you because she was sitting right there in that chair the whole time!"

"It's okay, really."

"I thought about getting up to use the ladies' room and then calling you from in there, but right about then you showed up and it was too late."

"Honestly, Helga—no harm done. It was just kinda awkward, that's all. Although now I'm thinking we should have some sort of system for next time."

"Next time? Honey, there ain't gonna be a next time if I can help it! I want this place to go back to normal peace and quiet like before!"

"Let's say this then: if I'm coming up the stairs again and I should just turn and leave, what signal could you give me?"

She grinned. "Semaphore flags? Road flares?"

I laughed. "Yeah, something subtle like that. Something subtle like *you*." She snorted with laughter and we both let out the tension that had been building ever since I came in the door.

CHAPTER 26

SETH SAT ON THE COUCH with the day's newspaper spread open on both sides of him. Vlad was vexed as he stood on the floor by Seth's feet, hoping to find a clear spot on the couch on which to jump, so he could be nearer to Seth, the giver of love and treats and seemingly unending walks in the park. But Seth was too busy with the newspaper to notice Vlad hopping from one doggy foot to the other, and then the third and fourth feet, panting in shallow doggy eagerness for something that just wasn't going to happen. I stood in the kitchen with the coffee can in my hand watching the subtle interplay—or not so subtle—between them, trying not to laugh and spoil what was rapidly becoming a bad comedy routine.

Finally Vlad could stand it no longer, and he hoisted his body into the air, hoping to land next to Seth on the couch. Instead, he hit a section of newspaper that was spread open next to Seth and slid right back down onto the floor, calling out with a shrill "Yipe!" as he hit the floor. He stood soundly on all fours, uninjured except for his pride, and snorted loudly at Seth, then sauntered down the hall toward the bedroom. I burst out laughing, joining Seth who was already howling with laughter at Vlad's expense.

"Poor little guy," I said sympathetically. "You were torturing him with that newspaper."

"I didn't even realize he was there," Seth confessed.

"He's easy to miss."

I flopped down in the recliner and put the footrest up. "What's so interesting in the newspaper that you were ignoring the dog for it?"

"I was looking at apartments. Sean called and said he's got a lead on a place that's looking for a graphic designer and he gave me their number. If it works out, we'll be able to get back out on our own."

"Where's Sean been staying for the past month?"

"With his folks." He laughed. "They're driving him nuts."

"Not like your dear old mother, right?" I said, baiting him on purpose.

"You're the easy one, and you know it."

"But I'm such a . . . nitpicker, was it?" I smiled and winked.

"Just about some things. But, for a mom, you're okay."

"Thanks for the vote of confidence, I guess," I said, taking whatever passed for a compliment from the mind of Seth. When they're his age, a mother takes all the positive feedback she can get. "Find anything worth taking a look at?"

"We're not that ready to move out. I'll have to interview for the job—early next week is the soonest they can get me in. But, apart from that, it's just a matter of saving up for that security deposit. We'll need that on top of the first and last months' rent."

I thought wistfully of the extra money that Francine's manuscript editing would have brought in. But, all things being equal—and they weren't in this case—it was better to keep Seth around a little while longer so he could save up the money himself than to deal with Francine for as long as it would have taken to tweak her manuscript.

"I'm not going to be much help with that, Seth. Sorry." I pushed the headrest back on the recliner and it flattened out enough for me to feel extremely comfy.

"That's okay, Mom. Really. You've done plenty already just letting me crash here for the past few weeks. My guess is that, if this job works out, I could be out by about Thanksgiving."

"Speaking of which, we're having Thanksgiving here this year. Did I mention that already?"

"Probably. Sorry if I forgot. You mean, 'here' as in with you rather than Dad, or 'here' as in here instead of Grandma's house?"

"Both. Annie's going to be here too. She seemed grateful to have an excuse not to have to spend all day at your dad's house."

Seth chuckled. "Yeah, they're not getting along much these days." He thumbed through the first section of the newspaper, holding it aloft so that it covered his entire upper body and I could no longer see his face.

"You say that like it's news," I added, tapping the uplifted newspaper with my toe, which barely reached from the end of the recliner to Seth's end of the couch. He tipped the corner of the paper down and smiled at me.

"Hey, here's something interesting. I've been scanning the want ads in this newspaper every day for two weeks now. Faithfully. Regularly. Religiously, if I can use that word. And not once in that time have I seen one of those anonymous letters to the editor from that guy you and Helga called . . . what was his name?"

"Dirt Boy?"

"That's him! Yeah, no letters from him at all. So I did a little research and checked—and he hasn't written one letter since the murders. Don't you think that's a little strange?"

I sighed. "People in this household should be prohibited from using the sentence, 'Don't you think that's strange?' in my presence. Every time someone asks that question, something bad happens. Now, what were you saying?" I looked at him boldly, almost daring him to bring up that topic again. A topic, I might add, I'd managed to sublimate quite nicely over the past few weeks.

He frowned. "I never know if you're serious when you get like this."

"What's your best guess?"

"All I'm saying is that it seems a little weird that there haven't been any letters by this guy in so long. Doesn't he usually write at least once a week?"

I pulled the headrest back up straight and yanked on the handle for the footrest, sending it disappearing back into the recliner. I leaned forward to look Seth in the eye.

"Seth, you're one of the people who told me I had to let this go, and I have. So, the last thing I really want to talk about right now is Dirt Boy. My first guess is that he's not writing right now because of all the publicity surrounding the murders. And possibly also because the *Bugle*'s still without a permanent editor-in-chief. The guy doesn't have anyone to complain about right now. Don't worry—he'll be back, as soon as they put a new guy in that corner office."

My cell phone rang from deep inside my purse, and I got up from the recliner to retrieve my purse on the side table by the front door. I pulled it open and thrust my hand inside, reaching around and finding everything but the phone. I grabbed it on the fourth ring and answered just before voice mail would have kicked in.

"Hello?"

"Mags! Hey, howdy, girlfriend. Is Seth there?"

"Helga?"

"Yeah, toots. It's me. Is Seth around, or is he walking that dog again?"

"Helga?" I repeated, trying to process the fact that she was passing me by and asking for Seth.

"Yes, Helga is correct. Maggie, remember that strappin' young man staying at your house? Is he there?" she asked again. It obviously hadn't occurred to her that I'd find this request—without much acknowledgment of me—a little odd coming from her.

"Sure, he's right here," I said, confused, handing Seth the phone. "It's for you," I said to him quietly. "It's Helga, for some reason."

"Oh, great!" he said, too enthusiastically for me to interpret. "Let me talk to her!" He reached out and took the cell phone and sat back on the couch. "Helga! Show me the money!"

I sat on the edge of the recliner listening to this one side of their conversation. Unfortunately, Seth's half of the conversation consisted primarily of phrases like "Really?" and "Wow!" and "That's just what I thought you'd say!" and "Okay, now I'm curious!" At some point he finally hung up and tossed the phone back to me.

I blinked at him a few times and waited. After an interminable amount of time, I could see the light bulb going off above Seth's head. It had dawned on him that I might be curious about why my friend—a woman somewhere between my age and my mother's age—would call me on my cell phone and ask for my son.

"You'll never guess." The kid was brilliant.

"What gave that away for you? The blank look on my face?" I continued to stare at him blankly, frustrated for being this clueless.

"Helga double-checked my hunch that Dirt Boy hasn't written any letters since the murders. Because it occurred to me that just because the *Bugle* wasn't printing them doesn't mean Dirt Boy wasn't writing them. Heck, there could be a whole drawer of unprinted, unsigned letters from this guy sitting there wasting away because there's no editor to give them a thumbs-up or thumbs-down."

"Seth, I'm not entirely sure the editor-in-chief picks out the letters to the editor—even though, yes, they're called 'letters to the *editor*.' Last I heard, someone in Gerber's job would approve them but not necessarily read every single letter that comes in just so he could handpick them. He'd have more important things to do than read letters to the editor all day."

"But what about during a transitional period like this one? You know, one with a power vacuum like this? Couldn't something like this fall between the cracks?" He had moved up to the edge of the couch and was leaning forward, eager to hear my assessment of whatever pathway he was leading me down now.

"I suppose it could happen, yes. Especially in a case like this one where the transition of power came on suddenly and because of a . . . trauma."

"Precisely," he said triumphantly.

"I'm still not getting your point, though."

"Helga and I were wondering about letters to the editor, and we both thought Dirt Boy might be writing again, but that perhaps nobody's putting his stuff in right now."

"And?"

"And Helga checked and found out that no, nothing's been printed—so she confirmed that for me. But she also found out that most of the stuff like that is currently locked up in Gerber's old office. The police are done with it, of course, but after Helga opens the mail every day, some office flunky's been sorting the mail and putting letters to the editor and other stuff into the filing drawer in Gerber's desk—and locking it up tight."

He sat back, looking victorious in his still-incomprehensible theory.

"And?" Either he and Helga were concocting something really stupid or I was getting a little dimmer than I cared to admit.

"And," he said, with an exasperated sigh, "who knows *what's* in that drawer? Grandma may not want you to pursue this, but this time I think she's wrong. Helga and I agree with you that the mail clerk just couldn't have killed Gerber. And killing Brenda makes even less sense. We checked all the articles and short blurbs on the case—not just in the *Bugle* but in other papers—and nothing's really been clear on his status. And nobody's really come up with a good motive yet. But Dirt Boy—now there's a guy who's a walking motive, if you ask me!"

He looked away in order to fold the newspaper a little better, so it would lay flat on the couch in a smaller pile. At some point Vlad was going to want that space and it wasn't fair to have it totally covered in newspapers as if we were still housebreaking him. It was probably an offense to his little doggy ego.

"Wait, so you're telling me you're—that you and Helga think—" I was too stunned to continue, but Seth finished my thought for me.

"Yup. Helga and I are reopening our case! Get out that white board, Mom!" He beamed as he managed to get the last section of newspaper properly folded and set down neatly on the couch. At that moment, Vlad ran in from the bedroom where he'd probably been sulking and leapt up deftly onto the couch, like a dog half his age would have done. He turned to face us both, wagging his tail and lapping at Seth's face with his tiny tongue. Seth blinked and pulled away, not wanting quite that much dog spit on his face. It had never been proven clinically, but I always suspected Vlad had overactive salivary glands tucked into his cheeks somewhere.

"See?" Seth said, laughing as Vlad's tongue tickled his face but grimacing at the accompanying saliva. "Even Vlad's excited about it!"

I would have laughed along with Seth, but I wasn't liking what I was hearing.

"You're telling me you and Helga have been playing detective again?"

"It's not like that. Not really. It's only a little research into something that feels like a loose end, that's all."

"There's no halfway here, Seth," I said, wanting to sound firm but not angry. My voice shook a little bit, but mostly out of fear and some anxiety, not out of anger. "If the cops were right and they have the right guy, then what you're doing is pointless and could even end up hurting someone. And if the cops are wrong and the real killer is still out there, it's not a job for amateurs like us. I think I'm more convinced of that than I ever was." Firmness, not anger.

He pulled Vlad away from his face and set him gently on the floor. Vlad sat at Seth's feet for about a nanosecond before leaping back up onto the couch. This time Seth guarded his own face with his arm outstretched to fend off Vlad's spit-wielding forces.

"Down, Vlad!" He grabbed Vlad a second time and placed him a little more firmly onto the floor, saying "No!" as he did it. Vlad, knowing a brush-off when he heard one, slunk back to the bedroom without so much as a whimper. He'd been stunned into silence.

"Mom," Seth continued when his face was done being slobbered on, "we've got a hunch here. We'd like to either put it to rest or go with it, depending on what we find out next. It's not a big deal. I was joking about reopening the case. It just sounded more dramatic that way. I thought it'd freak you out, but in a funny way. Didn't mean to upset you." He folded his hands in his lap and waited for my verdict.

"What do you mean, depending on what you find out next?

What are you two doing next?" I had to admit a certain amount of curiosity by this point. Helga and my son had found some sort of common denominator. I had to know what it was.

"We're going to sneak into the editor's office and open the desk and look at the files!" he blurted out, sounding proud of their achievement, as if he had just told me they'd won the Nobel Prize for Literature. Oddly, my reaction was not what I would have anticipated. I could forgive Seth this sort of youthful indiscretion, but what was I supposed to think about Helga's involvement?

"Seth, this is insane. How did you get Helga to agree to this?"

He laughed. "Get her to agree? She was the one who talked me into it! She's the one sitting in the middle of Gossip Central there at the *Bugle* office. It was bound to start bothering her sooner or later."

"What was?"

"The combination of the mail clerk having no motive and Dirt Boy having plenty. If you compare the two, which one would you arrest?"

"It doesn't work like that, Seth. You don't assign guilt based on a sliding scale. They could *both* be innocent."

Now I'd done it. I inadvertently came down on the wrong side of my own argument. Seth was grinning widely, arms folded, waiting for me to try to back out of it now. He continued to watch me, waiting patiently.

Finally, I smiled back. "I got nothin'," I admitted. "Let me call Helga and talk to her myself, okay? No traipsing off for a little breaking and entering without me, you hear?"

Now I'd *really* done it. I hadn't meant to put it quite that way, but it was out there now and I couldn't really unsay it. Seth looked like a kid let loose at the carnival with a fistful of quarters. He pointed at the cell phone still clutched in my hand.

"Call her."

With a few button-presses, the number at Helga's desk at the *Bugle* rang. She picked it up on the second ring, as she always did.

"Brighton *Bugle*. How may I direct your call?"

"Helga. It's me, Maggie."

"Mags!" she said excitedly.

"So, now you're leading my son into his very own life of crime?"

"Aha, I see you've talked to Seth since I called then."

"You bet your sweet felony I did, girlfriend." Firm, not angry. Just firm. Was I coming across accurately? Hard to tell with my voice trembling like this.

"Felony?"

"I'm pretty sure breaking and entering is a felony, yeah. And I know I wanted Seth to find his own place and move out soon, but I wasn't really thinking 'jail cell,' Helga."

"Aw, but Maggie, he's got a cause now. Think of this as a sort of project he's working on. And look at how excited he is about it."

She was making no sense. And I decided to stop feeling sorry for her that she'd never had children. "Helga! Volunteering at a soup kitchen is a project. Protecting the environment is a cause. This is . . . well, it's a crime!"

"I can see why Seth says you're a stick in the mud when you get like this, Maggie. It's very unbecoming."

"Helga!"

"What?" she asked, as if I'd actually been getting ready to ask her a casual question.

"Helga, promise me you won't take my son on a crime spree. You don't have my permission!" I looked over at Seth and saw him frowning at me. The last time I saw that look on his face I had just told him I wouldn't teach him to drive until he'd brought his grades up to B's. I frowned back at him—hard, trying to look stern and unyielding—and actually wiggled my finger at him in a "shame-shame!" sort of way. He turned away, grabbing a throw pillow and holding it to his chest. I think he was pouting.

There was still nothing from Helga's end of the conversation. "Helga? Promise me."

She sighed. "All right. He won't go with me."

I relaxed. "Good. I'll work on keeping *you* from doing this stupid thing later."

"Maggie?"

"Yes?" I asked, almost afraid of what she was going to say next. Turned out I had good reason for my trepidation.

"I'm going to do this anyway. It's bugging me. I think the police are wrong. I can't let that innocent man sit in prison. I want to see what I can find out about Dirt Boy and his letters."

I said nothing for a long time. Helga also said nothing, although I could hear the room noises from her end of the phone.

"Maggie? Are you still there?"

"Yeah, Helga. I'm here. Is there anything I can say to keep you from going through with this insanity?"

"Nope."

More silence from both of us. Finally, I spoke up, but immediately wished I hadn't.

"Then I'm going with you."

CHAPTER 27

RESISTED THE URGE TO DRESS AS A CAT BURGLAR—all in black, tights, turtleneck sweater, gloves, ski mask. Why announce the obvious? If we got caught, I certainly didn't want my mug shot to have me looking like some bad unemployed mime down on his luck. Helga's plan was straightforward and simple enough: I'd meet her at the *Bugle* office sometime late in the afternoon, before everyone had gone home for the day. The two of us would then wait until everyone had left—we'd walk around the place and double-check to make sure no one was on the main floor—and then we'd hastily sneak into the editor's office to check out that desk drawer. The two hitches in her plan, at least the ones I could see from my perspective, were that the desk was apparently locked and the press operators downstairs worked through the night printing the morning edition.

When I arrived at the *Bugle* that afternoon, I waved at Helga through the glass doors and she smiled broadly. It looked like an all-systems-go smile, so I strode in and right up to her desk, plopping my usual manila envelope on the counter.

"Hello there, sunshine!" she said over the desk. "It's a lovely day when you come in and grace us with your presence!"

"Well, well. Somebody's having an easy time quitting smoking this week!" She was positively beaming.

"Ha, don't let the smile fool ya. It's plastered on. I'd kill an elephant with my bare hands for a cigarette right about now." She chomped loudly on some gum and pointed to her mouth. "Nicotine gum."

"Yummy."

"Not exactly. Tastes like shoe leather."

I laughed.

"The bottom of the shoe."

I laughed again.

"After a rain storm."

"That bad?" I asked, still laughing despite the underlying nervousness about our insane plan. I was no thief. I couldn't even muster up a good fib without flop sweats, let alone break into a locked desk to steal documents. It was all feeling mighty . . . well, Watergate-like.

"You have no idea. Don't ever take up smoking, Maggie. The cure's worse than the disease."

"I've heard that," I said, nodding.

She looked left and then right, ascertaining quickly that no one was within earshot of the desk. "Listen, as soon as five o'clock hits, everyone here scatters. Especially on a Friday. We'll have the place to ourselves by five-oh-one."

The mental picture of dozens of cartoonish people dashing for the door in droves as a cartoon whistle blew, Flintstone-like, yelling "Yabba dabba doo!", made me smile despite my nerves. "Well, we won't be *entirely* alone," I added.

"Meaning?"

"Won't the press guys downstairs just be coming in at five?"

She shook her head. "Don't worry about them. They come in around three, so they're already here. And they never come up here. They have their own breakroom down there—a full kitchen, really—and there's nobody up here for them to come up to talk to anyway. We'll be completely alone up here. Not to worry."

Too late for that, I thought. I was already worrying. "Helga, ever hear of Murphy's Law?"

She snorted with laughter. Behind her I saw people milling about their work areas, grabbing purses and straightening up piles of papers on their desks. I looked at my watch. It was coming up on five o'clock already.

"Yeah, hon. I think I invented it. If I didn't know better, I'd guess my name was Murphy!"

I leaned in a little closer over the top of her counter. "Then why aren't you nervous about this? You can plan something like this till the cows come home, and something will still go wrong. Doesn't that bother you?"

She smiled sweetly. "God grant me the serenity to—"

"Oh, no you don't!"

"Footprints in the sand?"

"Helga, get serious for just a moment." I patterned deep breathing for her—*in, out, in, out*—and she matched it, still smiling. "Now, I realize you're not as anxious about this . . . *enterprise* as I am, and I guess that's about par for the course. But honestly, since you don't work at night, how can you be so sure none of the press operators will wander up here while we're in that office rifling through the drawers?" I gestured bluntly toward the editor's office as I spoke. Helga calmly took my hand in hers and gently brought my arm back down so that I wasn't pointing right at the future scene of the crime. It was, after all, only 4:57, and the place was still crowded with people.

"Now, now. Let's point somewhere *other than* the big bad office door, shall we? Hmm?" she said soothingly, winking at me and looking around to make sure everyone was still busy tidying up and more concerned about getting out of the building as soon as humanly possible. I put my arm down to my side and looked around for snoops too. No one was paying any attention to us. According to the wall clock, it was now 4:58.

"Helga, there's another thing—a more important thing. Didn't you say those drawers in the desk are usually locked?" I raised an eyebrow at her, certain I'd caught her in an obviously overlooked dilemma. As usual, she merely smiled.

"No problem there either. The copy editors have the key."

I paused, waiting for the rest of her explanation, since that couldn't be all of it. But she said nothing. I suppose she assumed telling me something simple like the copy editors have the key would placate me. Oh, how wrong she was.

"Well, therein lies the problem, Helga: The copy editors have the key. And last time I checked, neither one of us was a copy editor here. So, how do we get the key from the copy editors?"

She shook her head and laughed at my simplemindedness. "Maggie, Maggie, Maggie. You're so cute when you're being bone-headed."

"Keep talking. You haven't explained anything yet."

"The key is in one of their desk drawers."

Again, a pause. She was waiting for the supposedly obvious to dawn on me, but it wasn't coming.

"And their desks aren't locked?"

"Nope."

"So you're telling me they lock the desk at this end of the floor, then walk to that end of the floor and put the key in an unlocked desk?"

She nodded. "Yup." That omnipresent smile was beginning to annoy me.

"How do you know they don't have the keys with them at all times?"

"What is this, Fort Knox? Maggie, we're talking about a simple desk drawer key. Nobody's really dying to get in there anyway—except us. Locking that desk up at night is just a habit that's been around for a long time. It pre-dates several editors, and nobody really knows why it's still locked every night except that probably some editor a long time ago had an ego the size of a horse and thought his personal papers were too important to leave out for prying eyes."

"And the subsequent editors just kept locking the desk?"

"Of course. Train the new guy, tell him where the cafeteria is, and don't forget to tell him to lock the desk drawers. It's really just that simple."

"Huh." I was a bit flummoxed. Could it really be something that stupid? Murphy's Law in reverse?

"Actually, this is the first time locking the drawers makes any sense. Now—since Gerber Baby, well, you know—there are all kinds of people in and out of there. It gives things some sense of order to have someone unlock the desk at the beginning of the day and then lock it back up when the day is over."

"Speaking of which . . ." I added, glancing around the room. The wall clock had just hit exactly five o'clock, and people were herding themselves up and rounding themselves up out the doors. Just a tad faster and it would have looked like a full-fledged stampede.

"Quittin' time!" Helga added, watching everyone stream past her desk and out the glass doors. Various forms of "Good-bye, Helga!" were muttered as folks flowed past the desk, and Helga calmly nodded at each one, waving calmly and pretending to fuss with her purse and pack it up. Pockets of people traveling in waves bumped into me on the unprotected side of the desk, and I grabbed the countertop and hung on for dear life. This was like herding cattle, only without the bad smell. Mostly.

"Is it always this crazy right at five o'clock?" I asked, speaking loudly so Helga could hear me over the light crowd noise.

"How the hell would I know?" she yelled back. "It's the one up side of working right near the front door—I'm usually the first one out the door!" She grinned, waving at a few more people and snapping her purse closed, slinging it onto her shoulder. Looking behind her, I could see that the main floor was already almost empty. Most everyone had streamed out onto the front steps and toward the parking lot across the street by now, dispersing slowly and fanning out to find their cars.

Once the dust had settled, Helga and I stood at her desk and surveyed the huge room. Empty desks as far as the eye could see. The only sounds on the main floor now were the light buzzing of the remaining fluorescent lights and the click of the large industrial wall clock directly behind me. We looked at one another. Naturally, Helga smiled first, letting her purse slip off her shoulder and back onto her desk. I smiled back, still nervous but at least happy to see Helga was entirely right—so far. There was, however, still plenty of time left for something to go wrong. I tried to shrug off this worry, still smiling at Helga.

"So," I said cheerily. "Did you bring your cat burglar suit?"

* * * * *

"What do you mean, it's not there?" I whispered as Helga continued to dig in the head copy editor's desk drawer. I was standing watch over Helga's feverish rummaging, making sure a stray press operator didn't show up and catch us. Helga had pointed out earlier, though, that a press operator wouldn't have any idea whose desk was whose, and that she could very well be rooting around in her own desk for all he'd know. This would have been little comfort to me if we had been caught, of course, because everyone else in the place knew this was a copy editor's desk and that Helga's desk was all the way out front.

"I said, I can't find the desk key," she said quietly through clenched teeth, her arms still buried in the wide middle drawer nearly up to her elbows. "Maybe it's at the back here."

"What's that again, Miss *Murphy*?" I asked, not bothering to rein in the sarcasm. As a proofreader I usually enjoyed being right, in catching people's mistakes. In fact, it was probably a chief reason I was a proofreader in the first place. Guilt-free error-pointing, and I got paid for it, too. But this situation was entirely different. I'd been counting on Helga to know her own place of employment, and her earlier confidence was now draining from her body like water through a broken dam. She slammed the middle drawer shut, opened a side drawer, and began her search all over again. I saw a few granola bars in the drawer, a partial roll of stamps, some loose change—it wasn't looking so good for the desk drawer key, in my opinion.

"Maggie, why don't you try the other copy editor's desk across the aisle?" Helga asked curtly. She indicated the desk with an upward nod of her head. I glanced at the desk, a mirror image of the one Helga was raiding except for personal touches like family photos and knick-knacks, and then looked back at Helga.

I wagged a finger at the other desk. "Do you mean to tell me I could have been searching in this second desk the whole time?"

Helga looked up from her archaeological dig in the desk drawer and glanced from one desk to the other and then to me. "Well, yes, of course. But you were pretty clear you wanted to keep watch in case somebody showed up from downstairs."

"So you let this take twice as long—and you didn't mention the other desk?"

She shrugged. "I was pretty damned sure we'd find the key right here in this first desk. It never occurred to me we'd still be looking for the dumb key!"

"Right you are, Miss Murphy. Remember this moment later, would ya?" I said, walking around to the other desk and opening the middle drawer as Helga plunged her arms back into the side drawer of the first desk.

"Fine, fine, fine," she muttered, rearranging the miscellaneous contents of the drawer as if there were some purpose to her skittish movements that I couldn't quite fathom. It was all or nothing with Helga, feast or famine. "Just look for that key!"

I looked straight down into the drawer I'd just opened. "You mean this key?" I asked, holding up a single, small, unmarked key in my hand. Helga stopped abruptly, both her hands still shoved in the drawer the way a cat will thrust its paws under the edge of a rug, looking for nothing in particular but pretending it's having fun anyway.

"Where did you find that?"

"Helga, you're losing your cool. I found it in the middle desk drawer of the desk you just asked me to search." I held the key up and it caught what little light we'd left on and gleamed, winking slyly at both of us.

Helga bolted upright, her arms coming out of the drawer. She closed it with a solid thud—and I answered with a hasty "Shh!"—and came around the desks to take it from me. She inspected it meticulously, holding it up close to her eyes. I was half-expecting her to bite down on it to see if it was real, the way gold prospectors always did in the movies. Instead, she drew it away from her face and held it tightly in her hand.

"This is it, all right."

"How can you be sure?" I asked. It occurred to me that, since Helga was never the one to lock and unlock that desk, she might not even know what the key looked like.

She smiled—the first smile since the key search began. "All this week I've been finding reasons to call over whichever copyeditor was doing the locking or unlocking. So, they'd always stand right in front of me by my desk twiddling that stupid key around in their fingers. Instead of listening to a word they were saying, I'd be studying that key instead."

For all her faults, once in a while Helga pulled a proverbial rabbit out of her hat. This was one of those times. "Nice going," I said.

"Now, quick, let's get that desk unlocked and get to work!"

CHaPTer 28

I N SOME WAYS, RIFLING THROUGH THE DESK in the editor's office—
the one I'd seen Lee Gerber slumped over not so very long ago—
was surprisingly uncomplicated. And yet, in too many other ways,
it was like searching for a needle in a haystack, if clichés were per-
missible in this context. Helga had never been bold enough to follow one of the copy editors into the office to see exactly what was in
the desk and where things were being kept, and so we were largely
going on instinct trying to find letters from Dirt Boy. Helga opened
the left-hand drawer, and I took the right side. Both side drawers
held hanging file folders stuffed tight with files. I wondered how
anyone could keep coming in here every day to add more papers
to this already overstuffed drawer. Shooting a glance toward Helga,
I saw that she was having the same issues. She finally gave up and
yanked a bunch of the folders completely out of the drawer, plunk-
ing them onto the top of the desk.

"There! Now I can look through these things properly!"

I gawked at her boldness. "Did you at least make note of where
those files were in relation to all the other ones?"

She pointed to the top folder on the stack. "Alphabetical," she said simply, something I hadn't yet noticed in the drawer on this side because I'd been too busy trying to wedge more than a finger or two between any of the folders.

"Smart aleck," I said quietly, hoisting a group of folders out of the right-hand drawer and pitching them onto the desk as neatly as I could so the contents wouldn't spill out.

"Grab a chair and let's sit here and go through these right away."

Within minutes we were both shuffling through folders, hoping to find recent letters to the editor. I was working more slowly than Helga, who seemed to have an efficient method for eyeballing the stack of papers in each folder and making mental judgments on whether or not digging deeper would yield results. I think my tortoise speed to her hare came chiefly from me gawking at the familiar mahogany desk, long since cleaned up and polished to a beautiful shine again, as Gerber himself would have kept it every day. The ink blotter was gone, but it was essentially the same desk in the same state. It was the desk I saw in my dreams whenever the incident replayed itself in my subconscious without my permission.

Those dreams were far more infrequent now, but I'd had the dream again just last night: Gerber's upper body slumped over this very desk, dark red blood pooling on the rich red mahogany, that horrid letter opener jutting out of his back—the same letter opener that I'd noted was conspicuously absent from the desk set when I came in a few minutes ago. Staring at the desk now, both sides covered with stacks of file folders and no sign that anything untoward had ever happened here, I felt a little bit woozy. I closed my eyes to keep the room from spinning, my hearing sharpening in response to my eyes' lack of stimuli and picking up the sound of papers being sifted through, one paper turned, then another, methodically, rhythmically, over and over as Helga continued to make short work of her own stack of folders.

"You okay over there?" I heard her voice from far away, although she sat no more than three or four feet from me shoulder to shoulder.

"Fine," I answered weakly. "Just a little vertigo. Probably the memories, images."

She knew what I meant. "Oh, sorry. I hadn't even thought of that. Kinda like I feel whenever I have to go into the prepress room where . . . where Brenda used to sit."

I nodded, eyes still closed, and inhaled deeply, trying to relax and exhale slowly so I could open my eyes and feel a little more grounded again. "Keep going. I'll feel better the faster we get done with this and get out of here." I heard the papers start rustling again: *thwip, thwip, turn, turn, crinkle, crinkle, thwip-thwip-thwip* . . .

At some point as I was inhaling deeply and exhaling slowly—and hoping I didn't hyperventilate in the process—I heard the paper noises stop. "Psst! Maggie!"

I exhaled one last time and opened my eyes. The room wasn't spinning, and I relaxed a little bit. "What?"

"I think I found the right one," she said, holding up a single folder in one hand. She was smiling.

"Good. I wasn't making much progress anyway." The folder was marked "LTRS TO ED," and I quickly deduced that there probably wasn't a guy named Ed in the building to whom people were sending letters.

"Let's put all these other folders away and take this one little folder out to my desk to look through it. That way we'll have almost everything back where it belongs, and if anyone does come upstairs, at least we'll look like we're where we're supposed to be. None of the press guys are going to care or know whether we're looking at files we shouldn't look at or not."

She was already stuffing the other hanging folders back into the drawer in the right alphabetical spot. I grabbed my own folders, which were virtually untouched, and crammed them back in place as well. Her plan certainly had its good elements, and this was one of them. I was going to feel a lot better once we were safely out of this dreadful office. We got Gerber's office back to normal—or, as close as we could reasonably remember—and tiptoed out to the front desk with our one folder. Another perk to her plan was that several people had the ongoing task of coming in this office during the work day and pillaging the desk for different items. So, no one person would know offhand if some small folder were slightly askew or if the papers inside any given folder weren't as neatly arranged as they had been previously. I was beginning to loosen up a little bit.

Helga laid the folder on the countertop at her desk, which was a good height so we could both look through it while standing side by side. She opened the folder and turned to each letter slowly, deliberately. The letters were arranged in the folder with the most recent ones on top, so we started there and worked our way backwards in time. Most of them were the garden-variety letters to the editor, griping about this or that zoning ordinance or congratulating this or that local sports team for yet another good season, rah rah rah.

We were looking at each letter together, with Helga flipping the pages over when she saw I was done perusing them, when suddenly Helga gasped a loud intake of breath and dropped the paper she was holding. I turned in Helga's direction just in time to see Francine Stettler standing directly behind her, holding something into her back up near her shoulder blades and now reaching her other arm around the front of Helga's waist. Helga's eyes showed the panic and irrationality of a wounded animal, and I stood still, rooted to the spot by what I was seeing, trying vainly to process it as part of reality. It seemed to be part of a horrendously bad dream.

"Francine?" I squeaked out, partly to let Helga know exactly who was holding her prisoner. Helga closed her eyes and didn't move, except for the uncontrollable quivering of her entire body.

"Miss Velam. Right where I was told you'd be."

"Helga—are you okay?" I asked, ignoring Francine for a brief moment and hoping to focus in on Helga in order to find out what was going on behind her back.

"Knife . . . a big knife. I can feel it—"

"Shut up!" Francine interrupted, and judging from the fear and anguish on Helga's face now, her eyes open wide and her mouth gaping, I knew Francine had wedged whatever large knife she was wielding a little bit closer to Helga's back.

I stood stock still, not daring to move a muscle in case it sent Francine totally over the edge—although I suspected she was already most of the way there just by our current predicament. "Francine, what are you doing here?"

"Your son told me you would be here. Lucky for me your home phone number's listed."

Everyone on the planet had dropped their landlines but me—I still needed mine for faxes, and the cell signal in my building wasn't anything to write home about. My mind snapped in a quick mental reminder to change my number to unlisted as soon as we got out of this mess. Assuming we did, of course.

Suddenly I felt queasy. Helga looked ready to pass out. She was blinking through tears, which had begun to trail down her cheeks. I was in agony watching her, helpless against a total freak of a human being. Why hadn't any of us seen *this* coming? Dirt Boy and the mail clerk had both been joke suspects in comparison to this. We were fools, all three of us.

"He told you we were here?" I asked, incredulous, before remembering Seth had no way of knowing Francine was a nut job.

"Sure. Once I told him I had a manuscript for you and that I'd driven all the way from Ohio, he took pity on me and said you'd be down here with this person—whatever her name is. Working late, he said. Lucky for me."

She pulled Helga a little closer to her, and Helga winced noticeably. I grimaced at having to watch the terror mount on her face each time Francine pushed the knife in tighter between her shoulder blades. I wondered whether it had yet pierced the skin. My control-freak nature was reeling from my complete and utter lack of control in this situation. There was absolutely nothing I could do that wouldn't endanger Helga. Francine was even more unpredictable than I had originally guessed. And I certainly didn't have the lightning reflexes of a television detective or some movie star on an impossible mission, so grabbing for the knife myself was out of the question. I bit my lip to try to alleviate some of the escalating tension but it only served to make things worse.

"Francine, what did we do to you? Please, if you just stop this before someone gets hurt, Helga and I will go back to our work and forget you were ever here." I wasn't sure why I thought playing hostage negotiator with someone as unreasonable as Francine was a good idea, but it was all the ammunition I could muster. And I couldn't do *nothing*—not with Helga standing so close to me and yet so far from any help I could offer.

"Don't think I'm not onto you, Miss Velam. *Maggie*. I went back to Deerpark Press like I said I was going to. And do you know what they told me? Seems you'd been there not too long ago yourself. Looking for work, they said."

My heart sank. I knew where this was going.

"And yet you'd told me just a little while ago that you couldn't help me because you had *too much* work and couldn't squeeze me in. Isn't that right?"

She was making herself angrier, and all this meant was that she grasped Helga even more tightly. Helga was sobbing silently now, and I could see her legs were shaking. I wondered what would happen if her knees gave out and she collapsed. I tried willing Helga to be strong and steady, to not do anything that Francine would interpret as a sudden movement.

"I was trying to be . . . nice," I said weakly, my voice trembling under the strain.

"By lying to me? Is that how you're nice to people?" She was looking straight at me from over Helga's right shoulder, the venom plainly seeping from every muscle in her face.

"B-B-But why are you here? Because I lied to you?" In some remote corner of my mind, I was still hoping this was mostly a joke— just a bad day for Francine because I'd fibbed to her to get out of working with her. But deep down I knew nobody, not even Francine, held someone hostage with a knife—or worse—simply because she was mad about being lied to by a stranger. Francine was off her rocker, but even I knew there was more to this than that. Gerber. Brenda.

"Don't make me laugh. Like you're worth all this! You're just another loose end. Like the girl."

My own knees felt weak, and I tried making eye contact with Helga again. Her lips were quivering and her body was shaking. *Stay strong a little while longer, Helga. I'll figure something out!*

"But why Lee Gerber?"

She clicked her tongue in disgust. "I'm not even going to dignify that with an answer. You're just stalling for time. Time for me to wrap all this up and move on."

"Move on?"—I wasn't sure how or why I'd said this—I was in total reaction mode now, and my heart was fluttering so fast I was sure I'd slip into a coma any second. For now, though, I knew I didn't want to keep egging her on, and yet yes, I was stalling for time, wasn't I? But, that wasn't going to change any time soon. I couldn't reach for a phone, or anything else, without triggering Francine's already heightened panic reflex. The only thing to do was to stand still, speak when spoken to, and pray for a miracle.

"Yes, move on. Life. The novel. Everything."

"Oh," I squeaked.

"I'm thinking of self-publishing," she said, almost triumphantly. She stood quietly, firmly, and it became clear she was waiting for my response.

"I . . . think you're the perfect candidate for self-publishing," I said, hoping I'd struck the right balance of truth mixed in with exaggeration and understatement. In any other context, the line might have been humorous.

I looked back to Helga, just in time to see her eyes roll back up under her eyelids and her knees buckle suddenly. She went limp—so completely limp as she lost consciousness that Francine was caught off-guard for a split-second and Helga slipped quietly to the floor at her feet. Francine was left exposed, holding a large, obscenely sharp kitchen knife in one hand. Stunned, she looked from Helga's prostrate body at her feet to me standing in my original position a few feet away from her. In the time it took for all this to register on Francine's face, I did almost nothing. I was too frightened to attempt any sort of daring rescue, and I silently cursed myself for not working out at the gym like I'd been promising myself I'd do for years.

As my scattered thoughts raced from one pointless topic to another within a matter of seconds, I heard the glass doors behind Francine swing wide open, the voices and scuffling of several large, heavily outfitted men rushing into the building.

"Freeze right there! You're under arrest!"

My arms instinctively shot straight up in the air. Amazingly, so did Francine's, and I heard the clanking of the knife as it hit the floor just next to Helga, missing her by inches. Francine's shocked face etched itself on my memory as the officers rushed in, grabbed her upstretched arms, and yanked them quickly and efficiently behind her back. I dropped to my knees in a massive wash of adrenaline leaving my body with an almost audible whoosh, and I crawled the few feet over to Helga, turning her over to see if the knife had penetrated the skin. A small slice in the back of her shirt scared me, until I saw just a very tiny, superficial puncture and only a few small drops of blood at the site.

"Officers, here! This woman needs help!" I yelled, holding Helga in my arms, her head in my lap as I sobbed uncontrollably and realized that I very desperately wanted my mommy.

CHaPTer 29

P ASS THE GRAVY, PLEASE," SAID ANNIE, handing the oversized
bowl of mashed potatoes to my mother sitting on her left.

"It's coming, Ann!" said Seth, with a bit more annoyance in
his voice than I would have liked. It had been a while since I'd had
both kids here at the same time, and I realized I wasn't used to their
clipped interaction with each other anymore.

"Maggie, dear," my mother added as she scooped potatoes onto
her plate. "The turkey looks marvelous!"

"Thanks." Mom had started complimenting me on everything
I did or said since the episode in the *Bugle* office not so long ago.
I wasn't entirely sure it was all sincere—to me the turkey looked
a little bit overdone and dry—but I wasn't going to spoil her fun
either. Perhaps she was just making up for lost time, or learning
to appreciate something while you have it, or any manner of other
platitudinous stances she'd adopted in recent weeks. Ultimately it
didn't matter why she was being so kind when I didn't deserve it—I
was going to bask in it anyway while I could.

The gravy traveled past Seth to Annie, and Helga asked for
it next. It seemed good and proper—almost necessary—to invite

Helga to Thanksgiving dinner this year. Her extended family desperately wanted her with them, but something unspoken between Helga and me made her eagerly accept my invitation, which came the very next day after Francine was arrested. Suddenly I wanted family and friends as close as possible, and Thanksgiving seemed to be perfectly timed to make that happen.

Vlad sat quietly under the table—at Seth's feet, of course—thumping his little tail on the floor as a dead giveaway of his actual intentions. He wasn't here for family or friends—only for food. But, this early in the meal none of us were "accidentally" dropping scraps on the floor for the dog. The turkey, potatoes and trimmings really had turned out halfway decent this year. Or maybe it was the company that made everything that much more delicious.

Dad said little, but he smiled a lot. He carved the turkey, enjoying being at the head of the table, even if it was in my apartment, and one by one we passed our plates to his end of the table so he could gingerly lay a sliced wedge of turkey onto each plate.

Helga beamed at me. "Mags, this is just great. Thanks for inviting me."

I reached my arm around her shoulder and pulled her in close. "No sweat, *toots*. My pleasure."

She laughed. "Hey, that's my line!"

"Well, I kinda like it. I think I'll borrow it."

Helga turned to Seth and patted his hand. "If it hadn't been for you, Seth, figuring out what Francine was up to and calling the police, well . . . who knows?"

Seth blushed crimson. "If I hadn't told her where you were in the first place, though . . ."

"Seth," I chimed in. "We've had this discussion before. You didn't know she was crazy. Plus, if all this hadn't happened, maybe she'd still be out there roaming around with all the normal people."

Helga snickered. "Normal people? Speak for yourself, hon. I resent the insinuation that I'm normal." She slipped a forkful of turkey into her mouth after dipping it into a little puddle of gravy. Her eyes closed and a serene smile passed across her face. It was therapeutic to see her enjoying herself like this, unabashed and unafraid, the way I knew and loved her best.

"Mom," Annie said between bites of food, scarfing it down so fast I wondered if she'd eaten real food at all in the past month. "When are you going to start dating again?"

I choked on my potatoes. "Dating? That's totally out of left field, young lady!"

"*Motherrrr*," she said, rolling her eyes. "You have to start dating again. You're going to turn into an old maid soon!"

Ah, I so loved teenagers. "I'll date when a really nice guy sweeps me off my feet. And not a moment sooner." Another creamy bite of mashed potatoes found its way into my mouth, and I ate it slowly and enjoyed it immensely.

Seth cleared his throat after swallowing a morsel of stuffing. "I heard she's been getting these anonymous love letters from somebody named Dirt Boy."

Everyone stopped in mid-forkful and turned to stare at Seth, who broke into a wide but sheepish grin.

"Kidding! I'm *kidding*!"

"Next time, try saying something *funny* when you're kidding," I cautioned. Everyone laughed—everyone but Annie, who, at her own request, still hadn't heard all the details of my big adventure as a crime detective. I turned to Helga just in time to see her surreptitiously slipping a small chunk of turkey to Vlad under the table, who abandoned Seth and became Helga's new best friend, at least for the duration of the meal.

And me? I looked around the table and fought the urge to quote Dickens and cry out, "God bless us, every one!" There was so much to be thankful for this year. Even for a nitpicker like me.

THE END

If you enjoyed Maggie's first adventure, or even if you simply had a chuckle at poor Vlad's expense, please consider reviewing *The Scarlet Letter Opener* on places such as Amazon.com and Goodreads. Struggling authors rely on positive reader reviews!

Thank you!

aBOUT THe auTHOr

I N THE EARLY 1980S, Linda pursued a writing degree from Carnegie Mellon University in Pittsburgh, Pa. She pursued it but it kept getting away.

She has since worked behind the scenes in publishing as a proofreader, typesetter, and copy editor. She's worked with publishers, big and small, and with individual authors, big and small. (The big ones really ought to get a little more exercise.) She's also an 8th grade composition coach for WriteAtHome.com.

Linda is currently on the board of the St. Davids Christian Writers' Association and also the board of education and publication of the Reformed Presbyterian Church of North America. She also serves as author liaison for the Beaver County BookFest in Pennsylvania. She sounds really important and busy, doesn't she? She's not, but it's still a shame she doesn't get paid for any of these things.

Her favorite writing challenge since 2004 has been the yearly contest known as National Novel Writing Month: writing 50,000 words of a single new fiction project during the month of November. She loves the pressure of a ridiculous, forced deadline.

Linda also enjoys comedy, computer gadgets, office supplies, reading, movies, adventure games, crocheting—and her office guinea pigs, who keep her company while she's working. She currently lives in western Pennsylvania with her husband, Wayne Parker. They share six children between them, all of them now grown and living their own humorous stories.

Visit Linda online:
www.lindamaubooks.com
www.lindaau.com

Follow Linda on Twitter:
www.twitter.com/LindaMAu

Stalk Linda on Facebook:
www.facebook.com/pages/
Author-Linda-M-Au/119278508108217

43007583R00145

Made in the USA
Charleston, SC
11 June 2015